DEATH'S BRIGHT ANGEL

DEATH'S BRIGHT ANGEL

by
William Kerr

Narwhal Press
Charleston, South Carolina

Copyright © 2001 by William Kerr

First Edition

ISBN: 1-886391-52-1 (hardcover)
ISBN: 1-886391-54-8 (paperback)

Library of Congress Control Number: 00-136724

LIBRARY CARD CATALOG CLASSIFICATIONS (suggested by the publisher): adventure novels; Berkeley, Matt (hero of novels by William Kerr); Kerr, William (author of Matt Berkeley adventure novels)

COVER & TITLE PAGE DESIGN & PHOTOGRAPHY: E. Lee Spence

IMPORTANT NOTICE: This novel, *Death's Bright Angel*, has been copyrighted for both compilation, characters, and composition. As in all of the Matt Berkeley novels, except for historical figures, if any, who may have been loosely drawn upon, all other characters are fiction and any resemblance to persons living or dead is purely coincidental. Some of the central characters, such as Matthew (Matt) Berkeley appear in other novels by the author and all rights to them have been claimed and reserved by the author. Except when such use is not otherwise in violation of the Act, no part of this work may be reproduced or transmitted in any form or by any means, electronic or mechanical, including scanning, placement on the Internet, photocopying and recording, or by any storage or retrieval system, except as may be expressly permitted by the Copyright Act as currently amended or in writing by the Narwhal Press Inc. which holds those rights by assignment from the author. The only exception to the foregoing is for brief excerpts (maximum length of one page per review) used solely for review purposes. All correspondence and inquiries should be directed to Narwhal Press Inc., 1629 Meeting Street, Charleston, SC 29405.

Printed in the United States of America.

DEDICATION

To Women, Everywhere

This novel reflects the wrenching, often life-altering decisions women must make during the reproductive years of their lives, regardless of their station in society.

Death's Bright Angel

**OTHER NOVELS
by William Kerr**

The Collector

Judgement Call

Path of the Golden Dragon

The Red Hand

ACKNOWLEDGEMENTS

While their leanings toward pro-life or pro-choice within the sensitive and highly divisive subject of abortion was never discussed, I do want to express my sincere appreciation for the expert technical assistance rendered in their respective fields:

Dr. Jojo Gorospe

Sgt. R. Scott McLeod
Jacksonville, Florida, Sheriff's Office
(Detective Division - Homicide)

Death's Bright Angel

Eyes shut tight
Tiny clenched fists
A pink cradle-womb
Life's breath denied.
                —*Ann Sims*

William Kerr

DEATH'S BRIGHT ANGEL

Death's Bright Angel

William Kerr

PROLOGUE
Jacksonville Beach, Florida
October, 1952

Breakers, driven by the powerful nor'easter, thundered across the beach, their spray flung high in the wind, mingling with low-flying clouds racing in from the Atlantic. Only the concrete seawall provided a barrier between the raging surf and the boardwalk, its carnival rides, hot dog and cotton candy concessions already closed for the winter.

Past the boardwalk, a line of mom-and-pop souvenir stores sat hunkered down against the autumn nor'easter and its intermittent rain squalls. The stores, their front windows normally crisscrossed by the late morning shadows of an aging roller coaster and Ferris wheel, were deserted by tourists and townspeople alike. Salt spray formed a halo around a single lighted neon sign – *RxMORE SODA FOUNTAIN & DRUG STORE*. A woman, short, poorly dressed for the weather and hesitant in her movements, hovered in the drug store's doorway, her eyes nervously glancing up and down the street. Satisfied no one was watching, she pushed open the door and slipped inside.

• • •

Even though Sam Moreland wasn't a real-life doctor,

everybody that was anybody in Jacksonville Beach called him "Doc." The poorer side of the community called him "Dr. Sam," a formality he'd never discouraged. They'd done it for years. During the war, as owner of RxMore Soda Fountain and Drug Store, he'd been the only pharmacist at that end of the beach, filling prescriptions written by the few elderly doctors not taken by the Army or the Navy. They were physicians whose writing was so bad, half the time he had to ask customers to describe their symptoms so he could work up what he thought was the right medication. Whether they survived or not, he'd never gotten a complaint.

Doc was a tall, big-boned man in his late fifties with a voice slightly less harsh than the foghorns you could hear late at night if you lived along the beach. It was his granddaughter, however, sitting on a high stool at the rear of the pharmacy, who could bring out the tenderness in the old man's heart. She was the absolute love of his life.

"Be careful, sweetheart, or you'll dribble that stuff all over your dress," Doc warned as he counted out the last of twenty pills and slipped them into the packet for customer pickup later that day.

Eight-year-old Samantha, named after her grandfather by parents who had died in an automobile crash in Georgia when she was six, clutched the Coke float even tighter in her hands. "No I won't, Granddaddy. See." She held up the glass with two hands.

The brownish-black bush of a mustache on Doc's upper lip tilted up slightly in the closest thing to a smile he could muster. "That's good. Why don't you go back to the stock room and help one of the clerks unpack the Halloween candy we just got in, and don't you eat it all. Hear?"

"I was going home after I finished my Coke float."

"That nor'easter outside's blowing harder and harder, and I wouldn't want it to blow you away. Go on back to the stockroom, and we'll go home together at lunch time."

"Just a little piece?" Samantha asked, slipping from the stool.

"Of what?"

"Halloween candy."

Doc chuckled. "Just one, but don't tell Grandmomma."

Samantha laughed. "I won't," she said and headed for the stockroom.

Doc looked out over the store from the prescription counter, searching the aisles of cosmetics, the eye, ear, nose and throat over-the-counter medicines, the tobacco section, Halloween masks already on the shelves. Except for the cashier at the front, the store looked empty.

"Damn nor'easter," Doc grumbled to himself. It was like this every fall. As Atlantic waters chilled in anticipation of winter, winds blew out of the northeast, sharp and biting, bringing the first hint of changing seasons. Unfortunately, what it did not bring were customers and the ring of the cash register to his ear.

The counter, built on a platform about two feet higher than the surrounding floor, enabled Doc to oversee the entire store and, at the same time, feel a little like God, looking down on his people and dispensing lifesaving favors to the masses. He liked that most of all, the God part, that is.

"Dr. Sam?"

"Wha—?"

"Down here."

"Who's that?" Doc leaned over the counter and peered down at the woman who stood about a foot shorter than the top of the counter.

"It's me. Clara Mae Johnson. I got a problem."

Doc Moreland shook his head. If it was the Johnson woman, that could mean only one thing. "Which one this time, Mrs. Johnson?"

"My youngest one, and you can call me Clara Mae. Everybody does."

Doc eyed the woman, remembering their last encounter, and decided he had to draw the line on familiarity. "How far along, Mrs. Johnson?"

"Not sure. Six, maybe seven weeks. She missed her second period and tried to take care of it herself."

"Herself?" Doc blurted.

"Yes, sir, but now her whole body's in a cold sweat and she can hardly walk for the pain in her stomach."

"Damn! That means she didn't get it all." Doc's frown turned into a wrinkled question mark. "I don't know. I can usually take care of things before they get too far, but cleanin' up something after a coat hanger job?"

"Nobody else we can go to."

"I can't guarantee the outcome on this one. This is different from your other daughter... when we did the abortion." The last words were hushed, almost inaudible, even though there were no other customers in the store. When saying the word *abortion*, he always said it soft and whispery so others couldn't hear. It just seemed better that way to Doc Moreland.

"When can you do it?" Clara Mae asked.

"Ten o'clock tonight, my house, and come in the back alley like you did before," Doc warned. "Somebody see you, they'll start asking questions, and questions mean trouble. Understand?"

Clara Mae nodded. "Back alley at ten o'clock."

• • •

Samantha pushed deeper into the covers. The nor'easter, if anything, had grown stronger, more violent as the night lay heavy across the small beach community. Bands of rain, fast-moving curtains of water along the darkened streets, swept in from the ocean. They splattered like buckshot against the windowpanes. It was not the rain, but the screech of tree limbs driven by the wind, tearing and clawing at the weathered shingle siding outside Samantha's second-story bedroom, that startled her awake.

Bolting upright, Samantha clutched the blanket close to her throat and waited for the next blast to shake the house, but it was neither wind nor rain that sent the cold chill through her body, filling her head with a million pinpricks of fear. It was a scream, a shallow scream from far away. From the attic? She listened, almost afraid to breathe, and again, a cry, even more piercing, followed immediately by the gruffness of her grandfather's voice. "Keep her quiet,…" The wind and the rain, lashing at the windows, momentarily drowned out his voice, until, "… or so help me God, I'll stop right now."

"Grandmomma," Samantha cried, but only the wind answered her call.

Samantha threw the covers away from her body and shot across the room into the pitch-black hall. Turning right, away from the painful moan filtering down from the attic, she stumbled through the open doorway of her grandmother's bedroom. "Grandmomma, what's happening? I heard somebody scream, and—"

"It's your grandfather," Norma Moreland interrupted as she raised herself on one elbow and reached for Samantha's hand. "He's extracting the sins of the world. Go back to bed and pray that God will bless your grandfather for all the good he does."

"But, Grandmomma, I'm scared."

"There's nothing to be afraid of, Samantha," Norma said, the sternness in her voice overcoming Samantha's fear of the unknown. "Do as I say." Norma pointed toward the door. "To bed."

Samantha stood for a moment, uncertain, then turned and shuffled timidly back into the hall. As she reached her room, she heard that same pathetic little moan filter through the wind sounds. "It's your grandfather," Grandmomma's words echoed in her thoughts. "He's extracting the sins of the world," and if it was all right with God, Samantha thought...

Looking back to make sure her grandmother had not followed, Samantha slipped past her own room and tiptoed down the darkened hallway until she reached the door to the attic stairs. The door was ajar.

Waiting for a particularly loud blast of wind to rattle the house, Samantha eased open the door and squeezed onto the landing at the foot of the narrow flight of steps. One step, two, like a cat creeping on all fours, then a third. She was careful to make as little noise as possible, afraid the wind whistling around the eaves of the house might suddenly cease and give her away. Samantha stopped just below the tenth and final step. Lying almost prone, her feet dangling three steps below, she could barely see above the horizontal line that marked the attic floor.

The single overhead light, its yellowish glow creating long shadows around the attic, and the continuous moans of someone in pain, dredged up the earlier fear, but Samantha was as much afraid to go back as she was to stay.

Blinking the room into focus, Samantha saw her grandfather, his body wrapped in a large white apron, his hands covered by plastic gloves, the kind her grandmother wore when cleaning the bathroom. A mousy little woman, not much taller than herself, stood next to an old kitchen table that had been in the attic for as long as Samantha could remember. It was what lay on the table, however, that took her breath away — a girl, partially covered by a sheet, her thighs, pale white, spread wide and angled upward. The raised crosspieces of two crutches, each crutch secured firmly to the end of the table, provided a rest beneath the girl's knees. Each leg was held fast to its respective crutch by long strips of white adhesive.

"You say she tried to do herself," Samantha heard her grandfather say. "When?"

"Tuesday," the woman answered in a matter-of-fact voice. "Three days ago."

Doc Moreland shook his head. "God only knows why she's not already dead. The penicillin shot I gave her oughta help, but what she needs more is a real doctor."

"You know they wouldn't've touched her unless she was willin' to have the baby. Anyways, all they'd do now is say this was God's way of punishing her and report her to the State."

To the State? For the woman to say something like that, Samantha thought, the girl must have done the most terrible things, and for God to make her hurt so much... Samantha prayed she'd never do something that bad.

Doc sighed, adding, "Put this rag in her mouth so she can bite down when it hurts, and Mrs. Johnson, you'll have to hold her down. I don't have anything to give her for the pain, but I'll be quick as I can."

"Yes, sir," she answered, then, "Hold tight, Mary. It'll be over soon as Dr. Sam gets you cleaned out."

Mary gripped Clara Mae's arm and groaned, "But I hurt so bad already. Don't let him hurt me anymore."

"Like your mother said, Mary, this might be God's way of punishing you for killing your baby, but for now, I want you to pray like you've never prayed before. Pray to God, Mary, that He'll forgive you of all your sins and guide my hand to cleanse you of your wicked ways."

Samantha watched as her grandfather switched on a swivel-neck lamp and aimed its beam between the girl's legs, illuminating the oval-shaped opening, the surrounding nest of light brown hair and pinkish lips already spread, her buttocks pulled forward, even with the end of the table. A thin line of urine trickled from the base of the opening into a large wash pan placed on the floor. It was all Samantha could do to keep from gagging, but she could not force herself to turn away.

Wiping away the blood and using something that looked to Samantha like one of her grandmother's smallest measuring spoons, its metallic edges cupped to resemble a miniature ice cream scoop, its handle attached to a narrow length of highly polished wood, Doc Moreland spread the girl's opening with gloved fingers and inserted the spoon, slowly, deliberately. Within seconds, he stopped as if meeting some kind of resistance. The girl moaned; her body strained against the force of her mother's grip.

"I'm at the entrance to the womb. I don't have anything to dilate the opening, so this is going to hurt. Hold her, Mrs. Johnson. Hold tight."

"I got her."

Samantha's hand involuntarily moved to her own female parts, pressing hard as though she, too, could feel the pain that Mary felt, anticipating the pain that was yet to come.

"Here goes," Doc said, and with a short grunt, he pushed the spoon forward. The girl spit the rag from her mouth and screamed. Her tortured cry cut through the nor'easter's fury and filled the room with an animal-like, ear-piercing squeal. Samantha gritted her teeth and squeezed tight the facial muscles that controlled both eyes and ears, trying to shut out the sound until abruptly, the scream stopped. Only the rising stench of stale urine and dead flesh remained, suddenly filling the attic, penetrating everything with its putrescence.

"Good God!" Doc cursed, using his shirtsleeve to cover his nose.

"She fainted," Clara Mae reported.

"Keep holding," Doc ordered. "I'm going to scrape out the infection and whatever part of the baby she left."

Dazed at what she had already seen and heard and

smelled, Samantha felt as though she was living a nightmare as her grandfather manipulated the instrument in the girl's body. Round and round, back and forth. It was as if she could feel and hear the scraping of the spoon's edge against her own insides, and then the spoon emerged, bringing with it blood and mucous and blackened, rotting flesh, minuscule lumps that splashed into the pan beneath the table.

In Samantha's mind, each lump represented a tiny hand, a tiny foot, the heart and soul of an unborn baby. Tears flowed from Samantha's eyes for the baby that would never be. No wonder God made the girl hurt so bad. Samantha suddenly hated the girl, and told God as she crept down the stairs and back to the safety of her bed, "When I grow up, I won't kill my baby, God. I promise, and I won't let anybody else kill their baby, either."

Death's Bright Angel

CHAPTER 1
Jacksonville, Florida
October 24, 1992
Saturday Morning

Although the digital clock on the dashboard showed half past ten in the a.m., the sun had finally begun to burn holes in the river fog that so often blanketed St. Johns Bluff in late October. There was, however, enough visibility to see the National Park Service entrance sign: *TIMUCUAN ECOLOGICAL AND HISTORIC PRESERVE — FORT CAROLINE NATIONAL MEMORIAL.*

Matthew Berkeley gunned the engine and did a quick spin of the steering wheel, expertly maneuvering the white Jeep Cherokee through a narrow opening in the oncoming traffic, an endless stream of cars, pickups and sport utility vans headed toward downtown Jacksonville's Gator Bowl and the annual universities of Florida and Georgia football game. As he drove past the Park Service sign and along the tree-shaded asphalt road toward the park's Visitor Center, Matthew glanced at the three forty-yard-line tickets mocking him from the normally unused ashtray. His anger grew like a spreading rash at the thought of Jackie, his sister, and Tony, her husband, waiting for him to pick them up for the game that was known throughout the country as the "largest outdoor cocktail party in the world."

Muttering through the scowl that lined his face, Matthew vowed, "This better be good, or somebody's ass—" The promise caught in Matthew's throat as he pulled into the Visitor Center parking lot.

"Holy Christ!" Automatic reflex forced his foot down hard against the brake pedal as he counted two, three, four patrol cars, two with red, white and blue roof lights blinking their silent warnings. The forward side doors of each car bore a blue and gold emblem which read, *OFFICE OF THE SHERIFF, JACKSONVILLE POLICE.* A uniformed police officer, who looked to Matthew like he should be playing linebacker for one of the teams at the game that day, stood talking to an unseen face through the driver's side window of a van marked, *CRIME SCENE UNIT.*

Matthew eased off the brake and allowed the Jeep to roll toward an empty parking space next to one of the cruisers until the policeman shouted, "Hey!" The officer stepped in front of the Jeep, the flattened palm of one hand raised in an immediately recognizable gesture. Matthew stopped. Approaching the Jeep's open window, the officer said, "Park's closed today."

Matthew noted the stripes on the officer's sleeve and asked, "What's the problem, Sergeant?"

"Not at liberty to say, but..." The sergeant hesitated for a moment, then read aloud the writing painted along the Jeep's side. "*North American Archeological Research and Preservation Association. NAARPA.* You Berkeley?"

"Last time I looked."

"Park your car. Lieutenant Taylor wants you down at the fort."

"I know that, but what for?"

The sergeant brushed aside the question, asking, "Is

there another way to the fort besides the two nature trails?"

"Work road back through the woods."

"The crime scene guys need to get their truck down there. You can ride with 'em and show 'em the way."

"Sure," Matthew said with a chuckle edged with cynicism, "but what the hell kind of crime scene have we got down there? Somebody steal the fort?"

"Just go with the truck, Mr. Berkeley. The lieutenant's waiting."

• • •

As the Crime Scene Unit van rolled to a halt, Matthew opened the door and unfolded his still athletic, nearly six-foot frame from the crowded front seat and stepped to the ground, made damp by the now thinning fog. Even though just short of his forty-eighth birthday, still a young man, at least by his own constantly changing definition, his knees creaked from the cramped position. He wished he'd worn his work khakis and boots instead of the slacks and loafers he'd put on for the game.

Alertly, and yes, with an ingrown reserve of suspicion carried over from his Vietnam years, Matthew's eyes quickly took in the scene. To his right, massive oak trees towered along the banks of the St. Johns River as it lumbered its way toward the Atlantic, some six or seven miles to the east. In front of him loomed the arched entrance to an earthen re-creation of Fort Caroline, built originally by French colonists during the sixteenth century. To his left lay a marshy area and an archeological dig site with which he had grown intimately familiar over the past months, but where was the hotshot lieutenant who wanted to see him?

One of the crime scene technicians, the name, *BURGESS*, sewn onto the chest of his blue, short-sleeved shirt, opened both of the van's rear doors and pulled out two large boxes. The one labeled *Evidence Collection Kit*, Burgess kept himself. The other, marked *Photographic Kit*, he handed to his partner. "Which way's the dig site?" Burgess verbally tossed over his shoulder at Matthew.

"I thought it was the fort you were —"

"The dig site," Burgess repeated.

Matthew gave a so-okay-I'm-stupid shrug of his shoulders and led the way along a narrow but well-trodden path that skirted the shallow moat surrounding the fort. As he rounded the southwestern edge of the fort, Matthew stopped short.

"What the hell's going on here?" Matthew said, loud enough for his voice to carry across the corner of the marsh to several piles of dirt and oyster shells excavated from rectangular pits during the summer. "And where the hell're my people?"

Two uniformed officers and another three, who Matthew took to be plainclothes officers, one a woman, all in a group on the far side of the largest and most distant mound of dirt, snapped their heads in his direction. Without a word, the group opened ranks as a sixth man rose from what Matthew assumed to have been a kneeling position behind the mound.

He handed a small shovel to one of the officers and moved very slowly in Matthew's direction. Dressed in civilian slacks and jacket, the man was heavily built, well over six feet and somewhere close to Matthew's age, or so Matthew judged. His close-cropped hair was edged with a hint of gray; his skin a satiny black. "You Berkeley?"

Matthew nodded.

"Stay where you are," the man ordered. The haggard roughness in his voice reflected annoyance at Matthew's questions.

Matthew watched the man approach. Law enforcement or not, he was tired of taking orders from people who had so far refused to tell him what was happening or why he had been called.

Death's Bright Angel

As the man drew near, he reached into his jacket pocket, pulled out a black leather wallet, opened it and held it up for Matthew to see. Hazy sunlight danced off the gold and blue badge for only a moment, and then the wallet popped shut. "Rich Taylor, Jacksonville Sheriff's Office. Detective Division. You can call me Lieutenant."

"Fantastic! Just met and already we're on a first name basis," Matthew said, sarcasm dripping from his voice, followed by, "To be honest, Lieutenant, I'm getting a little tired of asking, but what's this all about and,..." looking past Taylor toward the dig site, "where are my people?"

"Being questioned up at the Visitor Center, all three of them. Should there be more?"

Matthew shook his head. "Only three. We finished the dig this past week. Those are grad students from Florida State, assigned to fill in the trenches."

"You head man for the dig?"

"No. Dr. Judith Webster, head of the Archeology Department at Florida State University and member of the Florida Division of Historical Resources. She left yesterday. I've been in charge of security for the dig."

One of the plainclothes officers near the dirt pile taunted, "Some security." This was immediately followed by a round of laughter cut short by a withering glance from the lieutenant.

Ignoring the remark, Matthew continued, "Since I'm staying in the area for another week or two, I volunteered to make sure we left everything the way we found it when we started the project."

"And the project was?"

"Location of artifacts left by the French, Spanish, and Timucuan Indians. An annual project whenever the State or the Park Service has the funds. And speaking of the Park Service, where's the park superintendent? Why isn't he here?"

"Said he didn't have anything to do with the dig and

gave us your name. Since he had tickets to the Florida/Georgia game, we let him go." The lieutenant looked at his watch. "Hope he made it. Game oughta be starting in about an hour."

Matthew laughed bitterly, thinking of the three tickets resting in the ashtray of his Jeep. "Thanks a helluva lot, Lieutenant. My sister and brother-in-law thank you, too."

"What do you mean?"

"Forget it, but I'd appreciate it if you'd tell me why I'm here."

Lt. Rich Taylor turned on his heel and moved toward the dirt mounds, explaining, "Your people found it when they were filling in the holes."

Hurrying to keep up with Taylor's jumbo strides, Matthew, with growing impatience in his voice, insisted, "Found what, goddamn it?"

As they clambered up and over the largest of the mounds, the circle of officers, which had been augmented by the two crime scene technicians, widened to give them room. Taylor stopped and pointed. "That."

"Aw, shit!"

Lying prone in the dirt and shell mixture, legs spread wide apart, was the partially uncovered skeletal remains of a... what? Man? Woman? Matthew moved closer.

"Watch it, buddy," Burgess the technician said.

"Watch it yourself, *buddy*. I didn't ask to come down here. You people sent for me, remember?" Turning from the technician, Matthew dropped to one knee next to the remains. "From what I can see of the pelvic area and the overall height of the skeleton, five feet or less, it looks like a woman."

"A regular Sherlock Holmes," Burgess whispered to a responding chorus of chuckles.

"When did you people start the dig?" Taylor asked.

"Late June. This pile would be material from one of the earlier pits."

Death's Bright Angel

"Find any bones, human or otherwise?"

Matthew shook his head. "Not human. Fish bones, deer, bear, pottery shards, tools and utensils made from conch and turtle shells, but what you've got here is much more recent than anything we found."

"How can you tell?" the female plainclothes officer asked, obviously questioning Matthew's reasoning.

Matthew cocked an eye in the direction of the voice, a figure hidden beneath a full-cut checked blazer and flared skirt, hair swept back in a bun, bifocals giving a scholarly appearance that seemed out of place with a crime scene. "And you are?..."

"Sergeant Bartelow. Homicide."

Matthew grunted acknowledgment and explained, "First of all, she couldn't have been in this pile of dirt any longer than the end of June."

"And you didn't smell anything?" Bartelow pressed.

"No, but besides being buried, there was a period back in July and early August when we had to abandon the dig because of heavy rains. Maybe that's when it happened. In warm, moist weather, with insects doing their thing, three to four weeks and all you've got are bones and little else."

"So I'm told," Bartelow muttered with indifference.

"Second," Matthew said, continuing with his original line of thought and pointing to the skull, "I'm sure you've already noticed, the dental plate she's wearing is twentieth century, not sixteenth century, and if you check out the ring finger on the left hand, that's a wedding band and a modern-day engagement ring with a diamond as big as a walnut. If nothing else, the rings indicate robbery wasn't the motive."

Taylor continued the test Bartelow had started. "Motive for what?"

"Murder. That's what you and your people think, isn't it?" Matthew shifted the weight of his body to his other knee.

Pulling a ballpoint pen from his shirt pocket, he pointed. "First, the nasal bone has been crushed and forced inward. The right temporal bone has also been cracked."

"Fell and hit her head."

"I doubt it. I'll bet you tickets for next year's Florida/Georgia football game there's a rock or something around here that was used to cause that kind of damage. Probably when she didn't die from the other wounds."

"What wounds?" Bartelow asked.

Still using the pen as a pointer, Matthew continued. "The rib cage. See the scrapes and scratches along the lower edges of the sixth and seventh ribs and on the base of the sternum? Like a knife blade trying to get at the heart, but look down here, and this is the strange part."

Everyone crowded close as Matthew pointed out deep gouges and scrapes in the forward part of the lower pelvis. "Somebody butchered the hell out of this woman, cutting up her sex and reproductive organs, and I hope to God she was dead when it happened."

"What the hell do you think you are?" Taylor growled. "A fucking medical examiner or something?"

Matthew laughed softly and stood up. "A former naval officer providing security for archaeological digs in Canada, the U. S. and Central America. I also have a degree in archeology and the opportunity to observe skeletal remains under the worst of conditions over the past ten or so years, but back to the subject. Why perform what looks like an amateur hysterectomy on a woman that's more than likely already dead or dying?"

"I don't know, Berkeley, but if it really was murder, it had to be some kind of kook to have done something like that. Where can I get in touch with you? Right now, you and this dig site are the only links I've got to that skeleton."

"Evergreen Apartments in the Arlington area. Lease is

up in two weeks."

"Extend it. You don't leave Jacksonville until —"

"Whoa up, Lieutenant," Matthew interrupted. "I'm not—"

He stopped, suddenly focusing on something grayish-white at the base of the skeleton's pelvis, something caught by the increasing brightness of the sun. "What's that?"

"What?" Taylor asked.

Matthew turned to Burgess and pointed to an object in the dirt between the skeleton's thighs. "Dig it out."

The technician glared at Matthew.

"Dig it out, damn it!" Matthew snapped.

Rich Taylor nodded. "Get some photographs first and let's take a look."

"C'mon, Lieutenant," Burgess argued, already working rubber gloves over his hands. "Medical Examiner's investigators aren't here yet, and you know—"

"Do it, Burgess," Taylor ordered. "M.E.'s office can't get anybody out here till after two this afternoon, and I want to see what it is. If there's any flack, I'll take responsibility."

After the second crime scene technician took some carefully aimed shots, Burgess scraped dirt away from the object, gradually working far enough down to get a finger hold. Tugging gently, he pulled it free from the surrounding debris and brushed it off with a small paintbrush he took from one of the many pockets in his utility trousers. "It's a... a baby doll." Burgess squeezed it to show the softness of the doll's plastic skin and flesh. "Head's too big in relation to the rest of the body, but —"

"Let's see," Matthew said, moving closer.

The technician held up the foot-long doll, its waxy looking, milk-colored skin stained with reddish-brown splotches, its eyes shut tight, thumb pressed against tiny lips.

"It's a doll, all right," Matthew agreed, "but not a baby.

At least not one that would've made it down the birth canal under normal conditions."

"Goddamn it, Berkeley," Taylor blasted. "What're you saying?"

"It's the replica of a human fetus, somewhere around the twenty-fourth or twenty-fifth week of development, near the beginning of the third trimester of pregnancy. And unless I miss my guess, those rust colored stains are —"

"The woman's blood," Bartelow inserted.

"More than likely," Matthew agreed. "And in the position we found the doll, I'd say the killer probably considered the woman as the doll's surrogate mother. What do you think, Lieutenant?"

Rich Taylor shook his head and grunted. "I think if what you say is true, whoever did this is some kinda gene pool retard, and I hate to think what he might do next."

CHAPTER 2
October 24, 1992
Saturday Afternoon

The noonday sun was hot as it so often is during the initial days of autumn along northeast Florida's *First Coast*. Heat waves, barely visible to the human eye, rose from the recently laid asphalt along Beach Boulevard. The odor of tar still clung to the air, swept along by the movement of traffic in front of the two-story brick building.

Clinic Director Dr. Debra Wagoner stood at the window, studying the fifty-to-sixty demonstrators and the signs they carried, her face and blouse shadow-striped by the heavy wrought iron bars that protected the clinic's reception area from the outside world. The heat and weekend traffic, augmented by the continuous caravan of cars en route to the "big game," many carrying flags picturing either the ferocious Florida gator or the pugnacious Georgia bulldog, were the least of Dr. Wagoner's worries.

The doctor, tailored and attractive, not a day over thirty-eight, forty at most, her admirers said, swept the lock of light brown hair from her forehead and sighed. Though frustrated and often angered by their actions, she was resigned to the demonstrators as they paraded back and forth in front of the building. What irked her most, however, were the two police officers in the cruiser parked across the street. Since the clinic opened at 8:30 that morning, they had done nothing to assist or protect the patients who had braved the throngs of Save the Unborn demonstrators. To Dr. Wagoner, that was a complete misdirection of justice.

Thank God, she thought to herself, touching the double-insulated windows. At least the staff was shielded from the constant harangue of prayer circles and hymns and the so-called street counselors, the ever-present Truegood Foley and his wife, Samantha, being the worst of the lot. Dr. Wagoner looked at her watch.

"Quarter 'til one," she said over her shoulder to the three women and one man standing near the building's entrance. Each wore a yellow armband inscribed with the word, ESCORT. "She should be arriving any minute."

The lone male escort grumbled, "And if that Truegood Foley character sticks that megaphone of his in my face one more time, I'm going to ram the damn thing straight up his–"

"That's exactly what he wants, Ernie," Dr. Wagoner cautioned. "This is the last appointment of the day, so keep it cool."

"Her husband coming?" one of three female escorts queried, a woman Dr. Wagoner guessed to be in her seventies.

"No. She's not married."

"Boyfriend?" Ernie asked.

"She'll be alone," Dr. Wagoner answered, shaking her head sadly. "A real shame. The father is her married employer. He's paid in advance. Thoughtful, huh?"

• • •

The signs, some professionally printed, others hand-painted in blood-red hues, delivered an unmistakable message, exactly what the Reverend Truegood Foley wanted.

Death's Bright Angel

ABORTION STOPS A HEART BEAT
EQUAL RIGHTS FOR THE UNBORN
JESUS LOVES YOUR BABY

While the adults, mostly housewives accompanied by a smattering of highly energized, well-dressed men, marched silently in front of the Jacksonville Women's Clinic for Family Planning, Truegood Foley gathered the group of kindergarten-aged children into a circle immediately outside the clinic doors.

"All right, young people," the hollow-eyed, anemic-looking man said, "sing as loud as you can. When she arrives, I'll have to leave you, but keep singing."

Small heads nodded their understanding, but why not? They'd been doing the same thing over and over all morning.

"Ready?"

Heads nodded again, accompanied by a tired muttering of, "Yes, sir."

Reverend Foley, his scarecrow of a body towering over the children, his nearly bald head glistening with beads of sweat, raised his arms, counted, "One, two, three, four," and led the children's chorus in:

"Jesus loves me! this I know,
For the Bi-ble tells me so;
Lit-tle ones to Him be-long,
They are weak, but He is strong.
Yes, Jesus loves me!
Yes, Jesus loves me!..."

From the corner of his eye, Reverend Foley saw a black Mercedes pull to the curb and the now-familiar four escorts hurry from the clinic to the car. The car door opened, and a young white woman, early twenties, pretty in a scrubbed, Ivory Soap kind of way, stepped to the sidewalk, wide-eyed and obviously frightened by the massed demonstrators.

"Keep singing, children," Foley ordered, quickly

picking up the megaphone at his feet and hurrying toward the car.

"... The Bible tells me so.
Jesus loves me! this I know,..."

As soon as the car door closed and young Chris Atwell was surrounded by the clinic's four escorts, the car's tires spun against the hot pavement. Its engine roared and it was gone as quickly as it had arrived. The driver, an older man with a thick mane of silver white hair, never looked back.

While the children sang, huddled as close to the clinic doors as possible, the adults pushed forward. Some waved signs, while some shouted, their words meant to create doubt in Chris's mind about what she was about to do. Others threw verbal stones, designed to demean and hurt, to cut deep into Chris's psyche and destroy her ability to make her own decision.

"Don't kill your baby!" they yelled, one face after another, jutting forward, magnified and distorted by Chris's growing fear.

"Most women will get pregnant only once," Chris heard. "Don't kill the only baby you'll ever have."

"Jesus loves your baby!"

"Don't let your womb become a tomb!"

Ignoring the protesters, the four escorts, holding hands with Chris in the middle of their protective circle, moved against the crowd, their forward progress measured inch by inch.

"Let us through, please. Thank you," the escort named Ernie said above the demonstrators' words. "Thank you. Let us through, please. Thank you."

What was taking on more the fervor of a mob than a peaceful demonstration grudgingly opened ranks, just enough for Chris and the escorts to move forward until the Rev. Truegood Foley planted himself in their path, his megaphone blaring.

"Escorts?" he shouted. "Ha! *Deathscorts* who drag women to the slaughter of their innocent babes. And you, young lady,..." The megaphone extended past the linked arms of the escorts, not more than two inches from Chris's face. "Five minutes of your time is all I ask so that you can know the child you carry is God's own and not yours to destroy."

Emotionally torn by what was happening, Chris pushed the megaphone away from her face, forcing Truegood Foley back against the crowd and cutting his lips on the megaphone's mouthpiece. "Get away," she cried as tears spilled down her face, her upper body wracked by great wrenching tremors.

"God will damn you for that," Foley shrilled through bloody lips, at the same time, raising the megaphone as if to strike at Chris.

"And goddamn you, you son of a bitch," Ernie shouted. Jerking his hands free from the other escorts, Ernie grabbed Foley's shirt collar and slung him to the sidewalk. "I oughta stomp your goddamn ass into the —"

"Make way! Make way!" voices cried over the melee.

Ernie turned just in time to see two blue uniforms rush through an opening in the crowd; to see the fiberglass baton strike down against his shoulder. He screamed and grabbed his shoulder as the force of the club sent him to his knees.

Truegood Foley, already on his feet, pointed at Ernie and shouted, "Did you see what he did, officer? He attacked me. He interfered with my right of free speech. Arrest him, officer. Arrest that man!"

Accompanied by the shouts and catcalls of Foley's disciples, the police officers grabbed Ernie and half-dragged, half-carried him to the far side of the street, shoving him roughly into the back of the patrol car.

Already exhausted and on the verge of emotional meltdown, Chris didn't feel the hand at her elbow, the elbow that Ernie had guarded. It was, however, the voice, little more than a forced whisper, yet harsh and commanding, that caught her attention. "Is this what you want, Chris?"

She turned her head. It was a man, broad shouldered and taller than herself. He was immaculately dressed in coat and tie with long but neatly combed black hair and a matching-color mustache that curved slightly just above his upper lip. She wanted to draw away, but something in his eyes demanded an answer to his question.

"I have no choice," she whispered, tearfully. The fact that this stranger knew her name bypassed her for the moment.

One of the remaining escorts stepped boldly in front of the man. "Who are you?" she demanded. "Do you know this lady?"

"Azrael, John Azrael. If this is what she truly wants," the man added, nodding to Chris, "I am willing to assist. Clasp hands and we'll proceed."

With no further words, Azrael joined hands with the other escorts, reforming the circle around Chris, and pushed forward, past the smug-looking Truegood Foley and the accusing looks of Foley's flock. Except for the children's chorus and their plaintive voices, the demonstrators grew silent when Chris and her protectors reached the clinic doors.

As though on cue, the doors opened, but the man with the mustache, the man who called himself John Azrael, held back. Taking a plain white card from his coat pocket, he placed it in Chris's hand.

Chris turned the card over and silently read *747-CARE*. A puzzled look clouded her face. "I don't understand."

"After it's over," Azrael explained, "if you feel lonely and in need of God's love, call that number, and help will be waiting."

Chris wiped the tears from her eyes and smiled. "Thank you, but..." She hesitated, remembering something that had initially escaped her, then asked, "How did you know my name?"

Azrael chuckled softly, answering only, "God works in mysterious ways," then turned and walked toward the demonstrators, pausing for only a moment before the children who sang,

>*"Je-sus, ten-der Shep-herd, hear me,*
>*Bless Thy lit-tle child to-night;*
>*Through the dark-ness be Thou near me;*
>*Watch my sleep till morn-ing light."*

William Kerr

CHAPTER 3
October 31, 1992
Saturday Afternoon

It had been a full week since finding the skeleton at Fort Caroline, a week with virtually nothing to do but wait for the Jacksonville Sheriff's office to remove the crime scene designation from the dig site. Thank God for Peyton, Matthew thought as he steered the NAARPA Jeep along Third Street, Jacksonville's beach community's main thoroughfare.

Jax Beach, as he had called it for so many years, was nothing like Matthew remembered as a boy, visiting his aunt on Fourth Avenue North. Walks to the beach, the boardwalk, the sharp sugary taste of cotton candy on his lips, Coke floats at Doc Moreland's RxMore Drug Store. And of course, that wonder of all wonders, the boardwalk Ferris wheel that seemed to reach to the clouds. From the top of its arc, he could see forever, or at least to the seaward horizon extending ten to twelve miles to the east.

Though he still felt that same boyish wanderlust, to always know what lay beyond the next horizon and the next, that was forty years ago. Except for the beach itself, all was gone — his aunt's house, the boardwalk, Doc Moreland's, even the Ferris wheel. They were replaced mostly by hotels and condominiums, the remaining beachfront a latticework of bars, seashell and surfboard shops, everything designed to loosen the purse strings of unwary tourists.

"Damn," Matthew cursed, almost missing the turn, at the same time working the brake pedal and nosing the Jeep onto the narrow side street and the hard-packed shell-and-gravel parking lot. Switching off the ignition, he sat for a moment, staring at the small, white clapboard cottage, an anachronism amidst surrounding stucco and pastel storefronts. The words, *Knowledge and More, Books, CDs and Jewelry* were scrolled in Old English across the broad picture window that stared down at the parking lot.

Was he early? Was the reading Peyton had spoken about still going on? If the number of cars in the lot were any indication, yes, he was early.

It was the first time he'd come to Peyton's place of business, the converted beach house, the books and friends she'd talked about so often, and to be honest, he was a little unsure of what to expect. Peyton was one thing, but a room full of psychics and psychic wannabes? She'd said her customers were normal, everyday people, like herself, but he still envisioned a group of weirdos, wearing 1960s hippie-like clothing and spouting metaphysical jargon that only those who lived in some psychic never-never land could understand.

What seemed even more amazing to Matthew, and to Peyton, was how their college romance, many years dormant, could be revived to such intensity after an improbable meeting at one of the local hardware stores. He smiled, thinking of the blush on her face as they practically stumbled over one another, reaching for the same shovel. The immediate recognition, the clasp of hands and the sudden embrace were as though their last, bitter good-bye had never happened. He'd known other women during the intervening years, but Peyton had always held a special place in his thoughts.

With a strong sigh of uncertainty, Matthew got out of the Jeep, climbed the cottage steps and eased open the door. He was right. The reading was still in progress, in a room to his left, partitioned from the main book display area. It was Peyton who alerted him with a finger to her lips. That same finger quickly beckoned him to come in and shut the door.

Peyton Chandler, at forty-nine, a year older than Matthew, had retained the smile that had first attracted him. A little broader in the hips and waist than in college, she was still a damned good-looking woman. What Matthew liked best was the natural auburn hair, more red than brown, a deep lustrous sheen styled in a short bob, the hint of bangs in the front, the taper at the back of her neck somewhat less severe than his own. A little old-fashioned, he thought, but on Peyton? Perfect.

From the adjacent room, he heard a man's voice ask, "Can you provide a concrete, factual explanation for your experience and your, uh... talents?"

A woman replied, "To be honest, no. Some who find it hard to believe call anything to do with the paranormal, the Barnum effect, after P. T. Barnum of circus fame. Others call it the giggle factor. At the same time, they accept the virgin birth, not on hard, factual evidence, but on the strength of their religious faith. Why and how anesthetics work on the human body is still a mystery, but no one questions anesthesia. Belief in and use of powers of the sixth sense, the psychic, is something you either accept or reject. Any more questions?"

A moment of silence, and then applause from the more than a dozen men and women who, Matthew noted when he peered past the partition, looked and dressed like a cross-section of people you might see at a shopping mall. His idea of a hollow-eyed subculture, languishing in the hazy world of séances and hypnotic trances, quickly evaporated.

Within moments, the babble of individual conversations

Death's Bright Angel

spilled over into the bookstore, many of the customers questioning Peyton about particular books dealing with astral projection, clairvoyance, telepathy and other areas of psychic phenomena. Matthew watched, intrigued by the interest and excitement he guessed was generated by the reading.

"Yes, they are, aren't they?" The woman's voice came from behind his left shoulder. Matthew turned. She was a short, rather portly woman, the one he'd heard answering questions in the reading room.

"Are what?"

"Excited. That's always the way, especially for those on their first visit, whether they believe or not."

"Don't know what you told them, but it sure turned them on."

"I'm Helena, and you must be Matt, the one Peyton can't say enough about," the woman said. Closing her eyes and putting her hand to her forehead as though sinking into a trance, she tilted her face toward the ceiling and mumbled, "I see a future filled with wonderful times for you and Peyton." Her eyes popped open and her mouth spread in a wide grin. "Is that prophetic or not?"

Matthew laughed. "Whatever it is, I hope you're right."

"Attention, everyone," Helena called. All heads turned. "Make your decisions, pay your money and be gone," she ordered, the smile on her face reflecting the twinkle in her eyes. "This beautiful man is Peyton's friend, waiting to carry her off on his magic carpet, and if you don't hurry, I might spirit him away for an erotic out-of-body experience that would be a waste of his time and Peyton's." She ended with a bow that would have made any Thespian proud.

After a flurry of applause, the customers completed their purchases and within minutes, the bookstore was empty except for Matthew and Peyton.

"Hi, lady."

"Hi, beautiful man." Peyton put her arms around Matthew's neck. "I think Helena liked you. You must have passed her test."

"I'm thrilled, but forget Helena." Matthew pulled Peyton close and kissed her, savoring the taste of strawberry lipstick and the sensual movement of her tongue against his. Just as quickly, she broke away and hung the *CLOSED* sign on the entrance door.

"Sure you want to go?" he asked.

"If there's anything serious about our relationship, and after the past two months, I should think there is, it's time, don't you think? They are expecting me, aren't they?"

Matthew looked at the clock on the wall and laughed. "Yes, in about ten minutes to be exact."

"Oh, God! Look at me. I've got to change clothes and —"

"Don't sweat it," Matthew said. "It's what's called being fashionably late."

• • •

Early Evening

Although the first hour had been punctuated by the arrival of Halloween trick-or-treaters, everything had gone well. Peyton, warmly accepted by his "little" sister and brother-in-law, appeared to be enjoying herself, but beneath it all, there was an undercurrent of something gone wrong. Matthew had noticed it from the time they arrived. Jackie's face, usually perky and upbeat, was drawn, her attention span about as long as his little finger.

The meal finished, their after-dinner coffee growing cold, Matthew found himself more and more concerned. He didn't like the direction the conversation was taking, and by the look on his brother-in-law's normally placid face, he knew damned well Tony felt the same way.

"I realize this is a family matter," Jackie said, her eyes

Death's Bright Angel

troubled as she reached across the narrow dinner table and touched Peyton's hand, "but the way Matt has talked about you the last several weeks, I feel as though you're already part of the family, or at least I hope so."

"My little sister thinks its time I tied the knot," Matthew said to Peyton. "She forgets it takes two to do the deed."

Tony Serafina finished his coffee, adding, "And even if she was family, I doubt if she or Matt want to get involved."

"You're leaving me, Tony, and all I get out of you is 'I don't know, I don't know.' " Jackie turned back to Peyton.

"Tony's a structural engineer. His company's sending him to Saudi Arabia for two years. He leaves tomorrow, tomorrow night to be exact, and the Saudi government won't let me accompany him. 'Too dangerous,' they say. If it's that dangerous, why go at all?"

"You know damn well, Jackie. If I want to get anywhere with Connelly Engineering, I've got to go. No choice, and besides, I get six weeks leave to come home at the end of the first year."

"Goddamn it, Tony, we're going to have a baby. Not just me. It's *we* who are having this baby. In seven months. If I can't go, I need you here. I can't handle it by myself. Tell him, Matt. For Christ's sake, talk sense into the man's head."

"You're asking the wrong guy, Sis," Matthew said, holding up both hands to form a protective barrier between his sister and himself. "It's been, what?.., over fifteen years since the breakdown? You're stronger now than you've ever been."

"It's not just that," Tony said, biting his lower lip. "It's the whole thing about having a baby. When I get back from Saudi Arabia, we're going to be on the move, constantly. From one construction job to another. Florida this month, California the next, Brazil after that. A kid would only be in the way."

For the first time, Peyton entered the conversation, her words spoken softly but to the point. "You don't want the baby, do you, Tony?"

Tony stared into his empty plate and shook his head.

"You need to be more explicit, Tony," Matthew said. "If you don't want any children, what do you want my sister to do? Put the baby up for adoption, or..." Matthew hesitated, then added, "get an abortion?"

"Yes," Tony hissed, jerking his head upward.

"Yes?" Jackie challenged, her voice rising with frustration, her face suddenly distorted by a mottled pattern of red and white blotches, something Matthew hadn't seen since before she underwent psychiatric treatment. "Yes, fucking *what*, Tony? Adoption or abortion? If you don't want the baby, what do you want?"

Tony pounded the table with his fist and jumped to his feet. "Abort the goddamn thing, Jackie," he shouted through clenched teeth. His chair crashed backward into the glass-front china cabinet. Shards of glass exploded across the floor.

"Shit!" Matthew cursed as Tony stalked from the room. Reaching out to Peyton, he mouthed, "I'm sorry." To Jackie, he said, "I'll talk to him, Sis. He's upset. He doesn't know what the hell he's..." She wasn't hearing a word he said. She was stunned. Tears rimmed her lower eyelids, but more than that, he'd experienced that same silence before. The withdrawal. *Oh, God, not again.*

As though reading his thoughts, Peyton nodded her understanding, then made her way around the table and knelt next to Jackie's chair. Placing a hand on Jackie's arm, she whispered, "Matt and I both will be here to help. In whatever way you want or need."

Matthew waited. When his sister made no reply, he said, "Sis, don't do this. You'll only hurt yourself and all the people that love you. Like Peyton says, we're here for you, but don't shut us out."

Very slowly, Jackie turned her head and stared into

Peyton's face. "Matt says you're a special person with special powers. The future. What do you see? Should I —"

"Nothing, Jackie. I can't see the future, and if I could, I wouldn't tell you. From the pictures on the wall in your living room, you're Catholic."

"Tony is. I joined when we were married."

"Have you talked with your priest?" Peyton asked.

"Father Jerome? Tony said it would be a waste of time, but I didn't know how strongly he felt until tonight."

"So far as I'm concerned," Matthew argued, "you're pregnant, you're healthy, you have the baby."

"But Tony —"

"If Tony loves you, Sis, he'll accept it. I can't force you to have the baby. I would if I could, but as you and I both know, it's your decision. And very honestly, it's one you'll have to live with for the rest of your life."

• • •

Chris Atwell looked at the card the man with the mustache had placed in her hand. "Seven-four-seven-C-A-R-E," she said to herself, still debating whether to dial the numbers or not. Had the demonstrators been right? Their voices still rang in her ears.

"Jesus loves your baby."

"Don't let your womb become a tomb."

"Don't kill your baby."

And to Chris, that's exactly what she had done. She had killed the life inside her. Had it sucked and scraped from her body. She had killed her baby, and even the antidepressant her doctor prescribed had done little to erase the thought from her mind.

"God forgive me," she prayed. Tears of self-recrimination spilled from her eyes, blurring the numbers on the telephone's keypad. She punched the seven, the four, a six. Wrong. She wiped her eyes with the sleeve of her sweater and started again. Seven, four, seven,...

Chris waited. One ring, then two. After the third ring, a click sounded against her ear and a recorded yet familiar voice answered, "Hello, Chris. I know how deeply you hurt. Just say, 'help me,' and I'll lift this burden from your shoulders."

Chris's heart swelled with grief as she whispered the words, "Help me."

CHAPTER 4
October 31, 1992
Saturday Night

Chris paced the apartment's living room floor, around the sofa and back to the window. It had been the longest seven days of her life. No matter how hard she tried, the trauma of giving up her baby, of giving up part of herself, had settled a guilt the size of Mount Vesuvius on her shoulders.

With the combination of Valium and several glasses of wine, she'd forgotten it was Halloween until the laughter and voices at the door had brought chorus after chorus of "Trick or treat!" Scavenging a box of chocolate chip cookies and a package of miniature Snickers stuck in the back of the freezer from she couldn't remember when, Chris weathered the storm.

It was the children, however, that brought more tears to her eyes. Their tiny bodies clothed in different costumes, some with monster faces, some with fairy wands and angel wings — each child alive, happy and loved by a mother who stood at the edge of the light spill, smiling, protective and proud. Could they... did they know that only a week earlier, she had...

The children were gone, the remaining cookies and candy scattered on the table next to the front door. For the thousandth time, or so it seemed, Chris stared through the window into the night. "Seven-four-seven-CARE, damn it," she cursed, looking for the man with the mustache, the man called Azrael, or some sign that God was about to lift the burden from her shoulders. "Where are you? I need you so much."

A soft knock at the door. Chris turned and, slightly dizzy from the wine and Valium, crossed the room, picked up several Snickers bars in gold-colored wrappers and opened the door.

"Oh," she said, startled at first, then relieved. "It's Halloween, and I thought it was one of the children. I didn't think..." The words escaped her.

The man with the mustache smiled. "May I come in?" His voice was deep and throaty, bordering on unpleasant, yet reassuring in its calm masculinity.

"Yes, yes, Mr. Azrael, please. I'm sorry." Chris held the door wide as the man passed close by, the fragrance of his after-shave lotion heavier than she would have expected, but if he could help, who cared?

"Do you have a tape player?" Azrael asked. He pulled a tape cassette from a leather case he carried. Not a briefcase exactly, but slightly larger and shaped similar to the case Chris had used for her clarinet during high school band days.

"Uh, yes." The thought of listening to a tape didn't seem the kind of thing that would lift her burden.

"Not what you think," Azrael quickly added as though reading Chris's thoughts. "Background music, only. To help us concentrate on what needs to be done. Here." He handed her the tape. "Put it in and let it play."

At first Chris couldn't find the tape deck opening, or were there two? Was she seeing double? Must be the Valium. Another try, and the cassette entered the tape deck as Azrael went to the window and closed the blinds. Chris watched the

Death's Bright Angel

man lift a silver cross from the velvet-lined case and place it on a low coffee table in front of the sofa. On either side of the cross, he positioned two small clay bowls, each holding the barest remnants of a candle.

"I'll light the candles," he said, "if you'll turn off the lights and join me in front of the cross."

The music began as a melodic hum, soothing and restful. Its melody sought out the corners of Chris's consciousness, already dimmed by the mixture of wine and tranquilizers. It filled each painful crevice, flowed like a gentle stream, washing and cleansing. Chris switched off the lights, leaving only the candle glow and the sudden smell of incense to guide her toward the cross. Two candles. Their light flickered and danced against the curtains, hypnotic beacons offering redemption from the tightening bondage of her sin.

"Already I feel like God is here, all around me," Chris whispered, each word a sigh of relief.

"Good," Azrael said. "Here, beside me, on your knees before the cross." Choir voices emerged from the hum of music. Their plea floated on the air like feathers of a bird, soft at first, each line slightly louder, more pronounced.

"In my hour of tri-al,
Je-sus plead for me,
Lest by base de-nial
I depart from Thee;..."

"I am your guide," Azrael said close to Chris's ear. "Take my hand, close your eyes, and we'll pray."

Chris knelt before the cross and closed her eyes. She felt Azrael's hand lift hers to the top of the table, a soft hand, yet large and filled with what she hoped to be the forgiveness of God.

"Almighty Power, Father of our Lord Jesus Christ, Maker of all things, Judge of all mankind, Chris acknowledges and bewails her manifold sins and wickedness, which she has committed by thought, word and deed, against the life in her body and against Thy Divine Majesty. She does earnestly repent and is sorry for her misdoings. The remembrance of them is grievous unto her; the burden is intolerable."

"Yes, God," Chris moaned, her breath, labored, almost painful. "My burden is intolerable. I feel such pain. Take it away, God. Please." And the pain was real. Azrael's hand tightened around her wrist. It hurt, but she was afraid to speak, to interrupt the prayer and the music. And the choir sang,

> *"When my last hour com-eth,*
> *fraught with strife and pain,*
> *When my dust re-turn-eth*
> *To the dust again;..."*

Azrael's voice lifted above the choir. "Have mercy upon her, have mercy upon her, Most Merciful God. Forgive her all that is past, and grant that she may ever serve and please Thee in that new life which You are about to give. To the honor and glory of Thy Holy Name. Through Jesus Christ our Lord, Thy son who loved the little children. Amen."

The pain coursed from Chris's wrist, up the muscles and tendons of her arm and into her shoulder. "Please," she begged, "you're hurting me."

" 'Tis the hand of God that hurts you, Chris. To lift that burden, God must punish before He loves. Keep your eyes closed, Chris. Keep them closed and pray."

Without warning, Azrael jerked her arm downward and pulled her to the floor as the five-inch, serrated knife blade plunged deep into her chest. At first, no pain. Only the force against her body, the scrape of metal against bone, and then the fire, a blowtorch inside her lungs. Chris screamed, but the choir sang louder.

> *"On Thy truth re-ly-ing,*
> *Through that mor-tal strife,*

Death's Bright Angel

Je-sus, take her, dying,
To e-ter-nal life."

"No-o—o-o," Chris wailed. A second blow, and another, each a red hot branding iron in her chest, each driving her deeper into the floor, the carpet like quicksand, tugging and drawing. Chris tried desperately to get away, to fight with her free hand, to kick, but the weight of the quicksand held her down, or was it the man called Azrael?

"You can't fight the hand of God," Azrael's voice cut through the pain. "Your child will be reborn in God's likeness. Rejoice Chris, rejoice."

Chris felt the blade cut deeper, gnawing at her ribs; its tip, eating the flesh in search of her soul. She tried to cry out, but a froth of air and blood flooded her mouth, only to be sucked back into her lungs as she fought for life. Her mind's voice cried out, "Why, God, why?"

From far away, she heard the choir's dirge-like song.

"A-sleep in Jesus! far from thee
Thy kin-dred and their graves may be;
But Thine will be a bless-ed sleep,
From which none ever wakes to weep."

Suddenly, the pain was gone, blown away by a swirling wind, but the candlelight? Chris had never seen candles so bright. Blinding! Their flames like a giant beacon, merged into one. She wanted to close her eyes, to shut out the glare. She tried, but she couldn't. Brighter and brighter, until...

• • •

The tape deck clicked silent as Azrael slipped on the black, heavy latex electrician's gloves and pulled back on the knife. He grunted as the blade came free from Chris's chest. "O God," Azrael offered, "I, your bright angel of death, will return your image to its rightful place."

Working in the candlelight, Azrael raised Chris's skirt and tugged at her urine-soaked underpants, pulling them down along her thighs, past her knees and finally over her feet. He then spread Chris's legs as wide apart as possible and, with expertise developed from practice, rammed the knife blade into the flesh just below the pubic arch and sliced downward through clitoris and urethra. The tip of the blade bit into the bladder, drawing out what urine was left and mixing it with the blood that spilled and soaked into the carpet.

Azrael's breath came heavy as muscle resistance in the vaginal canal forced him to push down harder, to move the knife in a sawing position. His fingers slipped from the knife's handle, but he continued, twisting and carving into the cervix and uterus, ignoring the odor of urine and blood, still hot from a once-living body. With a final grunt of redemptive anger, Azrael cut through the perineum into the rectum.

"There, Chris. Plenty of room."

Wiping the blood from his gloved hands on Chris's skirt, Azrael reached into the leather case and removed a package, unwrapped it and held up a fetal doll. "How beautiful you are," he whispered. "Your chalk-white skin, tiny feet, eyes closed, oh, so tight, a thumb between your lips, preparing you for Mommy's breasts."

He nodded to the gaping wound between Chris's legs and said, "Mommy's ready, little one. In you go." Spreading the opening as wide as possible, Azrael shoved the doll, feet first, into the mass of torn and bleeding flesh until only the head could be seen.

"How well you fit." Azrael stared at the doll head for a moment, then asked, "A lullaby? Why certainly, my lovely." Gathering his arms as though cradling a baby, Azrael rocked back and forth, gently crooning,

> *"Rock-a-bye baby, in Mommy's womb;*
> *Human in making, not for the tomb.*
> *If the knife scrapes, baby will fall,*
> *But Mommy will suffer, her sin cursed by all."*

CHAPTER 5
November 1, 1992
Sunday Morning

Lights flashed and cameras clicked as Lt. Rich Taylor, latex gloves stretched over his hands and light blue fibrous booties covering his shoes, edged his way into the apartment just far enough to see the body — skirt pulled above its waist, thighs spread, knees bent to form awkward triangles with the floor, hands already bagged. A doll's head protruded from what was left of the vulva and anal region.

"Jesus fucking Christ!" Taylor groaned, at the same time pulling a handkerchief from his pocket and holding it to his nose. The odor of drying blood hung like a suffocating vapor in the air, something Taylor had never gotten used to. "When?" he asked.

Dr. Fay Lundgren, the Duval County Medical Examiner, who Taylor long ago had decided was the perfect model of spinsterhood, a woman who considered her profession far more exciting than any man she would ever meet, looked up from the body. "Sometime last night. Rigidity, which is really not a very accurate indicator, body temp and advanced lividity indicate between eight and ten p.m., maybe eleven."

Taylor eased his massive bulk past the uniformed officer

at the door. "Got a name?" he asked, his question directed to the investigation team's leader, standing behind Fay Lundgren.

Sgt. Polly Bartelow, mid-thirties, pleasantly attractive despite the necessity of bifocals and the sweep of dark hair screwed into a tight little knot at the back of her head, resembled more a woman on her way up the corporate ladder than a police detective. Taylor often wondered why, with the list of social science and business degrees on her résumé, she had chosen law enforcement as a profession.

"Atwell," Bartelow answered. "Chris Atwell."

"Who found her and when?"

"Neighbor woman. This morning. Around 6:30. They usually go jogging together. Front door was unlocked. She stuck her head in, and that's what she found."

"In the words of *Dirty Harry* Callahan, the world's greatest detective, bet that made her day," Taylor said, lifting his eyebrows in disgust. "Anybody hear or see anything last night?"

"The team's knocking on doors," Bartelow responded. "Already have some people say they heard what sounded like church music coming from the apartment, but that's all."

Taylor grunted, then soft-stepped his way past the sofa and around the coffee table, at the same time nodding to Burgess, one of two crime scene technicians photographing anything and everything that didn't move. He was careful to avoid the wide spread of blackish crimson soaked into the carpet. "What about the hands?"

"Defense wounds on the left hand," Lundgren answered, "and a badly bruised right wrist, but no fingerprints on the skin. We'll do fingernail scrapings back at the office."

Taylor studied the body. "Posed like she was..."

"Giving birth." Bartelow supplied, finishing Taylor's thought.

"Whoever did it even supplied the baby," Lundgren added.

"Full term or fetus?" Taylor remembered the fetal doll found with the skeleton at Fort Caroline.

"Let's see." Fay Lundgren grasped the doll head with one gloved hand and pulled, but the surrounding flesh refused to yield. "Damn," Lundgren muttered. "Burgess," she called, "give me a hand."

Burgess stooped next to the body and pushed down on the lower abdomen as the medical examiner pulled. With a sucking sound and the rush of built-up gas and momentary flow of molasses-thick blood collected in the uterine cavity, the doll came free. The room suddenly filled with the fecal stench of body flatulence.

"Goddamn!" Taylor coughed as he swung away from the body and rushed to the window, the handkerchief pressed even tighter against his nose and mouth.

"Fetus," Lundgren said with some surprise. Over her shoulder, she asked Taylor, "You knew, didn't you?"

Without looking, Taylor continued, "Twenty-fourth or twenty-fifth week, with a thumb in its mouth?"

"Bingo, but how—"

"The doll with the skeleton at Fort Caroline." Taylor turned from the window. "You didn't see the report?"

"Just got back from California last night. Here." Lundgren handed the doll to Burgess, the technician. "Wrap it in paper, box it and make sure it gets to the lab. I want to... Hello, what's this?"

"What?" Bartelow asked.

Lundgren leaned closer to the open wound between Chris Atwell's legs. "I'll be damned."

"You'll be damned, what?" Taylor insisted.

"Look."

Taylor closed his eyes. "Just tell me."

Fay Lundgren moved a rubber-gloved finger along the apex of the opening, immediately below the pubic arch, then pushed inward. "It's gone. The glans clitoridis. The clitoris. It's been cut out, but they did a lousy job."

"Why the hell would they do that?"

"Assuming it was a man, I'd say he wanted a souvenir, and if not the breast,... It's what you men call the clit or clitty. What you think turns us on. Composed of erectile tissue like a miniature penis."

"A fucking souvenir, and I bet he's got at least two by now. One from her," he nodded toward Chris's corpse, "and one from Fort Caroline. Probably gets his rocks off playing with a piece of the woman he just hacked to death."

Bartelow shaped her fingers like the viewfinder of a camera and focused on Chris's body. "And he poses her, like he's telling us, 'I can do whatever the hell I want, and you can't stop me.' "

Burgess, the technician, speculated, "Looks like that guy at the fort mighta been right."

"That's all I can do here," Fay Lundgren said, standing and stripping the rubber gloves from her hands. "What guy?"

"Hey, Hal," Burgess called to the other technician. "Tell the M.E.'s people the body's ready for takeout."

"He's right," Taylor said, responding to Lundgren's question, his face screwed out of shape by the thoughtful scraping of his upper incisors back and forth across his lower lip and the memory of Fort Caroline.

Lundgren chuckled. "When was Burgess ever right?"

Taylor clamped his hand tight on Burgess's shoulder. "This time, he is. A guy named Berkeley, part of the archaeology team at Fort Caroline. When he looked at the scars and scratches on the skeleton we found, he described almost the same thing we got here, and that doll. A goddamn twin. If I didn't..."

Death's Bright Angel

The lieutenant stopped in midsentence and pulled out his wallet. "Where the hell did I put that thing?" He dug through the wad of papers in the back of the wallet until, "Here it is." He extracted a soiled business card and handed it to Polly Bartelow.

"Matthew Berkeley. This is his card. Temporary Jacksonville address and phone number on the back. Get him. I want him in my office at two this afternoon. And you," Taylor directed at Burgess, "tell your buddy with the camera I want prints of the body. ASAP! Closeups, Technicolor and fucking 3-D if he can do it. I want to see Berkeley's reaction when I show him what we got here. I'm betting he knows more than he's saying."

• • •

Sunday Afternoon

Matthew paused in front of the door marked, *DETECTIVE DIVISION —HOMICIDE*, turned the handle and pushed inward. He stopped, amazed at what he saw.

The room was filled with more than a dozen desks and worktables, each desk supplied with a computer monitor and keypad, along with a pile of files and assorted papers that made the local paper recycling plant look neat. In one corner stood a table with an automatic coffee maker, the contents in the accompanying carafe as black and as uninviting as the bottom of Matthew's shoes. Immediately adjacent was a water cooler, its upside-down, five-gallon glass jug empty and leaning at a Tower-of-Pisa angle that defied gravity.

It was the men and women at various desks, some staring vacantly at computer monitor screens, others scribbling on note pads as they listened over telephones cupped between shoulder and ear, that drew him up short. At a glance they looked like average people doing an average job, but closer inspection showed faces haggard and old sooner than their time, lined with the scenes of man's daily inhumanity to his fellow human beings. Unable to imagine that kind of existence, Matthew mouthed to himself, "No thanks."

Rich Taylor stood by one of the monitors while Polly Bartelow clickety-clicked the keypad at the front of the computer until Taylor asked, "That's it?"

"Yes, sir. The only other source would be Justice Department's 'Z' file, and we don't have clearance."

"I would of thought there'd be more than this. This guy might not be a surgeon, but he's had practice. I know damn good and well, somewhere, —"

"Lieutenant Taylor?"

Taylor's head swiveled toward the door. "About time. I said two o'clock. It's two-thirty."

Matthew chuckled sourly as he closed the door behind him. "Guess we oughta synchronize our watches, but I gotta tell you, your timing isn't worth a damn. You already screwed me out of the Florida/Georgia game. This time, a lady friend and I had Sunday afternoon plans that sure as hell didn't include a visit with you at the local lockup."

"Gee whiz, Mr. Berkeley," Taylor said in his best Amos and Andy dialect. "Ah's sho nuff sorry to bother you agin about sumpin' as unimpawtant as a lil' ol' murder, but if you'd git yo ass into that office ovah dere,..."

Matthew heard a smattering of chuckles and snickers behind his back.

Taylor continued, this time in his normal drill instructor gruffness. "... and I'll tell you why you're spending Sunday afternoon at the local lockup, as you call it." To Bartelow, he said, "Keep trying, Polly, and keep pinging on the Intelligence Unit. Let me know if you find anything."

Matthew's head shook in resignation as he followed Taylor past a door marked *UNIT COMMANDER* and into a corner room that was much smaller, but totally different from the outer office — an aging mahogany desk, graced with a gold-framed photograph of a woman and two teenage girls; a single, death-gray file folder in an IN box, and a Cartier pen and pencil set, polished as though varnish had just been applied. The bookshelves behind the desk were neatly lined with criminal law books and bound copies of the Florida statutes. Several framed police academy graduation diplomas and award certificates for meritorious service spoke volumes about the man who made the office his home. Even the two leather-bound chairs facing the desk actually looked clean, comfortable and inviting. Matthew was impressed.

"Not bad for a po lil' ol' black boy from Ocala, Florida," Taylor said, reverting to accent. "That's what you're thinking, isn't it, Berkeley?"

"What I'm thinking is, why me? The dig is finished at Fort Caroline, and I had nothing to do with the skeleton. And let's get something else straight. I don't play the 'po lil' black boy from Ocala' game. In fact, I don't give a damn what color you are or who you are, but you've apparently got a thing about me, so let's get it out in the open."

"You read the papers?" Taylor asked.

"If you mean the skeleton, yes. Identified from dental records. Justine Crowley, age thirty-one, separated from her husband, lived in one of the ritzy houses on the other side of the park boundary. Disappeared in early July, and you think I coaxed her into the park, killed her and buried her at the dig site. *My* dig site, no less. C'mon, Lieutenant, even if I'd killed her, I'm not that dumb."

Rich Taylor picked up the file from the *IN* box and shoved it across the desk in Matthew's direction. "Take a look."

"Why?"

" 'Cause I fucking said so, goddamn it!"

"You need to clean up your language, Lieutenant,"

Matthew shot back, at the same time flipping open the file. "Holy shit!" He jerked his hand back as if the file was bathed in acid. The pale, waxy consistency of Chris Atwell's face jumped at him from the photograph.

Taylor laughed. "Seems like I'm not the only one with a language deficiency. Go on. Look at 'em. Every one of 'em. Up close. Here." Taylor pulled a magnifying glass from a drawer and slid it across the desk. "What do you see?"

Matthew studied one photograph, then another, each more lurid, more graphic than the one before. Halfway through the stack, he stopped. "That's enough."

Taylor thrummed the desk with his fingers. "I asked, what do you see?"

Matthew stepped back and sank into one of the leather-bound chairs. "Other than the work of a pathological killer, what am I supposed to see?"

"The goddamn Fort Caroline skeleton, only this one's got flesh on it," Taylor snapped. "Two different women, but when you saw that skeleton, you described, to a T, exactly what happened to the woman in those pictures there. I think you know something you're not telling me."

Matthew sat forward in his chair. "And you're full of it, Lieutenant. In terms of a forensic examination, what I gave you was an archaeologist's opinion of what I thought happened to the skeleton, that's all. You're trying to make it more than it was." Matthew got to his feet. "Forget it." Pointing at the photographs of Chris Atwell, he added, "I never saw that woman before in my life. I never —"

"And what about this, Berkeley?" Taylor reached into the same drawer from which he'd taken the magnifying glass and brought out a cardboard box, lifted the lid and tilted it for Matthew to see.

"The doll we found with the skeleton."

"Uh, uh," Taylor grunted. He placed the box on the

desktop and quickly shifted through the photographs until he found one of the doll's head protruding from Chris Atwell's body. "That's where this one came from. What've you got to say about that?"

Before Matthew could answer, Polly Bartelow pushed open the door and barged in. "Lieutenant, I think we got something."

Taylor's eyes lit up. "The 'Z' file?"

"No, but at this point, something just as interesting. In addition to the fetus dolls, looks like we've got a possible link between the Fort Caroline case and Chris Atwell. Looks like..." Bartelow stopped, her eyes slanted suspiciously in Matthew's direction.

"Don't worry about me, Sergeant," Matthew said, a dark chuckle edging out from beneath his words. "I'm practically one of the team. Right, Lieutenant?"

Taylor rolled his eyes and spread his hands in a why-the-hell-not gesture. "Go on, Polly."

"The doll thing is so obvious, on a hunch, I decided to check with the State Department of Health and Rehabilitative Services in Tallahassee."

"So?" Taylor urged, leaning forward over his desk.

"We'll need a court order to get the full reports, but from what I did find out, I think I can say with some assurance that both women had an abortion within a week of their respective deaths."

William Kerr

CHAPTER 6
November 2, 1992
Monday Afternoon

A stroll through the largely African-American neighborhood north of Jacksonville's downtown business district would reveal a number of fine old homes, recently renovated and freshly painted, a stained glass window or two, with small, but neatly kept lawns. Not far down the block, however, you'd inevitably find a house, abandoned, its windows boarded over, roof sagging, paint chips on tongue-and-groove siding begging to be scraped away, yard filled with garbage and weeds. Nine times out of ten, burned-out marijuana roaches, dirty bloodstained syringes, small see-through plastic envelopes and empty wine and beer bottles would litter the narrow front porch and steps.

With the fallback from Daylight Savings to Standard Time, light was already fading when Lavonna Mayes stepped off the JTA bus and started north along Holland Street. She had no idea how many times she'd walked this street since her father had gone to prison for selling drugs and she, her mother and little brother, Kenza, were evicted from the city housing project. That was five years ago when she was only thirteen. The tempo of her pace quickened as she passed the deserted house.

Death's Bright Angel

"Hey, baby," a voice called from a window where the plywood covering had been smashed and torn away. "I got the best shit in town, an' I love yo ass. Gimme some a yours, and I'll give you some a mine."

Refusing to acknowledge the voice, Lavonna kept her eyes straight ahead and hurried across the street and up the steps of a small, clapboard house. The front door was ajar. Pushing inward, she entered the tiny living room, slammed the door behind her and called, "Momma, you home?"

"Your momma's not here," a man's voice answered.

"Damn!" Lavonna cursed under her breath, switching on lights as she moved through the living room and down the hall to the back bedroom. "What're you doin' here, Darrel? I thought you were on the late shift."

Darrel swung his feet over the side of the bed as Lavonna entered the room. "Budweiser fired me. Dumb-ass so'bitches!"

"What for? You've only been there two months."

Darrel shrugged his shoulders. "This 'n that. Fuckin' white guy."

"You didn't..." She studied his face and she knew. "You did, didn't you?" Lavonna let out a sigh and slumped into a chair that looked as tired as she felt.

Darrel raised his arms and stretched, watching the dresser mirror and smiling at the ripple of muscles across his chest and stomach. Lavonna watched also, but for once, she wasn't impressed. "D'you hear me, Darrel?"

"Coupla joints during break. Muthafucka had me searched an'..." Darrel hesitated.

"And what?"

"Two rocks. What the hell."

"You took crack to work?" Lavonna jumped to her feet and ran to the kitchen, cursing, "Goddamn, you, Darrel Jones! Just goddamn you! You promised."

William Kerr

Lavonna stood over the sink, her body shaking as tears ran down her cheeks. "Everything happenin' in one day. I can't take it. Where's Momma?"

"Fuck your momma," Darrel said from the doorway. "Whaddaya mean everything in one day?"

Lavonna turned toward the man she loved and wanted someday to marry. Wiping the tears from her face, she said, "I'm pregnant, Darrel. I got off work early this afternoon and went to see the doctor at the women's clinic over on Beach Boulevard. I missed my period and I'm pregnant."

Darrel stood in the doorway, thoughtful for a moment before his lips spread in a wide grin. "That's great, baby. That's —"

"Great?" Lavonna cried. "You think it's great when you just got fired? You think it's great after I finally got a job of my own to help support Momma, to save up something for us, to maybe get us outta this shit hole of a neighborhood?" Lavonna jabbed a finger toward the street. "The crackheads, and the pimps and whores out there every night. My little brother, Kenza, shot dead last summer 'cause a drug deal went bad at the corner, and all he wanted was a Popsicle from the ice cream man. You think —"

"Shut up!" Darrel lunged forward and grabbed Lavonna by the wrist. "Dumb-ass bitch. Sit down and shut up!"

"No I won't," she shot back.

"Yes, goddamn it, you will."

The power of his arms propelled her back against the sink, but it was the sudden blur of his hand and the impact against her face that sent her reeling. The kitchen table, a chair, the corner cabinet — their edges grabbed and tore at her ribs and breasts as she fell.

"Keep your mouth shut an' don't fuckin' get up 'til I tell you," Darrel ordered, his eyes on fire, the words exploding from his mouth like scattered shrapnel.

Death's Bright Angel

Lavonna wiped the blood from her lips. She knew if she did try to get up, Darrel would do it all over again, only worse.

"That's my baby, you carryin'," Darrel shouted, "an' don't forget it. Darrel Jones's baby. What you think the brothers'd say if you got an abortion an' got rida my baby? They'd say Darrel's not a man, or she wouldn't'a got rida his baby. That's what they'd say."

Tears from both emotional and physical pain rolled from Lavonna's eyes. "That's all you're worried about, isn't it? Your manhood. The baby's nothing more than a symbol of what a big man you are."

"Fuckin' bitch!" Darrel spun on his heel, but stopped as he got to the door, turned and pointed a finger in Lavonna's direction. "You kill my baby, I'll make you wish you were dead. Y'hear me? Fuckin' dead!"

As Darrel disappeared down the hallway toward the front of the house, Lavonna called, "Where're you goin', Darrel?"

"Got a new job," he yelled from the hallway.

Lavonna pushed herself from the floor and stumbled to the kitchen door. "Doin' what?"

"Whaddaya think? I need money, an' there ain't no other way."

• • •

Monday Night

"You next."

" 'Bout damn time," Darrel said as the three men watched through the holes they'd bored in the plywood window cover. He looked back at the room. The glow of a single kerosene lantern provided the only light, the remainder of the creaky old house dark and full of human waste left by the homeless.

"Man, this place smells like shit," he had said when he first walked in.

"Yeah, but shit happens," the older dealer had said, "so get used to it."

Darrel heard the sound of tires rub against the curb outside.

"Your turn, Darrel," one of the men said again.

"I'm gone."

Darrel eased through an open window on the side of the house and made his way in the dark, feeling the tongue-and-groove wall boards as he went. He stopped at the front corner of the house. "Shit! White guys."

The rust-on-rust Chevy pickup with a camper cover over the rear bed sat next to the curb, its motor idling. From what Darrel could see, there were two men seated in the front, the lights from the dash picking up the whiteness of their skin. Behind him, he heard a voice at the window, "Whatsa matter, Darrel? You punkin' out or sumpin'? Get out there 'fore they leave."

"Yeah, yeah," he hissed back. Checking one more time for the plastic crack vial in his pocket, Darrel moved to the sidewalk and the driver's side of the pickup.

"Took your own sweet time," the driver growled.

Darrel identified the accent — good-ol'-boy white trash — and knew there'd be trouble if he didn't make the sale as quick as he could.

Darrel couldn't see the passenger that well, but from what he could tell, the driver was a big man, filling up half the front seat. His beard covered what Darrel figured was the ugliest white man's face he'd seen in a long, long time.

The driver kept on. "When that five-gallon bucket on the front porch is turned upside down, that says you're open for business, an' I 'spect you to be out here soon as I drive up. ¿Comprende, amigo?"

"Hey, man, I'm new at this shit," Darrel tried to explain. "Next time, I'll recognize you. Okay? I got four rocks. How much you want? I can get more."

"Four's enough. Here." The driver handed Darrel a wad of bills. "This is takin' too goddamn long. Gimme the stuff." The man grabbed the plastic vial from Darrel's hand, put the engine in gear and pulled away from the curb.

"Hey, wait a minute," Darrel shouted, jogging to keep up with the vehicle. "You gave me forty. That's four rocks for eighty."

"Fuck off, nigger," the driver yelled back. "That's all you gonna get."

Darrel broke into a run, trying to catch the pickup before it turned the corner. "You white-ass so'bitch! I want my money." He stopped, out of breath, but still shouting. "I got your license tag, mothafucka, an' I'm gonna find you."

Darrel watched the pickup brake to a halt, then lurch into reverse, its tires spinning as it bore down on him. He jumped to the sidewalk, barely getting out of the way of the pickup's left rear fender. The pickup stopped.

"You gonna do what?" the driver demanded.

"All I want's my money, man," Darrel panted, trying to get his breath.

"No fuckin' burrhead's gonna threaten me."

Darrel saw the barrel of the pistol poke up over the edge of the window, heard two sharp blasts, and felt the impact, like sledgehammers against his chest and gut. He stumbled and groped the air for support, but there was none. His knees, suddenly jelly, buckled, and he crashed to the sidewalk, face down as the pickup's tires squealed against the pavement only inches from his head.

"Gotta,... gotta..." Darrel's body refused to respond. He couldn't believe it. Not Darrel Jones. Gonna to be a father. His first baby. He's a man. Already told the brothers.

Darrel's entire chest and abdominal region were suddenly on fire. His breath came in gasps as unconditioned reflex forced his one remaining lung to work overtime, trying to increase oxygen to the already reduced volume of blood in his body. His heart pounded, faster and harder, in an attempt to replenish blood lost from a hemorrhaging liver and a collapsed lung, but it couldn't keep up. Like a flood of mind-numbing opiates, endorphins washed over his brain, and all at once, the pain that ravaged his body disappeared.

"Lavonna," Darrel whispered, the sound more a cough than a name. "It's my baby.... Don't... don't..." The words, washed with the blood from Darrel's chest, spilled into the gutter as the night closed in and sucked him deep into its belly.

Death's Bright Angel

CHAPTER 7
November 3, 1992
National Election Day
Tuesday Afternoon

What the hell is wrong with this guy? Rich Taylor asked himself as he stared across the desk at Chief of Detectives James Michael O'Riley. "Goddamn it, Chief, we're not communicating, are we?"

"Sure we are, Lieutenant. The skeleton at Fort Caroline, whatever her name, —"

"Justine Crowley," Taylor reminded the Chief.

"All right, Justine Crowley and this second one, the Atwell woman. Both had abortions at the Jacksonville Women's Clinic for Family Planning, but they were what? Three months apart? If abortion's a factor, what about all the other women in between? Sixty-eight abortions, you said, performed at that same clinic, including these two, in a three-month period. Why haven't any of the others been killed?"

O'Riley frowned and shook his head, the heavy jowls beneath his jaw waddling from side to side, giving a Porky Pig look to the man's fleshy, pockmarked face. "Hard to believe. Sixty-eight abortions. Babies snuffed out like so much..." O'Riley looked over the top of his trifocals. "What do you think about abortion, Lieutenant?"

Rich Taylor had been waiting for this. He was well aware of O'Riley's strong — no, adamant — antiabortion feelings as well as those of most of the Department's hierarchy. If their attitude toward abortion clinics was any indication, he wondered how much support he would get if abortion really was a significant factor in the case.

"To tell the truth, Chief, I don't give it a helluva lot of thought. I've got too many live people being murdered to worry about something *Roe versus Wade* made legal."

"What if the Supreme Court made a mistake. What if —"

"Chief," Taylor said, cutting O'Riley off. "I've got two women murdered. That's what I'm thinking about. Both had abortions at the same place; both murdered and butchered the same way, or so the M.E.'s office thinks; and both with fetus dolls stuck up their —"

"Interesting," O'Riley interrupted, "but as yet, all you've got is speculation. A theory. No solid evidence. No knife, no known sexual penetration, no fibers or pubic hairs, no fingerprints, no blood other than the victims'. Face it, Lieutenant, abortion may or may not be the link, but we need evidence. Certainly more than you've got."

Taylor studied a line of pictures mounted on the wall above and behind O'Riley's head. Seven kids, stair-stepped in age, elementary school to college. *Sure as hell no abortions in that family*, Taylor mused before replying, "That's what I'm looking for, Chief. Evidence, and I need your help. Other than the Atwell woman's neighbor hearing religious music coming from the apartment that night and some candle wax on the coffee table, I'm hurting."

"Then how can I help?" O'Riley asked, his voice filled with growing impatience. "Besides getting out and doing the job for you, that is."

"We've checked the FBI's Violent Criminal

Death's Bright Angel

Apprehension System for unsolved murders with a similar M.O., but we've drawn a blank."

"Nothing in VI-CAP, huh? You check the state's system?"

Taylor nodded. "Same thing. Zilch."

"So what are you asking me to do?"

"Justice Department's 'Z' file on solved and unsolved serial killings. From what I'm told, it makes VI-CAP look like recess time at kindergarten. The baddest of the bad. Even Son of Sam and Ted Bundy weren't screwed up enough to make that list. I need to see if there's anything in the 'Z' file that's similar to what I think we've got here."

O'Riley thought for a moment, then, "All right, Lieutenant. No promises, but for you, I'll try."

"That's all I can ask," Taylor said, at the same time pulling his six-foot-two-inch frame from the chair and moving to the door. "I got a coupla hunches," he said over his shoulder as he reached for the doorknob. "I'll let you know soon as I get something concrete."

"What about the killing on Holland Street last night?"

"Two-bit drug pusher and a deal gone bad," Taylor explained. "I assigned that to Wilson."

"And Rich,..." O'Riley said, pausing as though searching for the right words.

"Sir?" Taylor answered, one eyebrow cocked at the sound of *Rich*. When had O'Riley ever used his given name? Somehow, it didn't ring true coming from O'Riley, but he brushed it aside. If the Chief could get him into the "Z" file, he could call him Rich or boy or anything else for that matter.

O'Riley leaned back in his chair, folded his arms over his chest, and continued, "I want you to keep your theory about abortion to yourself. It's a hot topic without prematurely tying it to the deaths of these two women. Understand?"

Laughing under his breath, Rich Taylor opened the door

and hesitated long enough to say, "You got it, Chief. Wouldn't want to alert the abortion clinics about a potential problem, would we?"

• • •

"Who the hell is this?" the voice boomed from the telephone speaker.

"James Michael O'Riley, Jacksonville, Florida, Sheriff's Department. Chief of Detectives, damn it!"

"Jimmy boy, why didn't you say? It's me. Larry Bailey. Long time, no see. When was it? FBI course at Quantico? 1989?"

"Roughest school I ever been to," O'Riley grumbled. "How's the family?"

"Two kids in college and a wife that likes to shop till she drops, but what's this about the 'Z' file?" Bailey asked.

"You get my message?"

"Yeah, but what you described and what you're asking for is *verboten*. No way Justice and the administration are going to admit this kind of thing's been happening. Might be interpreted like some kind of conspiracy within the pro-life movement, and politically, that's unacceptable to the President. In fact, there's talk if the Democrats and their abortion-loving candidate win the election today, the President's going to order Justice to erase that part of the 'Z' file."

"No shit!" O'Riley responded, a satisfied chuckle in his voice. The smile on his lips widened as he swiveled around in his chair and counted the seven loving faces on the wall behind his desk. "Guess I'd better go vote if I want to keep a pro-life president in office, hadn't I?"

Larry Bailey laughed. "Like all good citizens, but the best thing you can do is forget we had this conversation, or we might both get a visit from the wrong people. See no evil, hear no evil, speak no evil. Get my drift?"

Death's Bright Angel

CHAPTER 8
November 4, 1992
Wednesday Night

Anna turned off the *Tonight Show*, then moved softly on slippered feet from one lamp to another, gradually transforming bright to dim to darkness with each flick of a switch. Rich Taylor still admired the way his wife walked, the way she looked, her body still young and firm, her face lovelier than the day they met. All that, even after two daughters, both now in their teens, and a lifetime of sleepless nights and worry over the safety of her husband.

"Coming?" he heard her ask from the doorway.

"Yeah, but I can't see in the dark. You'll have to lead me."

"What's the matter, old man?" Anna teased. "It's been so long since you've been home at night, you forget the way?"

Taylor laughed. "Depends on what's at the end of the road. With Tisha and Devada at that slumber party, I was thinking..."

It was Anna's turn to laugh as she moved along the hallway toward the downstairs bedroom. To Rich Taylor, the sound of her laughter had always been a delicious invitation and always would be. "If you can follow my voice," she said with a lilt, "I think you know what's at the end of the road, and it's all yours."

"Just keep talking, baby," Taylor called out, feeling his way around chairs and tables toward the doorway. "You better believe —"

The irritating chirp, chirp, chirp of the pager on his belt cut through the darkened room like a fingernail on a classroom chalk board. "Aw, no," Taylor groaned, not believing what was happening. He wanted to ignore the damned thing. Wanted to go to the end of the road with his beautiful Anna, not hear about some wife cutting her old man's throat, or some husband shooting his wife's boyfriend.

The hall light switched on. "You might as well get it," Anna said, "or it'll beep all night."

"Damn," he cursed as he hit the pager's selector bar and shut off the incessant squawk. "We gotta get another life, Anna. Just you and me and no goddamn beeper phones and pagers."

Grabbing the telephone from the hall table, Rich Taylor punched out the numbers shown on the pager's digital display, numbers already indelibly printed on his memory, and shouted, "This is Lieutenant Taylor. Just one goddamn night I'd like to stay home like a normal human being. What is it this time?"

He listened, then, "Not again."

Taylor's head drooped as the distant voice said the words he didn't want to hear, described the scene he didn't want to see. He closed his eyes against the mental picture already forming, but the voice at the other end of the line refused to let him shut it out.

"Right," he finally said. "Address?" Using the pad and pencil always on the hall table, always waiting for a rapidly scribbled name, time, or location, he wrote down the street and house numbers. "I'll be damn. I never would've figured...

Death's Bright Angel

Yeah, I'm on my way, and one more thing. I wanna know where that guy Berkeley was tonight, all night. Every hour, every minute."

Taylor put the phone down and looked thoughtfully at his wife as she waited in the bedroom doorway. "Never would've figured," he repeated, slowly shaking his head.

"Figured what?"

"The address. A signal five on the North Side. Holland Street. Across from where we had a drug dealer shot Monday night. Probably no connection. This one's an eighteen-year-old girl named Lavonna Mayes and another goddamn fetus doll."

"Holland Street." Memory wrinkles creased Anna's forehead. "I know where that is. She black?"

"Yeah. Cut up like the others, but it does tell us one thing we didn't know."

"What's that?"

"No matter what else he is, this proves we've at least got ourselves an equal opportunity killer."

• • •

The light magnolia scent of Peyton's hair, the heated softness of her skin and the way her buttocks and thighs fit so perfectly into the curve of his body would normally have excited Matthew all over again, but tonight...

"You're here, but then you're not," Peyton murmured, turning her head slightly in Matthew's direction. "Physically, yes, but mentally, you're a thousand miles away."

Matthew rubbed Peyton's cheek with the crook of his fingers and snuggled even closer. "I'm sorry, and if you must know, it's not a thousand. More like ten."

"The skeleton?"

"Yes, and a second murder a couple of nights ago that looks like a rerun of the first. Worse for me is the fact that the Sheriff's people think I was involved, but,..." Matthew laughed softly, "You're a psychic. You probably know more about it than I do."

Peyton shifted her position until she faced Matthew, at the same time pulling a blanket up around both of them. "Whatever gift I have, I never use it to impose on someone else's thoughts or life."

"What if I asked you to do a little *imposing* for me?"

Peyton pushed herself to one elbow and rested her head in the palm of her hand. "What do you mean?"

"Psychometry, or whatever you call it. You've told me you can sometimes see things that happened in the past by touching something, an object belonging to somebody, or seeing a location where that person has been."

"Sometimes."

"Would you be willing to try it for me?"

"Depends on what you want."

Matthew threw back the blanket and swung his legs to the floor. "Let's get dressed."

"Now?" Peyton asked, surprised by the immediacy in Matthew's voice and movements. "It's almost midnight."

"I know, but if you think you can help, there's no way I'm going to get any sleep until you try."

"Have you got something that belonged to one or both of the women?"

"Not exactly, but if you can use what I do have, it might tell us something about one of the murders and get Lieutenant Taylor off my backside."

• • •

Holding the robe close about her body, Peyton snapped on the light over the oven, then padded in bare feet across the kitchen and pressed Mr. Coffee into service slightly less than seven hours earlier than usual. The almost instant staccato pop and gurgle of water heating and the pungent aroma of liquid coffee squeezed through a paper filter filled the room as

Death's Bright Angel

Matthew entered with a large brown envelope and dropped into a chair at the tiny dinette table.

"Okay, Captain Mysterious, what exactly is it you have and what do you want me to do?" Peyton asked, watching as the drip, drip, drip of coffee into the glass carafe turned to a steady flow.

"This. Took it when I was at Lieutenant Taylor's office Sunday afternoon. Not sure why. Impulse, I guess." Matthew opened the envelope, pulled out an eight-by-ten color print of Chris Atwell's face and upper torso and laid it on the table. "Probably be hell to pay when he finds it missing."

Peyton walked to the table and picked up the photograph. "I'm not... my God, Matt!"

"You oughta see some of the others if you think that's bad."

Peyton's lips drew tight across her teeth, her lower lip drawn downward to allow the swift inhalation of air through her mouth, an action that coincided with the final, high-pitched *shheeoowwww* from Mr. Coffee's inner workings. "I'll try, but..."

"Coffee first?" Matthew asked.

"No." Peyton shook her head, the fingertips of her right hand already touching Chris Atwell's face. They lingered, then, like reading the raised dots on a page of Braille, moved slowly over what would have been the curvature of Chris's cheek bones, lips, and nose, finally settling on the eyes, still open, pupils glazed in death. "The eyes. They're..."

"You want to sit?" Matthew asked.

"No," Peyton said, closing her own eyes. "I want to see what she saw. Hear what she heard. Feel..."

Matthew's eyebrows furrowed as he watched Peyton's face. It was as if she suddenly slipped away to another time and place. "You see something, don't you?"

Peyton nodded. "A building. Brick. Two stories. A sign

near the door."

"What does it say?" Matthew asked softly, not knowing whether he should be asking Peyton or Chris Atwell.

"I... Jacksonville Women's... That's all I see. A crowd, taunting. They're angry. He knows my name and he wants to help. He —"

"Who wants to help?"

"A man with a mustache. Tall, dark hair, hypnotic eyes. He speaks his name, but I can't hear. So much shouting. Children singing. Hands leading. Into the building."

Tears seeped from between Peyton's closed eyelids as she lowered her head and raised Chris Atwell's photograph close to her face.

Matthew waited for a moment, not wanting to interrupt until Peyton lowered the photograph and once again touched Chris Atwell's eyes. "What happened in the building?"

"I... I didn't want it to happen. Want to forget. Halloween masks and children —"

"In the building?" Matthew cut in.

"No. Home. The man with the mustache, two candles, a cross. So hazy. Music. Hymns about death. Lift my burden, but the pain." Suddenly, Peyton clutched at her left breast and cried, "The knife, you're hurting me, no—o-o!"

Matthew lunged from his chair, slapped the photograph from Peyton's hand and wrapped her in his arms. "That's enough, Peyton. It's not your pain. It was hers. Sit down. I'll get you some coffee." Matthew lowered Peyton onto one of the dinette chairs as she wiped her eyes with the sleeve of her robe.

"Only a sip," Peyton said, her breath in short, rapid gasps. "There's still more to do."

Matthew looked at the oven clock. "What do you mean? It's almost one in the morning, and you're beat. In fact, I've never seen you so washed out."

"I'll be all right," she said, still catching her breath while accepting the cup from Matthew. "The skeleton at Fort Caroline. If we go there, I'm not certain, but I might see or feel something that would connect to the woman in the photograph." Peyton nodded to the crumpled picture of Chris Atwell, lying on the floor.

"You're sure?"

"I'm sure I want to go. As for whether I'll be able to experience anything, we'll have to wait and see, but we've got to go."

• • •

Matthew eased the Jeep Cherokee along the dirt road, tree limbs above and to the side forming a tunnel of evergreens and autumn golds in the glare of the vehicle's high beam lights. "Park super's gonna have a fit when he gets in and finds the park gate open and the lock busted."

Peyton's laugh was little more than a nervous grunt as the Jeep's headlights swung toward the hedge-covered stone arch leading to the replica of the sixteenth century Fort Caroline. Its wooden stockade door was closed and Christmas wrapped with yellow crime scene tape which stretched into the darkness on both sides of the entrance.

"Would you look at that," Matthew said. "They've cordoned off the fort, and that's not even where the skeleton was found. That means the whole place is off limits. You sure you want to do this?"

"Yes," Peyton answered, a slight hesitancy in her voice as she got out.

"You're the boss," Matthew said, clicking off the headlights and snapping on a halogen lantern before opening the driver's side door and getting out. "Take my hand. We go around the side of the fort to get to the dig site, and you don't want to step off into the marsh."

With the light beam acting as his guide, Matthew led

Peyton along the narrow path. They stooped to get beneath the crime scene tape extending from the side of the fort across the path to a tree on the edge of the marsh. Past the tape, they turned left along the earthen embankment, or levee, that held back the St. Johns River from the dig site and surrounding marshlands. "Watch your step," he reminded as they reached the mounds of excavation material Lieutenant Taylor had ordered left in place.

Night sounds from the marsh, accompanied by the intermittent slap of river water against the base of the levee, added to the uncertainty Matthew felt. "I'm not worried about myself, but bringing you out here... They catch us, and you're in as much trouble as I am. Maybe we oughta —"

"She ran this way."

"How do you know?" Matthew asked, stopping as they reached the final, partially dugout pile of dirt. "Maybe she came from upriver."

"No. She would have had to cross the marsh. She came this way, past the fort. When she realized where she was, she tried to double back. That's when he caught her."

"You're seeing this already?"

Peyton laughed softly. "No. Just common sense. We're standing where she must have stood. To her left, the marsh. To her right, the river. Ahead, a cut in the bank for drainage from the marsh. In her mind, she was trapped."

"Logical," Matthew admitted. "That's where they found the skeleton." He pointed the light beam into the depression that had been dug on the river side of the mound.

Peyton nodded and, with one hand on Matthew's arm for support, stepped into the shoveled-out area. She stood, staring across the river at lights on the far shore, some stationary, others moving along streets that paralleled the river.

"Anything?" Matthew asked.

"No. I feel a sense of urgency and fear, but that's all. I

Death's Bright Angel

thought there might be something, but it's been such a long time."

"What difference does that make? You said —"

"It's the emotional energy of a traumatic experience. It clings to a particular scene or location. Some can see and feel that energy, no matter how long ago it happened. For me, however, time causes the energy to unravel, like threads in a pattern. If I had something belonging to the woman, perhaps..."

"That I don't have."

Peyton turned from the river and pointed at the top of the dirt pile. "There."

Matthew swept the lantern's beam around the top of the mound. "Where? What?"

"Gold."

"I don't see anything."

"Just beneath the surface."

Matthew dropped to his knees and scratched at the dirt and shell mixture. "I still don't... I'll be damned." The yellowish glint of gold caught in the lantern's light. Very carefully, he dug around the object, swept away the dirt, and pried it out with his fingers. "A woman's hair barrette. The clasp is broken, but how do we know it belonged to the murdered woman? We had several college girls working the dig."

Peyton reached up and took the barrette. Turning back to the river, she closed her eyes and held the slightly curved, oblong clasp to her cheek. Suddenly, her breath became ragged, her teeth clenched, her face painted with the harsh brush of fear.

"What's happening?" Matthew demanded.

"The man... the man with the mustache. Please, let me go. Please! You're hurting me. Don't —"

"Goddamn it!" Matthew shouted, at the same time

tearing the barrette from Peyton's hand. "Stop it! No more!"

Peyton sank to her knees as tears spilled over and ran down her cheeks. "You're right," she sobbed. "I can't do this anymore. It's too much. I can't —"

"Don't move, either of you," a man's voice ordered from the darkness. Three separate lights flashed on as Matthew whirled around, pointing the halogen lantern in the direction of the voice.

"Police. Put your light down, and both of you, on the ground. Face down, hands on top of your heads."

"I can explain, officer. I'm Matt Berkeley and —"

"We know who you are. On the ground. Now!"

CHAPTER 9
November 5, 1992
Thursday Morning

"As nice as your office is, Lieutenant, we've got to stop meeting like this," Matthew said through a stifled yawn.

"Fun-*ny*," Rich Taylor mumbled over the top of his coffee cup, never taking his eyes off Matthew.

"And what about, 'You have the right to remain silent,' and whatever else it says. If you're arresting us, I'm sure the law books on your shelf tell you all about *Miranda versus Arizona*. If no warning about our rights, that means no arrest, and I want to see Peyton."

"Miss Chandler?"

"You know who I'm talking about. Your people have been running back and forth between Peyton and me since we got here this morning, and you and I both know she's told them the same story I have. The only thing we've done wrong is cross the yellow line."

"And the photograph you stole the other day."

"Borrowed. You'll get it back."

The door opened behind Matthew. Before he could turn in his chair, Taylor said, "Come in, Miss Chandler."

"Matt?" It was Peyton's voice.

Matthew pushed himself from the chair and took Peyton in his arms, ignoring Polly Bartelow as she followed close behind. To Peyton, he asked, "You all right?"

"I've been better," she said, "and no, they didn't use whips or put me on the rack, if that's what you mean."

"That's enough, you two," Taylor ordered. "It's been a long night, and we're all tired."

Matthew nodded before raising his right eyebrow in a question mark and asking Bartelow, "Any luck with the 'Z' file?"

"Whadda you know about the 'Z' file?" Taylor demanded.

"More than I'm supposed to. Take me off your hit list, and I've got a friend that —"

"People like you don't have friends," Taylor cut in, "and besides, 'Z' file's not your concern. What *is* your concern is the fact that you're not already sitting in a cell waiting for the next century to roll around. You ever disturb a crime scene again, that's exactly where you'll be. As for you, Miss Chandler, —"

"What about her?" Matthew interrupted.

Ignoring Matthew, Taylor continued, "Sheriff Whitelaw down in St. Johns County tells us you're the one who helped find the Wilson girl last year when she was kidnapped."

"Kind of him to say that, but really, it was his people. I gave them pieces of the puzzle. They put them together."

"Some of the stuff you told Sergeant Bartelow, the impressions you saw concerning the two murders. That was interesting, but if I told my boss, he'd laugh his..." Rich Taylor chuckled sourly, "He'd laugh me out of his office."

"That may be so," Matthew said, "but what about the man with the mustache? Peyton saw him both times. He was the killer."

Taylor exhaled his frustration in an extended rush of air.

"Even if I could spend taxpayers' money following up on Miss Chandler's psychic visions, how many white guys with mustaches and dark hair you think we've got in Jacksonville and the Beaches?"

"The Atwell woman's apartment," Peyton said. "Did you find a cross?"

It was Sergeant Bartelow that answered. "No."

Matthew saw what Peyton was getting at. "What about candles or candle wax?" he asked. "Anybody hear religious music the night she was killed?" He watched Taylor and his sergeant for any kind of reaction. Taylor's face remained a complete blank, but Sergeant Bartelow's eyebrows lifted and her forehead wrinkled upward, just enough to show surprise.

"Which was it, Sergeant? Candles, the music, or both?"

"Miss Chandler didn't tell us about that," Bartelow responded, the shock of what Matthew had said immediately erased from her face.

"Maybe you didn't ask, and I didn't remember until Peyton mentioned the cross. She probably also told you about the two-story brick building and the crowd."

"Jacksonville Women's something," Peyton reminded. "I couldn't see the entire name, but —"

Taylor cut her short. "Not important. As for you, Berkeley, your people at the North American Archaeological Research and Preservation Association faxed your file down from Charleston last night."

Matthew laughed sourly and grumbled, "What the hell ever happened to the Privacy Act?"

"Former Navy Special Warfare officer, Vietnam, twice. Small arms and assault weapons your specialty. Now in charge of security for archeological digs throughout North America. Involved in several cases of missing artifacts when you've had to kill."

"Or be killed," Matthew qualified.

"Like in Vietnam? Yeah, right," Taylor said, the sharp edge of sarcasm in his voice. "A man who knows how to kill. A man who can look at a woman's skeleton and tell us she was murdered and how. A man who returns to the scene of the crime like you did last night to find the dead woman's barrette. A souvenir, maybe, to remind you of something?" He didn't allow Matthew time to answer. "And both of you give an exact description of the scene where a second woman was murdered, though you both say you were never there."

"Chris Atwell's, you mean?" Peyton asked.

Sergeant Bartelow looked at Taylor. Taylor nodded his approval. "Yes," Bartelow answered. "Candle wax on a coffee table in two places and neighbors hearing religious hymns. That information's never been released to the public."

"Matt's only telling you what I saw from the photograph. What Chris Atwell's eyes told me she saw, and what I told Matt."

Silence settled over the room until Matthew said, "The last time I was lucky enough to be in this office," the word *lucky* awash with sarcasm, "Sergeant Bartelow said something about both of the women having had abortions shortly before they were murdered. What's abortion got to do with this?"

Rich Taylor lowered his head and slowly moved it from side to side, biting his lower lip in a moment of deep thought. Finally, looking up, he said, "So far as we know, nothing, but..."

"But what?" Matthew prompted.

Taylor took a deep breath and exhaled the words, "It's happened again."

Peyton was the first to respond. "Another murder?"

"Last night."

"And you think I did it," Matthew said, his words spoken as a statement of fact and not a question.

"All I can say is, once the Medical Examiner gives me a

Death's Bright Angel

time of death,..." Taylor wagged a finger in Matthew's direction and advised, "you'd better have some damn good witnesses to prove you were somewhere else."

"That's it," Matthew said, getting to his feet. "C'mon." He took Peyton by the arm and helped her from her chair. "I've had it with this place."

Taylor stood. "I'm not through."

"What now?" Matthew asked, his arms thrown wide in exasperation.

"Miss Chandler,..." Taylor hesitated for a moment, then, "the man with the mustache."

"Yes?" Peyton answered.

"If you saw him again, would you recognize him?"

"I think so. There was something strange about him, something I can't identify. Other-worldly, you might describe it, but yes, I think I would."

"I'd appreciate it if you'd come in this afternoon and go over some mug books to see if there's anybody that looks like your man. Sergeant Bartelow will be here to help."

"I'd be glad to."

"And Miss Chandler, I'd appreciate it if you didn't tell anybody. I..." Taylor paused as though searching for the appropriate words.

Peyton smiled her understanding. "I know, Lieutenant. Psychics and the so-called giggle factor. Don't worry."

"What about my Jeep?" Matthew asked. "When do I get it back?"

Taylor glanced at the calendar on his desk. "With the paperwork and everything, Monday at the earliest."

"Monday? You gotta be kidding. You people are..." Matthew bit his lower lip and took a deep breath, knowing it was useless to go on.

"Let's get outta here, Peyton," he said, taking Peyton's elbow and urging her across the room. As he opened the door, he stopped part way through and turned back to Rich Taylor. "If you and your people don't know how to get into the 'Z' file, give me a call. You decide I'm not your killer and give me back my Jeep, I might be able to help. Getting into and out of things is also one of my specialties."

CHAPTER 10
November 5, 1992
Thursday, Late Afternoon

The home, a ranch style with sand-colored stucco, sat comfortably beneath a cover of pine and oak trees in San Jose, one of Jacksonville's older but more affluent neighborhoods. With the beige Lincoln Continental parked in the drive, the flat tire on its right front giving the car a forlorn, down-at-the-mouth look, Peyton knew Jackie was home. She knocked again.

Should have called, she thought, but the murdered women and the impressions she had received, the grave where the skeleton had lain, the early morning interrogation — interview, Sergeant Bartelow had called it — and the past two hours staring at photographs of subhuman life forms capable of the most hideous crimes... All that had turned her body clock and thinking process into mush.

"One more time," she muttered to herself, this time pushing the button at the side of the door. The *bong-bong* of door chimes echoed from the foyer beyond.

Peyton shrugged her shoulders and turned to leave when a voice from inside called, "Please wait. I'm coming." Peyton stopped short. It was Jackie's voice, but in those few words, she sensed the woman's loneliness. When the door opened and she saw Jackie's face, she knew she was right. The immediately recognizable isolation and despair leaped at her along with Jackie's arms and embrace.

"Thank God, you've come," Jackie whispered in her ear. "Come in, please."

Unwrapping Jackie's arms from around her neck, Peyton ushered both of them into the house and closed the door. "Did you know you have a flat tire?" she asked.

"I know," Jackie responded, tightly clasping Peyton's hand in her own as though afraid Peyton might somehow suddenly disappear. "Matt'll fix it. Coffee?"

Peyton allowed herself to be led to the kitchen, laughing softly when she saw an empty glass and open bottle of Cutty Sark on the kitchen counter. "A good stiff Scotch on the rocks would be better." Peyton wondered how many "good stiff Scotch on the rocks" Jackie had already had?

"Me, too," Jackie agreed. Finally releasing Peyton's hand, Jackie spoke over her shoulder as she busied herself finding another glass, rattling ice cubes from an ice dispenser on the front of the refrigerator, and pouring out jiggers of Scotch. "Matt called. Worried about his baby sister. He didn't say so, but I know he thinks I'm on the verge of another breakdown."

"Are you?" Peyton positioned herself on a bar stool next to the kitchen counter and concentrated on Jackie's eyes, but they seemed cloudy, hiding what lay beyond.

Jackie continued as if the question had never been asked. "He said you'd be here, but didn't know what time. You apparently had one hell of a night."

"One to remember, that's for certain, but what about you?"

Jackie stared into her glass as she swirled the ice around with the tip of her index finger. Looking up, she asked, "I know you recommended I see her, but how well do you know Dr. Wagoner?"

Peyton sipped the Scotch, savoring the warming sensation it left on her tongue and throat in its downward journey. "Fairly well. Known her for four, maybe five years. We were members of the Beaches Women's Business Club until she closed her practice about six months ago and opened the new clinic in Jacksonville. She and a Dr. Russo. Paul Russo. I haven't seen her since she moved, but we still talk on the phone. I do know she's highly respected in the medical community."

"I saw her this afternoon. Along with Dr. Russo."

"And?"

"We talked. I liked her. Him, too. They explained my options. No pressure, one way or the other." Jackie took a long swig of Scotch, drained the glass, and quickly poured another jigger over what remained of the ice, adding at least another half jigger. "I appreciated that."

"Don't guess you've had a chance to talk with Tony?"

"No. There's nine hours difference between Saudi Arabia and here, and at this point, it really doesn't make much difference whether I do or not."

"Well," Peyton said, her right eyebrow notched upward in surprise, "from that little statement, should I assume you've made a decision?"

"I have an appointment with Dr. Russo. Tomorrow."

"For what?"

Jackie's eyes misted over as she downed the remaining Scotch in a single gulp. "You know damn good and well, Peyton. Tony's getting what he wants. What did he say that night?" Her voice began to rise; her face suddenly took on the pattern of angry red and white blotches Peyton remembered so vividly from her last visit.

Jackie answered her own question. "'Abort the goddamn

thing, Jackie.' That's what he said, wasn't it?" Her words almost a shout, she cursed, "Damn him to hell!"

Peyton watched, horrified, as Jackie whirled around and threw the empty glass against the tile splashboard behind the sink, shattering glass and sending long, spidery cracks through the tile. She immediately turned back to Peyton, slammed her fist against the counter top, and cried, "And that's what I'm going to do, Peyton. God forgive me, I'm going to abort the goddamn thing."

• • •

Chief of Detectives James Michael O'Riley looked at the clock. Six-thirty. He'd promised his wife he'd be home by six in time to go to the church supper. "Damn!" Three more case files to review for the next morning's briefing with the Sheriff and a quick meeting with Rich Taylor on the doll murders. He refused to call them the abortion murders as he knew some in the division were doing behind his back. The day had been hell on wheels, and he was already talking to himself. "Better call and let her know —"

The phone intercom buzzed and a male voice said, "Chief?"

O'Riley flipped a switch on the intercom and answered, "Tell them I'm not here."

"Justice Department in Washington. Line three. Asked to speak to Jimmy O'Riley like he knew you."

O'Riley's eyebrows crunched together in a question mark, then raised as he thought of the "Z" file and realized who it might be. "Got it." He pushed the button on line three and hit the phone speaker at the same time. "O'Riley."

"Jimmy boy, Larry Bailey here."

"Hadn't expected to hear from you again."

"Thought you'd be interested. The 'Z' file? Remember?"

"My lieutenant won't let me forget."

"With the Democrats winning the election Tuesday and a changing of the guard at the White House in January, the word's come down. That part of the 'Z' file you were interested in... even the code word for that section's got a cosmic top secret stuck on it," Bailey threw in for emphasis, "it'll be scrubbed sometime this weekend."

"I'll be damned," O'Riley said with more than a little wonderment in his voice. "Must be hotter than I thought."

"So hot, Jimmy, you wouldn't want to touch it with a ten-foot pole. Sure as hell not while the current Administration's still in office. Just thought you ought to know. Have a good Thanksgiving, Jimmy."

O'Riley turned in his chair and gave a smile to the seven O'Riley offspring spaced across the wall. "Already giving thanks, Larry. Already giving thanks."

• • •

"They won't let us in, Lieutenant," O'Riley said, moving his head from side to side as though to shake the crumbs of disappointment from his jowls. "I tried, but they kept saying no."

Rich Taylor gnawed at has lower lip as he usually did when things weren't going his way. "Any reason? I thought that's what VI-CAP *and* the 'Z' file were for. To identify certain criminal characteristics and patterns of operation. To look for similarities on a national scale. To help us little guys on the front lines."

"You're absolutely right," O'Riley responded with a what-else-can-I-do shrug of his shoulders and a sideways look-at-me,-I'm-helpless grin on his face, "but as the saying goes, when the man says no, you go with the flow."

Taylor wanted to slap the grin off O'Riley's Porky Pig face and say, "You know goddamn well what you can do, you fat-ass bastard." Instead, he said, "Tell me something, Chief. Why is it, the minute abortion is mentioned, you and half the other chiefs on the executive staff as well as most of the city council, stick your heads in the sand as far and as fast as you can?

"When one of the clinics has a problem with demonstrators, you ignore it, except maybe to arrest pro-choicers if they shout back. Why is that, Chief? We've got a case where three women have been murdered, each within days of having an abortion at the same clinic, and nobody gives a damn but me and Polly Bartelow."

James O'Riley leaned back in his chair and crossed his arms, resting them on the overfed stomach that Taylor wanted so badly to put a fist into and said with a near saintly air, "Life is a precious thing, Lieutenant, whether born or unborn. We have a duty to protect that life, now don't we? A duty to God, a duty to civilization, and a duty to ourselves."

"What about a duty to the law of the land?"

"Bad law. When we start aiding and abetting the killers of the world, that'll be a sad day, Lieutenant, whether they call themselves doctors, nurses or the freedom of choice generation."

"But somebody's killed three women and —"

"And we'll find him, Lieutenant, but we'll do it without glorifying the abortion clinics." O'Riley unfolded his arms and leaned forward, his stomach grinding against the top drawer of his desk. "We'll do it without giving abortion lovers the opportunity to feel oppressed and sorry for themselves. To cry for sympathy from the rest of the world.

"If you ask me, maybe those three women wouldn't be where they are today if they'd loved the life inside them enough to give birth. That's all, Lieutenant. Go find the killer, but leave abortion out of it. That's an order."

• • •

Rich Taylor bulled his way into the Homicide office and pointed a finger at Sgt. Polly Bartelow. "I wanna see

Berkeley," he barked, "and I don't mean next week. They won't let us into the 'Z' file, and if Berkeley says one of his specialties is getting into and out of things, we're gonna find out just how slick he really is."

William Kerr

CHAPTER 11
November 6, 1992
Friday Morning

    Taylor had heard the words before. How many times, he couldn't say, but the same dismal drone of Dr. Fay Lundgren's voice created an automatic wrinkle of his nose. Regardless of the mask and a liberal application of Vicks VapoRub inside his nostrils, he could still smell the penetrating odors of the autopsy room, even if only in his imagination.

    "This is continuation of case number 105-1192," Fay Lundgren said into the microphone attached to the front of her blue-green surgical scrubs. "Lavonna Mayes. The body is that of a well-developed, well-nourished eighteen-year-old Negro female with black hair and brown eyes. The body is sixty-four inches long and weighs 108 pounds. In addition to myself and technicians Unger and Raleigh, Lt. Richard Taylor, Detective Division, Homicide, Jacksonville Sheriff's Office, is present."

    "You know how I hate this, Fay. You could've at least sewn her up." Taylor's gaze slipped past Lavonna Mayes' body to Lundgren's tools of the trade: scalpels for cutting skin and muscle, pruning shears to snap the ribs, various sized ladles to scoop fluid for analysis, an electric saw for opening the skull and a large set of Toledo scales for weighing brain

Death's Bright Angel

and other organ tissues.

"Getting to you?"

"The killings? Yeah." Taylor wanted to turn away, to leave the frigid air conditioning that blanketed the room, to get as far away as he could, but his eyes returned to Lavonna Mayes' body, splayed in a gaping "Y" for internal probing and removal. The cut ran from shoulder to shoulder, down over the breasts, the arms of the "Y" meeting at the lower tip of the sternum and from there, a midline incision the entire length of the abdomen to the mutilated pubis. Lumps of brownish colored meat and short sections of rib lay in several clear plastic bags on a stainless steel dissection tray straddling Lavonna's legs.

Lundgren sympathized, "You see your own daughters or wife on the table and wonder how anybody can do something like this."

Taylor found it hard to speak even when prompted with, "Don't you?" His voice was wooden, masking the feelings that churned inside. "We didn't know at first, but it was her boyfriend, the drug dealer, that got blown away on Monday night."

"We did him yesterday," Lundgren added.

Taylor went on, "She was pregnant. Apparently upset over the boyfriend's death and had an abortion on Wednesday. Went home, and whoever killed her was waiting. Neighbors saw a white guy, well-dressed, dark hair, mustache. Little after seven that night. Thought he was a preacher when they heard church music, and after that..." Taylor blew out a loud swish of air. "Mother works late shift at Burger King. Came home between twelve and one and found her."

"Could have known the killer," Lundgren said. "No sign of struggle, but this is probably why." Lundgren turned Lavonna's head to the right for Taylor to get a better look. "Over here, Rich. She won't bite. I might not have noticed, but for the outer ear. First, a massive hematoma on the helix of the ear indicating some kind of blunt force. Second, in the concha or what I call the bowl of the ear, dried now, but cerebrospinal fluid indicative of a basilar skull fracture."

"Blow to the head," Taylor said, putting Lundgren's words into more familiar phraseology.

"Here." Lundgren parted the hair at the base of the skull immediately behind the left ear. "Bruising. Verified the location when we pulled the brain. Intracranial hemorrhage opposite that exact location, but that's not what killed her."

"What did?"

Fay Lundgren motioned to one of the packaged lumps of meat on the dissection tray. "Heart. Knife with a serrated blade. Ripped it open. Like the Atwell woman." To one of the technicians, she said, "You can put it back in, Unger, and close her up."

The technician nodded, added "Yes'm," and stuffed the plastic bags, one after the other, into Lavonna Mayes' abdominal cavity.

"In other words," Taylor said, acting as though he didn't notice the technician's offhanded manner in handling Lavonna's broken heart, "she was already dead when he cut up her... cut her up?"

"Undoubtedly. Want my opinion?"

"You're gonna give it to me, whether I want it or not, aren't you?"

Lundgren chuckled as she pulled a yellow, bloodstained latex glove from one hand, then the other, and tossed them into a trash container marked *BURN*. "She was otherwise a healthy woman, able to fight back if attacked. Like the skeleton at Fort Caroline, to prevent that kind of problem, he hit her in the head. A rock more than likely in the Fort Caroline case. In this one, a pipe, a club or a baton like your officers carry."

"What about the Atwell woman?"

"She fought to some extent as demonstrated by the defense wounds on her hands. The knife cuts between her fingers," Lundgren explained, "but with the large amount of Valium and alcohol in her blood, he probably figured she was pretty well immobilized to begin with."

Nodding to Lavonna, Lundgren continued. "After knocking her unconscious, knife to the heart to finish the kill. In all three cases, mutilation of the sex organs and placement of the fetus doll to show contempt for women. And regardless of what your boss O'Riley says, contempt for and hatred of abortion, the common denominator in all three murders."

"Souvenirs?"

"Same as with the Atwell woman. The glans clitoridis, but this time, the breasts."

"Damn! The way you got her cut, I couldn't tell."

"Only the mammilla or nipples from each breast, the surrounding areola and enough fatty tissue underneath to provide bulk."

Taylor's mind was feeling heavy. The air seemed colder than when he arrived, and the odor which he knew by now should have numbed his olfactory nerves was making him nauseous. "Bad odor, three minutes, and odor's gone," Fay Lundgren had always told him, but not for Rich Taylor. Not even with Vicks VapoRub.

"What about the fingernails? Skin, hair, fibers, anything?" he asked.

"Nothing. Fingernails like they'd been freshly scrubbed. Same with the Atwell woman, and no sign of sexual penetration. Only the doll."

The door to the autopsy room cracked open and Taylor heard a small voice. "Lieutenant?"

"C'mon in, Polly."

"Rather not."

"Get your butt in here, Sergeant Bartelow."

Bartelow edged her way through the door, keeping her eyes on Taylor and away from Lavonna Mayes. "I don't like —"

"I know what you don't like, and I don't either, but you'd better get used to it if you're gonna head up a homicide team. Where's Berkeley?"

"We can't find him."

"Why the hell not?"

"We checked Fort Caroline just in case, his apartment, Miss Chandler's house and bookstore. Woman named Helena said Berkeley and Miss Chandler were off somewhere, but didn't know where."

"What about his sister? Last name, Serafina. Lives in the San Jose area."

"Just came from there, and nobody home."

"Goddamn it, Polly! We got over 900 patrol and traffic cops in Jacksonville, and Lt. Rich Taylor's gotta pound pavement to find this guy? Let's go. I'm gonna teach you the fine art of locating a missing person. In particular, one Matthew Berkeley who knows more than he ought to." On his way to the door, Taylor called over his shoulder, "Thanks, Doc. Let's hope you don't have any more of these."

"Don't count on it, Lieutenant. I've got a real bad feeling about this one."

• • •

From a block away, Matthew could see the demonstrators shielding the entrance to the building, blocking the doors with their bodies and signs, and he knew automatically there could be trouble. Even though he opposed the act of abortion as much as the demonstrators, he also knew he had to protect Jackie from as much harassment as possible. "Is there a rear entrance?" he asked the taxi driver.

"Yeah, but the drive goes down the side of the building, and they got that blocked, too. No way I'm gonna get my windshield smashed. I'm droppin' you folks off right before we get to the crowd, and you're on your own."

"Thanks," Matthew muttered sarcastically, immediately angry at Lieutenant Taylor and himself for having to take a taxi as he pictured the impounded NAARPA Jeep and the flat tire on Jackie's car he had failed to change. Turning to Jackie and Peyton in the back seat, he instructed, "When we get out, ignore anything they say. Hopefully, the clinic'll send out escorts, but if they don't, we link arms and walk straight to the door."

Each of the women nodded and smiled, but he could see the concern in their eyes, especially Jackie's. *Help me take care of her, God,* he prayed under his breath as the taxi pulled to the side of the street.

"This is it, folks."

Matthew checked the meter and handed the driver a twenty, stepped to the sidewalk and opened the rear door for Jackie and Peyton. As Jackie took his hand, he could feel the tremors and knew how scared she was, of both the demonstrators and what she was about to do. It was Peyton, however, who surprised him. He could see the determination on her face, the set of her jaw, eyes narrowed, looking straight ahead at the thirty to forty demonstrators as though to say, "How dare you!"

He counted each step as they moved forward, arm in arm. One, two, three,... closer and closer to the "enemy's" front line, but something was different. Not like the televised newscasts he'd seen during the past several years, and then it dawned. Except for the traffic sounds along Beach Boulevard, silence. Silent men, silent women. No shouts, no catcalls, no prayers or beseeching. And the signs they carried. Not the usual change-the-mind-of-the-mother kind, but deliberately threatening signs, threatening more to the clinic than to the would-be mother.

William Kerr

THIS PLACE WILL BURN
ABORTION CLINICS ARE DEATH CAMPS — DESTROY THEM
ABORTION DOCTORS — OFF WITH THEIR HANDS

As they reached the front ranks, the unexpected happened. Without warning, the demonstrators suddenly put down their signs and sat on the sidewalk, each with legs and arms crossed, leaving only a narrow path to the clinic's doors, which in itself was surprising. It was Peyton's reaction, however, that forced Matthew to stop.

"What is it?" he asked.

Peyton stared at the building. Matthew had seen that look on her face only once before. *What's she looking at, and through whose eyes?* he wondered.

"I couldn't see it for the people and signs," Peyton said. "The name on the building."

A car horn bleeped. The car swerved to avoid a police cruiser as it made a sudden U-turn and pulled against the curb on the far side of the street, but the sound seemed a thousand miles away to Matthew. "Go on."

"What Chris Atwell saw. The name. *Jacksonville Women's Clinic for Family Planning.* She was here. This is what she wanted to forget."

"Oh, shit," Matthew whispered. "The fetus doll!"

"What are you two talking about?" Jackie asked, shaking her head in confusion. "You're scaring me."

"I'm sorry, Sis. We didn't mean to..."

Matthew's words died in his throat as a little girl of angelic beauty, her hair in golden curls, her dress white gossamer in appearance, stood and walked from the crowd along the open pathway, a single rose in her hand. She stopped in front of Jackie and held out the rose. As Jackie's trembling hand touched the flower's stem, the little girl pleaded, "Mommy,... please don't kill me," then turned away.

Jackie stood for a moment, staring after the child, her

eyes misted with tears. Clutching the rose close to her heart, she lifted her face to the sky and in one great sob, cried, "Dear God, forgive me, please."

Matthew tugged at Jackie's arm. "C'mon, Sis. Escorts." He pointed toward three women coming through the clinic's doors, each wearing a yellow armband inscribed with the word, ESCORT. "Let's get inside, but you can still change your mind. Maybe Peyton and I could take the baby. Maybe —"

He was interrupted by the sound of high-pitched voices. A children's chorus positioned on the far side of the clinic's entrance and led by a tall, scarecrow of a man sang:

"There's a Friend for little children
Above the bright blue sky,
A Friend who nev-er chang-es,
Whose love will nev-er die;..."

"Matt, it's him." Peyton pointed across the street.

"It's who?"

"The man with the mustache! The man at Chris Atwell's! The man at Fort Caroline!"

"You and the escorts get her inside," Matthew shouted above the singing. "I'm gonna damn well settle this 'man-with-the-mustache' thing once and for all."

Matthew dropped Jackie's arm and started across Beach Boulevard and its six lanes of traffic. He dodged a red and white pickup truck with lightning bolts streaked along its side; narrowly missed the front bumper of an eighteen-wheeler that sounded its horn, drowning out Jackie's cry of, "Matthew, come back." Two cars screeched to a halt; angry horns blared. One driver jabbed a knotted fist in his direction, the other a raised middle finger, as he reached the far side of the street and the arms of two police officers.

"What the hell do you think you're doing?" one of the officers, a female, demanded. "You could've been killed, not to mention causing half-a-dozen wrecks out there."

"Sorry, officer," Matthew panted. "Man with a mustache. On the sidewalk behind your car. D'you see him? I've gotta find him."

"You're not doing anything till we write a ticket," the male officer said.

"For what?"

"Jaywalking."

"For chrissake, officer, the man with the mustache. He's the man —"

"I don't care who he is." The male officer whirled Matthew around and shoved him against the cruiser. "You don't move till I say so."

With pen and citation booklet in hand, the female officer asked, "Name?"

"Matthew Berkeley."

Matthew didn't see the woman approach along the sidewalk from an RV, the name *CHILDREN OF CHRIST REFORM CHURCH — SAVE THE UNBORN*, painted on its sides. Glaring at Matthew over a number of antiabortion posters and several bundles of pamphlets stacked precariously in outstretched arms, she stopped and asked, "Was he disturbing the demonstrators, officer?"

Matthew turned his head toward the woman. She was large boned, nearly as tall as he was, with dark hair. Without the frown which he knew was directed at him, she had a face that could be pleasant, even attractive, and a voice that was iron-hard in a sensual sort of way.

"No, ma'am," the male officer said to the woman. "Just being a nuisance."

"Don't guess you saw a man with a mustache, did you?" Matthew asked the woman. "Standing on the sidewalk, tall, well dressed, —"

"Last name," the female officer cut in, glancing at Matthew from the citation booklet. "How do you spell it?"

"B-E-R-K-E-L-E-Y. Matthew Berkeley. Could we hurry? My sister's across the street and —"

"Address?"

"One-twenty Martin's Way, Apartment 816, Jacksonville, 32211."

"I used to know a Matthew Berkeley," the woman with the antiabortion placards said. "In Jacksonville Beach. Used to come to my grandfather's drug store across from the old Ferris wheel." The frown had disappeared and the voice had softened.

The female officer placed the citation booklet and a ballpoint pen on the patrol car's trunk lid and ordered, "Sign it. At the bottom."

Matthew scribbled his signature as fast as he could, at the same time asking the woman, "RxMore?"

After separating the multipart, Uniform Traffic Citation, the female officer handed Matthew his copy. "You can send in the fine, or go to court."

"Big choice. Thanks a lot. The man with the mustache? Did you —"

"Didn't see a man with a mustache or anybody else," the male deputy answered tersely.

"Nor did I," the woman with the posters said, "but yes, RxMore was my grandfather's. Sam Moreland."

"Dr. Sam, or Doc, as my folks called him, and you're?..."

"Samantha. Originally Moreland, now Samantha Foley. Everyone calls me Mother Sam. That's my husband across the street directing the children's choir. The Rev. Truegood Foley, pastor of The Children of Christ Reform Church."

"Small world," Matthew said with a forced smile, "but looks like we're on opposite sides of the fence at the moment." Matthew surveyed the front of the clinic and the demonstrators, still seated as another car arrived and another group of escorts came out to meet a young man and woman. Jackie and Peyton were gone. "I've got to get back to the clinic. My sister's already inside."

"If it's for an abortion, I'm sorry."

"So am I. My dislike of abortion might not be as vocal and visible as yours, but yes, I'm sorry, also."

As Matthew hurried across the street, cutting in and out of the lines of traffic and purposely ignoring shouts from the two police officers, Mother Sam called, "Children of Christ Reform Church, Mr. Berkeley. We'll expect you."

Without looking back, Matthew waved a hand and muttered to himself, "Don't hold your breath, lady, unless the man with the mustache is one of your boys."

As he reached the sidewalk in front of the clinic, moving rapidly toward the entrance, words sung by the children's chorus seemed directed, not only at the recently arrived couple, but at the heart of his own feelings as well.

> *"There's a rest for little children*
> *Above the bright blue sky,*
> *Who love the bless-ed Sav-iour,*
> *And to the Fa-ther cry;*
> *A rest from ev-'ry tur-moil,*
> *From sin and sorrow free,*
> *Where ev-'ry little pil-grim*
> *Shall rest e-ter-nal-ly."*

CHAPTER 12
November 6, 1992
Friday Afternoon

Taylor slammed the phone into its cradle with a loud bang and curse. "Goddamn it! What the hell kinda people we got working in this place? If we can't find Berkeley, how the hell are we gonna find a goddamn killer? We can't even —"

"Lieutenant." Sgt. Polly Bartelow pushed open the door.

"Whatever it is, forget it, Sergeant," Taylor shot back.

"Damm it, Lieutenant, he's here."

"Who's here?"

"Berkeley and Miss Chandler."

"Well why the hell didn't you... Bring 'em in."

Bartelow turned back to the open doorway and nodded, her gesture accompanied by a short, frustrated laugh as Matthew and Peyton followed her into the office.

"Where the hell've you been?" Taylor growled at Matthew. "We've been —"

"Back off, Lieutenant. I've had it with you and this whole goddamn outfit. The abortion clinic! Why didn't you tell me?"

"Abortion clinic, what? I don't have to tell you anything."

William Kerr

Matthew slapped the palm of his hand hard against the top of Taylor's desk. "The Atwell woman! The skeleton at Fort Caroline, and the murder you mentioned yesterday morning. It was in the paper last night. A black woman on the north side. They're all tied together, aren't they? How many fetal dolls have you got now? Three?" Matthew's eyes locked on Taylor's. "Yeah, three sounds like a good number. The murders, the clinic, abortion and the fetal dolls. And, oh, yeah, the man with the mustache."

"What *about* the man with the mustache?" Bartelow asked.

Peyton answered, "He was at the clinic. The Jacksonville Women's Clinic for Family Planning. We saw him."

"Sit down, Berkeley," Taylor ordered, at the same time dropping into the chair behind his desk. "You, too, Miss Chandler, please." To Peyton, he added, "This man you saw. Was he the same one in your so-called vision?"

"Yes," Matthew answered for Peyton as he held her chair before taking his own seat. "Across from the clinic. I went after him, but by the time I finally got across the street, he was gone."

"What were you two doing at an abortion clinic?" Taylor demanded.

"My sister, for chrissake. She had an abortion, but if you'd told me there was a connection,..." Matthew let the thought die. "It's all centered around the abortion clinic, isn't it? *That* abortion clinic."

Silence filled the room until Bartelow said, "You owe him, Lieutenant."

"I don't owe anybody. In fact, —"

"The 'Z' file," Bartelow reminded.

Rich Taylor leaned back in his chair, the air in his lungs doing a loud retreat through tightened lips while his fingers

Death's Bright Angel

beat a drumroll on the arm of his chair, gradually slowing to all-stop. "Where's your sister now?"

"At the clinic."

"We pick her up in an hour," Peyton added. "After they make a final check to insure there are no complications."

"Go on, Sergeant," Taylor said. "I know you're dying to tell, so get it over with."

Polly Bartelow gave a sigh that Matthew interpreted as both disbelief and relief. "Mr. Berkeley, Miss Chandler, there are certain people in the Department that refuse to believe that abortion has anything to do with this series of murders. For that reason, there's been nothing in the media linking the two."

Matthew interrupted. "Politically incorrect. Right?"

Bartelow nodded. "I guess," and continued. "Each of the three women had just had an abortion at the Women's Clinic. Each of the three were killed and butchered, their sex organs mutilated. A fetus doll like the one you saw at Fort Caroline was inserted into each woman's uterus. Body parts were removed, apparently as souvenirs, and yes, at the last murder, the black woman, Lavonna Mayes, neighbors did see a man with a mustache."

"Like the one Peyton described?" Matthew asked.

"Exactly."

It was Peyton's turn. "Has anyone looked into the group that pickets the clinic? Dr. Wagoner told me they're always the same people. Led by a man named Truegood Foley."

"And don't forget his wife, Mother Sam," Matthew inserted.

"Whadda you two know about Foley and his wife?" Taylor asked.

"Nothing," Peyton responded.

"Except for his wife," Matthew said. "Ran into her this afternoon while two of your cops were writing me an invitation to county court." He reached into his shirt pocket, fished out the jaywalking citation and waved it in front of Taylor's face. "Knew her when I was a kid visiting Jax Beach in the fifties. Back then, she was Samantha Moreland. I used to go to her grandfather's drug store across from the old Ferris wheel. Best Coke floats in the world, until he got into some kind of trouble and the drug store closed."

"Leave 'em alone," Taylor warned.

"Mother Sam and her husband?" Matthew asked, his face twisted into a you-gotta-be-kidding look of disbelief.

"You heard me."

"I think you're making a mistake, but if you tell me I'm no longer a suspect, I've got no reason to get involved with them or anybody else, but I still don't appreciate you not letting me know about the abortion clinic. Because of that, my sister's in danger of some jerk-off coming after her because she had an abortion. In fact, any woman that gets an abortion in Jacksonville is running the same risk, and they don't even know it. I don't understand how —"

"You don't have to understand," Taylor interrupted. "You take orders in your job, I take orders in mine."

"Interesting," Peyton said.

"What?"

"What you just said, Lieutenant. Makes me wonder if somebody higher up isn't —"

Taylor cut her off. "You can stop wondering, Miss Chandler. We've wasted enough time on psychic revelations, internal department decisions and all the rest. Whether Mr. Berkeley's a suspect or not has nothing to do with why we've been looking for him for the last two days."

"You missed my cheery personality," Matthew quipped.

"Cut it, Berkeley. I need help."

Matthew's mouth spread in a wide grin, his abbreviated laugh expressing the irony in what he'd just heard. "And I

Death's Bright Angel

need my Jeep Cherokee back. What kind of help?"

Matthew watched Taylor. The man's upper teeth bit into his lower lip as though the words he wanted to say were too unbearable, an admission of need that galled and burned like acid on the tongue. It was Polly Bartelow that answered. "The 'Z' file. You said you might be able to help."

Matthew looked at his watch, then at Peyton. "I think we'd better be going. Jackie's waiting."

"Damn it, Berkeley," Taylor exploded. "We've gotta get into the 'Z' file, and if you can help,..."

Matthew stood and leaned across the desk, almost in Taylor's face. "Ever heard of 'Let's Make a Deal?' You want my help, that's what we do. You tell the world about the tie-in between the murders and abortion —"

Taylor's fist pounded the desk. "I can't, goddamn it! Not yet, anyway. They won't let me."

"Then we will, Lieutenant," Peyton said, her voice calm and steady. "Now that we know for sure, Matt and I have no choice. To remain silent, regardless of what your superiors say or do to us, would be the biggest sin of all."

"And I want my Jeep."

Polly Bartelow asked, "You won't help unless you get your Jeep?"

"If it'll save more lives, I have no choice but to help, Sergeant, but I still want my Jeep."

CHAPTER 13
November 7, 1992
Saturday Morning

Even with air conditioning, heat from the television studio's lights had created beads of sweat on Matthew's forehead and along the collar line of his shirt, but it was the unmitigated anger he felt at the two men seated across from him that had raised his body temperature to near boiling point. Jacksonville Sheriff Danny Ryskowski, a large man with hands the size of ham steaks, and the droopy-jowled, Chief of Detectives James Michael O'Riley, whose earlier words had proven him an ardent antiabortionist. Both had played to the cameras like consummate professionals.

"Why is that, Sheriff?" Kevin Richards asked.

"While we appreciate Mr. Berkeley's sincere desire to keep the public informed, and you know, Kevin, that's something the Sheriff's Office has always tried to do,..."

Kevin Richards, the handsome, well-dressed moderator of WZYN's *Jacksonville Talks* news program, smiled and nodded his concurrence as Sheriff Ryskowski went on, "... he simply does not have access to our sources of information, many of which, for reasons I'm sure you understand, cannot be divulged without compromising the investigation itself.

Death's Bright Angel

"Mr. Berkeley has been most cooperative concerning the incident which took place at the Fort Caroline archeological dig site where he was working, but he has had no direct contact with the department's investigation of that or any of the other murders we've discussed today."

"In fact," O'Riley offered in elaboration of the Sheriff's words, "it appears that much of Mr. Berkeley's information comes from one of the many Jacksonville Beach psychics and not from any substantiated source. While that kind of thing might be of interest on the Discovery Channel with an exposé of the occult, it has no relevance in the mechanics of day-to-day police work."

Kevin Richards looked at Matthew. "We have one minute, Mr. Berkeley. Your response?"

"As with a number of other things," Matthew answered, "Chief O'Riley is either uninformed or, for whatever reason, providing only half-truths and half-information to the people of Jacksonville and surrounding areas."

"False, absolutely false," O'Riley countered. "I —"

Kevin Richards held up his hand, stopping O'Riley in midsentence. "Chief, please. One at a time."

Matthew chuckled at O'Riley's discomfort, then continued. "I'm sorry Dr. Wagoner of the Jacksonville Women's Clinic for Family Planning was unable to be here, but I'm sure she would agree that it is neither her place nor mine, as much as I dislike abortion, to dictate what any woman can or cannot do with something as personal as her own reproductive process. I also know from experience within my own family that women considering abortion at Dr. Wagoner's clinic are provided a full range of information, pro and con, before making their decision.

"It is a fact, which neither Sheriff Ryskowski nor Chief O'Riley can deny, that since July, three women have been brutally murdered in Jacksonville. In each case, the woman had been pregnant. And from what I've recently learned, each murder occurred after that woman had undergone an abortion at the Jacksonville Women's Clinic for Family Planning. Facts concerning the abortions themselves are documented in legally mandated reports provided by the clinic to the Department of Health and Rehabilitative Services. Finally, circumstances surrounding each murder give every indication that abortion very definitely was the underlying factor.

"Unfortunately, Dr. Wagoner was unable to provide this particular information to the clinic's patients for the simple reason, she was never told of the relationship. Had she been informed, there is a good possibility that, at the very least, the third victim might be alive today."

"If this is indeed the case," Richards said, watching the wall clock at the rear of the studio and obviously feeling the time constraints imposed for the program, "what are your final thoughts?"

"In my opinion, the murders have been well planned by someone determined to do whatever he or she thinks necessary to stop women having abortions. I realize in saying this I'm playing into the hands of the murderer, but until this person is caught, any woman considering an abortion in the Jacksonville area needs to know these facts. Failure by the Sheriff's Office to provide this information has, again in my opinion, been a severe dereliction of duty to the public."

"How dare you!" Chief O'Riley blurted, his face flushed with anger. "There is absolutely no —"

"I'm sorry, Chief," Kevin Richards cut in, "but we are out of time." Turning more to the camera, Richards ended with, "And there you have it, ladies and gentlemen, a no-holds-barred discussion concerning the recent trio of murders in Jacksonville. I hope you've found tonight's discussions informative, and until next Sunday evening, on behalf of our guests and the staff at WZYN, this is Kevin Richards saying, *Jacksonville Talks*, and we hope you keep listening *and* watching. Good night."

A woman's voice in the background called, "It's a wrap. Great show, Kevin, gentlemen. One of the year's best."

"Thanks, Donna," Richards said, "and thank you Sheriff, Chief O'Riley, Mr. Berkeley. As you know, this was recorded and will air Sunday night. Tomorrow night. A copy of the tape will be sent to your office, Sheriff, first thing tomorrow morning. If you would like a copy, Mr. Berkeley,..."

"I know where to get one if I need it," Matthew answered. "Thanks anyway."

As Matthew stood, O'Riley moved next to him and said in a low voice. "You're nothing but a troublemaker."

"Truth hurts, Chief, but sometimes you've gotta live with it."

"We'll catch the killer, Berkeley, but if it's the last thing I do, I'll get you."

"I'll tuck that away for future reference, but you know something? They were right."

"About what?"

"You do look like Porky Pig."

William Kerr

CHAPTER 14
November 7, 1992
Saturday Evening

Caught in the glow of burning logs in the fireplace, Jackie's shadow followed her, back and forth, step for step, as she paced across the room. Peyton watched from the edge of the sofa. It was Jackie's third drink, and though her feet were steady enough, Peyton wondered how many more it would take before Matt's sister would finally lose touch with reality. Already, Jackie was sinking into a morass of self-pity.

"You did what you had to do," Peyton said.

"Bullshit!" Jackie shot back, quickly downing the last of the Scotch in her glass and reaching for the nearly empty Cutty Sark bottle perched on the mantelpiece above the fireplace. She tilted the bottle and poured what was left into her glass, this time not even bothering to go to the wet bar for ice or water. "I should've stood up to Tony and told him to stuff Saudi Arabia and Connelly Engineering and all the rest. I wanted that baby like I've never wanted anything in my life, and he made me kill it."

Peyton wanted to counter with, "In the end, it was your choice, and you know it," but she knew that would only antagonize and push Jackie closer to the edge. Instead, she said, "Why don't you get some sleep. I'll be here in case they find Tony and he calls back. I'll wake you."

"Sleep?" Jackie replied, followed by a half grunt, half laugh. Lifting the glass, Jackie finished the last of the Scotch in a single gulp, then, "Easy for you to say. You didn't just murder your..." She stopped. "I'm sorry. With Tony a million miles away, guess I'm trying to hit at anybody and everybody I can find, even you and Matt."

Peyton stood and put her arms around Jackie's shoulders. "No harm done."

Jackie pulled away and moved with an awkward, one-too-many shuffle to the wet bar. "Oughta be at least one more." She opened one of the cabinet doors and pulled out several bottles, finally holding up an unopened bottle of Glenlivet single malt Scotch. She laughed. "Tony's favorite. A gift from his father. I'm not supposed to touch. Well, fuck Tony and his father. It's mine, now."

"Don't you think you've had enough?" Peyton asked.

Jackie ignored Peyton's question and twisted the top off the bottle, pouring until the amber-colored whisky spilled over the top of her glass. Sipping the level down below the rim, Jackie turned and said, "You didn't tell me where Matt went yesterday, and who was the man with the mustache he tried to catch? I never even saw the man."

Peyton stood with her back to the fireplace, staring at her own shadow, stretched across the sofa and up the far wall, outlining the breadth of her hips which seemed to be spreading more and more. "Just a man we know," she said, afraid any other explanation would create more problems than it would solve. "Nothing for you to worry about. It'll probably be another couple of hours before Matt gets here. Why don't we —"

The strident ring of the telephone cut through the air like the clang of a high-pitched alarm bell.

"Tony!" Jackie cried. She grabbed the phone before it could ring a second time. "Tony? That you?" Her face clouded as she listened. "She's here." Jackie held the phone in Peyton's direction. "For you. Somebody named Helena. Sounds excited."

"Wonder what?..." Peyton took the phone. "Helena?" Peyton's jaw dropped with an instant intake of breath. "Oh, no! I'll be there as quick as I can."

Peyton stood, frozen, her eyes locked on the flames that danced against the rear of the fireplace. "The bookstore. It's on fire."

Jackie took the phone from Peyton's hand and hung up, "Take the Lincoln. Matt changed the tire this morning."

"But you —"

"I'll be all right. I've got Glenlivet to keep me warm until and if Tony ever calls."

"Don't let anybody in, Jackie. Matt and I are the only ones you can let in. Understand?"

"Sure," she said, taking a swig of Scotch straight from the bottle as she handed Peyton the keys to the Lincoln, "but why?"

Peyton took the keys and rushed toward the front door, stopping long enough to warn even more forcefully, "Lock the door after me, and don't let anybody in. Not *anybody*. Promise."

"Don't know why, but okay. You, Matt,..." holding the bottle of Glenlivet up to the firelight, she added, "... and good old Mr. Glen here. The only ones, I promise."

• • •

Matthew steered the Jeep Cherokee into the parking lot just off Arlington Expressway and eased into a slot alongside the only other car in the lot. "I don't know how you do it, Lieutenant, but you've got a real knack for screwing up my personal life. Coming here this afternoon would've been a helluva lot better than tonight."

"I'm not supposed to be here, Berkeley, and I sure as hell can't afford to be seen in daylight with a guy who says the Sheriff and Chief of Detectives are derelict in their duty to inform the public."

"You heard about the taping, huh?"

"Yeah, and O'Riley says you're at the top of his suspect list. Half a chance and he's gonna nail you."

Matthew laughed. "Wouldn't you know it? Here I am, busting my ass to help, and I'm still a suspect. At least I got my Jeep back. One out of two ain't bad." Matthew pointed to a glass door at the side of the building, "That's him."

Just inside the door, in a small foyer illuminated by a stack of overhead florescent lights, stood a man of medium height and medium build, dressed in slacks and crew-neck sweater. As Matthew knew it would, it was the man's facial features that drew Taylor's immediate attention, a head marked by a receding hairline and a jaw, hooked noticeably left-of-center, on a face creased with the strain of too many killings and too much blood.

As both men got out of the Jeep, Taylor asked in a hushed voice, "What happened to his face?"

"Vietnam," Matthew answered, waving to the man inside the building as he moved toward the door. "Same time I was. Riverine squadrons. Took some shrapnel in the jaw. When they rebuilt it, the surgeon was standing at an angle."

Taylor grimaced. "You ever think of doing stand-up comedy, Berkeley, don't give up your day job."

Laughing softly, Matthew pushed the glass door inward, allowed Taylor to enter first, then followed.

The man with the off-center jaw extended his hand to Taylor. "Ray Houston, FBI."

"Rich Taylor, Homicide, Jacksonville Sheriff's Office."

Houston turned immediately to Matthew. "Matt. Been

awhile. How's —"

Taylor interrupted, at the same time, nodding toward the glass door. "You don't mind, I'd like to get outta the light, if you know what I mean."

"He doesn't like the idea of somebody seeing us together," Matt said. "Afraid they might think we've got something going for each other."

Houston laughed. "Same ol' Matt. You never change."

"He fucking well better change," Taylor threatened, part joke, part serious, "or I'm gonna put his ass under the jail first chance I get."

• • •

The unmarked patrol car sat in the darkness at the edge of the parking lot entrance. Rather than use official communication channels, the lone occupant punched out seven numbers on a cellular phone and waited until, "You're not gonna believe this, Chief. FBI off Arlington Expressway. He and Berkeley just went in."

James Michael O'Riley's "Shit!" was loud enough to force the phone away from the caller's ear.

• • •

Matthew looked around the office. Nothing impressive. Typical government, middle echelon metal-gray desk, metal-gray chairs, and carpet with a flecked pattern meant to annoy rather than relax the eye. On the walls, hand-me-down pictures some General Services Administration bureaucrat had turned in for disposal at least a decade ago. The only things of interest were the lack of windows in the room and five computer keyboards and monitors lined against one soundproofed wall. Each monitor displayed its own design of shapes and colors, all moving in and around like amoeba forms in petri dishes of rainbow plasma and soap bubbles.

"Matt gave me a heads-up why you wanted to see me, as well as what he knew about the three murders. Where do you want to start?"

"One thing you need to know," Matthew said, focusing on Rich Taylor, "Ray's in Jacksonville on a hardship transfer because of his parents. His real expertise is profiling for the bureau's Criminal Investigative Analysis Program at Quantico, Virginia. Ray helped me on a situation concerning artifacts stolen from archaeological sites with a couple of murders thrown in along the way."

Taylor grunted. "Quantico, huh? What they use to call the Behavioral Science Unit?"

Houston laughed. "Yeah. Better known as the BS Unit. Guess they thought CIAP sounded better."

"Since Berkeley seems to know more than anybody else on the case and he's already filled you in," Taylor said with an edge of sarcasm in his voice, "how 'bout a profile?"

Ray Houston sat for a moment, the off-center jaw working as though he had a mouthful of tobacco, then said, "A pathologically disoriented personality. Totally committed to something that's been building for years. Deep psychological scars. Anger demonstrated in both the killing and the mutilation is directed, not only at the victim, but at someone in the past. If the victims were posed in any particular manner, —"

"The last two were," Taylor interrupted. "Like they were giving birth. Hard to tell about the Fort Caroline woman, but it's probable she was. That's why I need to access the 'Z' file. To see if there's anything in the past that resembles what we've got here."

"What about VI-CAP?" Houston asked.

"We tried. Nothing."

Houston nodded his understanding and went on. "The fetus doll and the posing is part of the ritual, expressing hatred for someone or some thing. Probably the act of abortion itself as well as whatever happened in the killer's past. It leaves a signature showing the killer thinks he or she is all powerful.

What's perplexing is lack of the usual signs of sexual gratification from the mutilation and the blood, but Matt tells me there's been no sign of penetration or anything indicating sex."

"The bodies have been so cut up, we can't tell, but there's been no semen, hairs, or anything else," Taylor explained. "Whether he shoots off in his skivvies from butchering, seeing, touching or tasting the bodies and the blood, we don't know."

"A he or she?" Matthew asked.

"An interesting combination," Houston answered, his jaw still working as though an integral part of his normal thought process. "From the lack of evidence left at the scene, the perpetrator has the fastidiousness of a female, but it's the type of crime normally associated with a male. Whoever or whatever it is, there has to be a fair amount of strength, in the arms and upper torso, to inflict the wounds Matt says were present.

"My guess, a man. Late forties. Sometime in the past, got his wife or girlfriend pregnant. He wanted the baby, she didn't. She had an abortion. He's been thinking and agonizing about it for years, and finally flipped.

"The presence of candles at the crime scene and the church music heard by neighbors indicate it's become a religious pilgrimage. A way to erase the sins of the past. His wife's or girlfriend's for seeking an abortion as well as his own for not being able to stop it. He hopes the killings will pacify whatever god he serves and will stop others from getting an abortion."

Matthew glanced at his watch. "I've got to move, guys. What about the 'Z' file?" He looked at Houston and then at a computer screen that showed what resembled a school of rainbow colored fish swimming over pink and purple corals. "You said you knew how to get in."

Death's Bright Angel

Ray Houston took his seat in front of the computer and, with the index fingers of both hands, pecked out instructions which quickly devoured the fish and brought up a menu with the heading, *UNITED STATES JUSTICE DEPARTMENT ~ CRIMINAL INVESTIGATIVE ANALYSIS PROGRAM.* Of the menu's more than a dozen available selections, none meant anything to Matthew until his eyes settled on a lone "*Z*". To the side were the words, *SPECIAL CLEARANCE REQUIRED.* He watched as Houston maneuvered the mouse, sending the cursor arrow to the "Z" position.

"Before you do it," Taylor said, "two questions. How come you can get the 'Z' file and I can't, and why are you doing it for us?"

Houston shook his head. "First, it depends on what part of the 'Z' file you want and who you are. Not even the local agents can get what you want to see."

"So why you?" Taylor asked.

"I still have the 'Z' file *eyes only* clearance from Quantico," Houston explained. "As for your other question, Matt and I were in Vietnam together, and he did something for me nobody else has ever done."

"What?"

"Saved my life, and if you want me to do this, now's when you two go look at pictures on the wall."

Matthew laughed as he turned away and walked with Rich Taylor to the far side of the room. "How's that for trust? Don't know what this world's coming to when an old friend can't share his Vietnam buddy's code words."

Taylor studied Matthew's face. "And maybe you already know what's in there. Maybe you're the one they're talking about. Maybe that's how you know so much."

"You're sick, Taylor. If you weren't a cop, —"

"Knock it off, you two, and get over here," Houston ordered. "I think I've got what you're looking for."

"No shit," Taylor mouthed as he and Matthew raced each other across the room to Ray Houston's side. "What's it say? Can you print it?"

"No printouts. Not allowed on the 'Z' file, especially this heading."

"What's the heading?" Matthew asked.

Houston moved the arrow-shaped cursor to the top of the monitor page, stopping on a single word. *Azrael.*

Matthew's eyebrows furrowed. "Why Azrael?"

Houston shrugged his shoulders. "I don't know. Maybe it tells somewhere in the text."

Matthew followed the cursor in its downward journey, line by line, description by description. "Jesus Christ, I'm not believing this." As the cursor floated its way from one entry to another, Matthew read aloud the cities and dates. "Kansas City, 1989. Three murders, sex organs mutilated, and three fetus dolls. Buffalo, 1989, '90 and '91. Six more, each one a clone of those in Kansas City. Cleveland, Ohio, 1991 and '92. Three more, exactly the same, the last one in May of this year."

Rich Taylor let out a long sigh. "And we know in July, he moved south to Jacksonville and the woman at Fort Caroline, then October and November. He's traveling. Went somewhere between July and October. Keep going. Maybe there's a —" Without warning, the monitor screen went blank, then blossomed into the familiar scene of rainbow colored fish, swimming over pink and purple corals. "What the fuck?"

"What happened, Ray?" Matthew asked.

"Dunno," he answered, his fingers already punching at the key board. "Power outage in Washington, maybe, or somebody accidentally pulled the plug. Let's see if we can get back in." Almost instantly, the menu flashed on the screen. "I'll be damn," Houston said, sitting forward in his chair, a puzzled look adding to the wrinkles already scoring his face.

"The 'Z' file." He brought the cursor to the bottom of the menu. "It's gone."

Taylor leaned over Houston's shoulder. "You mean you can't bring it back?"

"Like I said, it's gone."

"What about Azrael?" Matthew asked. "Would that pull it up?"

Houston shook his head. "No. It's gotta be listed on the menu and answer to the daily code words. You'd have to access the 'Z' file before the word *Azrael* would do you any good. Somebody's deleted the 'Z' file. As for the word *Azrael*, I still don't know what it stands for."

"I do."

Both Ray Houston and Rich Taylor turned to Matthew. It was Taylor who spoke first. "And how the hell do you know?"

"I learned to read at an early age."

"Well, if you're so damn smart," Taylor growled, "how 'bout sharing. What's an Azrael?"

"Azrael is a creature with as many eyes and tongues as there are men in the world. Each time an eye closes, someone's soul is severed from their body and they die."

"What the hell are you talking about, Berkeley?" Taylor demanded. "That's a lotta crap."

"If you say so, but you wanted me to tell you, and I did."

"Then put it in plain fucking English, goddamn it?"

"Whether real name or only a code name, Azrael is death's bright angel, Lieutenant. In Moslem and Hebrew mythology, Azrael descends to earth as God's *angel of death*."

• • •

The doorbell was a distant nuisance, a three-note melody that mercifully broke through the melancholy of a sleep induced by Glenlivet and the weariness of her own mind and body. Jackie didn't know how long she'd been asleep, but it had dredged up everything she had wanted to forget — the abortion clinic and the smell of iodine solution, the stirrups, the tray of instruments.

She had asked for each instrument to be explained beforehand. Weighted speculums and retractors, chrome rods Dr. Russo had called dilators, the metal "dip stick" he had called a sound, for measuring the depth of the uterine canal, the pliers-like tenaculum and the curette, a rod-shaped instrument with a leaded handle at one end and on the other, a pinky-ring-sized loop with a sharp edge, for the final scraping and cleansing of the womb.

And then it was time. The intravenous drip of sugar water flowed into a vein in her left arm.

"You okay?" Russo had asked.

"A little scared, but I'm ready," she answered. Tony's words still rang in her ears. "Abort the goddamn thing, Jackie! Abort... abort... abort..."

Dr. Russo patted her arm and said, "You're going to be just fine."

Tilting her head at a slight angle, she could see the anesthesiologist turn a plastic butterfly screw at the Y-shaped junction of tubing leading to the needle in her arm. Sodium Pentothal. "If you'd count backwards for me, Jackie," the anesthesiologist had requested. "From ten."

She had closed her eyes and counted, "Ten, nine, ei... eight,..." and then she was swimming, effortlessly, through sunlight and soft white clouds. Everything quiet until she heard a distant sound, a steady, low-key hum that she knew intuitively was sucking Tony's unwanted offspring from her body, the tiny baby she had wanted to name Maria after Tony's mother.

The doorbell. Another three-note carillon, and another.

Jackie shifted on the sofa, the half-empty Glenlivet bottle clutched tight between her breasts. "Oh, God," she groaned as her eyelids scraped open. "If this is what Hell feels

Death's Bright Angel

like,..." The doorbell sounded like massive gongs vibrating inside her head.

"I'm coming," she whispered, "I'm coming." One foot on the floor, then another. The bottle fell, hit the brick fireplace hearth and shattered. "Damn!"

Stepping around the broken glass, Jackie shuffled her way to the door and looked through the peephole. "Matt? Peyton?" She switched on the outside light and a figure came into focus. Squinting through bloodshot eyes, she saw a man, his face toward the street, dark hair, clerical collar. A Catholic priest. "Yes?"

The man turned toward the peephole. "I'm from St. Paul's, Jackie. Father Jerome thought you might need a friend, but he was unable to come."

"I'm sorry, but Peyton said I couldn't let anybody in."

"After what you've been through, I understand," the priest said, still watching the peephole.

"You know?"

"Oh, yes, and if you'd like, we could pray together. It would take only a few minutes. A simple prayer can sometimes lift the greatest burden from our hearts."

Jackie shook her head, trying to clear away the shroud of alcohol and sleep. "You really think it could help?"

"Coupled with faith and love of God, prayer can always help."

As Jackie turned the metal toggle on the lock, forcing the bolt to slide free, she asked, "What's your name? I don't remember seeing you at church before."

"You may call me Father John. Father John Azrael."

William Kerr

CHAPTER 15
November 8, 1992
Sunday Morning, Predawn

As Matthew wheeled the Jeep into the driveway, the digital clock on the dash read 1:00 a.m., but it was the emptiness of the concrete drive that forced him to slam on brakes. The Lincoln? "Where the hell?..."

Immediately switching off the ignition, Matthew yanked at the door handle and swung to the ground, his feet already churning toward the lighted front door. Something wrong, and where was the Lincoln?

The sound of tires cornering on pavement, the roar of an automobile engine echoing along the deserted street and the stark white brilliance of dual high beams grabbed his attention. He stopped when the car pulled into the drive behind the Jeep. As the headlights blinked and faded to darkness, he recognized Jackie's Lincoln. The driver's side door swung open and a figure emerged.

"Matt!"

"Peyton?" he called, waiting for the door on the passenger's side to open. It didn't. "Where's Jackie?"

"In the house. I had to —"

"What do you mean, 'in the house?' You're supposed to

be with her, for God's sake."

"Oh, Matt," Peyton whispered, rushing into Matthew's arms. "The bookstore. It's gone."

"Do what?"

"The bookstore caught fire. It's completely destroyed."

Matthew held her close. "Anybody hurt?"

"No." Peyton pulled away and, taking Matthew's hand, moved toward the front door. "The fire chief said they'd be able to tell me more by tomorrow afternoon, but all indications are that it was arson. Helena was working late, getting ready for a Sunday afternoon reading, when she heard a noise at the rear of the building. Before she could get back there, the storage room exploded in flame, and with an old wooden building like that,... Let's get inside. I'm cold."

"You got a key?" Matthew asked as they reached the covered front stoop.

Peyton held up the car-key ring. "One of these."

Matthew took the key ring, examined the half dozen keys under the light, then tried several against the keyhole until the third slid home. He turned the handle, shoved the door open, and snapped on the foyer's ceiling light. "Sis?"

"Shhhhh," Peyton whispered. "She's probably asleep, and that's what she needs most of all."

As they entered the large family room, Matthew smelled the telltale odor of heated candle wax, still lingering on the air. The fireplace was cold. The room was dark except for the glow of small red, green and orange blips on the face of the stereo console. Some marked peak level indicators and cassette compartments on the tape deck, while others represented volume levels and graphic equalizer controls on the console's amplifier. "She forgot to turn off the stereo," Matthew muttered.

"To be honest," Peyton answered, "she'd been drinking so heavily, she probably went to bed and didn't even realize the thing was still on. I hope Tony called."

Matthew nodded, at the same time switching on a table lamp at the end of the sofa. It was the odor of wax that bothered him. Something familiar. Not the smell, but a relationship with the past. He shook off the feeling until he saw the remains of a broken whisky bottle on the brick hearth and a large wet stain on the carpet in front of the fireplace. "What the hell?"

"It's the bottle of Scotch Jackie opened just before Helena called about the fire," Peyton explained. "She must have dropped it."

"You check the bedroom and make sure Jackie's okay," Matthew said. "I'll put on some coffee, and you can tell me about the fire."

Peyton nodded and disappeared down a long hallway toward the master bedroom as Matthew turned on lights on his way to the kitchen. "Instant okay?" he called, remembering too late that Jackie was asleep. "Sorry about that," he mumbled to himself as he opened cabinet doors in search of a jar of Maxwell House instant he'd seen the day before. "Where did I —"

Peyton's scream sent chills through his body, and the scream didn't stop. It went on and on. "Peyton, what's wrong?" he shouted, already through the door and running down the hall toward the rectangular shaft of light that penetrated the hall's blackness and painted Peyton's shadow against the opposite wall. As he rounded the doorway into the bedroom, he shoved Peyton aside and stopped. Peyton's scream dropped to a strangled gasp. "It's... it's Jackie. She's —"

"Oh, Christ!" The impact of what assaulted Matthew's eyes and brain slammed against his chest like a ten-ton hammer. He couldn't breathe. Except for his lips and tongue, he couldn't move. "Sis?"

Matthew's eyes blurred; his body shook. His hands

tightened into fists, fingernails biting into the heel of each palm. No pain. Only shock at what lay on the bed and the splatters of dark crimson on walls and dresser mirror.

It was as though his spirit had suddenly detached from his body. A numbing sensation, and then the distant sound of his own voice when he saw... "The fetus doll!" And then his plea, "Oh, God, no," those last words broken by sobs from deep within his chest.

• • •

Matthew sat at the kitchen table, staring at the window above the sink. Outside, black was gradually turning to dawn gray. The rain, slow and steady, created a low, metallic gurgle as it flowed from the roof and down a nearby gutter spout. It was the steady shuffle of shoes covered with slippers of fibrous, light-blue paper, in, out and through the house, however, that kept him from shutting out the picture of Jackie on the bed, the soul-searing picture he would remember for the rest of his life.

"More?" Peyton asked, holding up the coffee pot.

"What?"

"More coffee?"

Matthew tasted the foul coating inside his mouth, like the odor of burned meat left in the bottom of a frying pan. "No. I just want all these people to finish up and get the hell out of here. I'm not thinking straight, and I need to get my brain in sync before I call Tony."

A voice, harsh and tainted with the sharp edge of weariness and frustration, answered, " 'These people,' as you call them, are doing what has to be done, goddamn it! They want outta here as much as you want 'em out."

Matthew looked over his shoulder at the doorway. It was Lt. Rich Taylor. Behind him, still in her white lab coat, bloodstains mysteriously absent, stood Dr. Fay Lundgren. "I'd like a cup," Taylor said to Peyton, "and one for the Doc here."

Taylor lowered the bulk of his huge body into a chair next to Matthew, muttering almost under his breath, "Sorry, Berkeley. No sense taking my frustration out on you."

"We've told you everything we know, Lieutenant," Matthew said, ignoring Taylor's apology.

Peyton placed two cups of coffee on the table. "Sugar, cream?" she asked.

"Sugar," Fay Lundgren answered, helping herself to the sugar bowl.

Taylor shook his head. "Take it black and bitter." Looking at his watch, he said, "Another two hours and we'll start knocking on doors to see if the neighbors saw or heard anything unusual."

"As a rough estimate," Lundgren added, "your sister had been dead only an hour or two when you found her. Most of the neighbors should have still been up when it happened."

Matthew eyed the medical examiner. "So far as Jackie's concerned,..." He hesitated, then went on. "Her body. Any change in the pattern of what he's done so far?"

"How do you mean."

"The mutilation. The souvenirs. Was everything the same as the others?"

"For the most part."

"You're waffling, Doctor. What's different?"

"Sure you want to know?"

Matthew nodded.

"Everything the same except there was what appears to be seminal fluid on the middle abdominal area, around and in the navel. Can't tell for sure until we run the necessary tests. Naturally, there was no such evidence in the case of the Fort Caroline skeleton, but neither was it present with Atwell or Mayes."

Taylor nodded. "And there was nothing in the 'Z' file like that, either."

Death's Bright Angel

Matthew looked at Fay Lundgren and then at Taylor. "I thought you weren't going to say anything about the 'Z' file, at least for now."

Taylor nodded. "Yeah, but the Doc hates O'Riley as much as I do, and she won't say anything. Anyway, it's a new wrinkle. Obvious sexual stimulation for the killer," Taylor explained. "Looks like he stood over the victim and masturbated. If we're lucky, this could give us DNA evidence for possible future identification."

"In other words," Matthew said, "he's graduating. Getting bolder. Next time, if there is a next time, God forbid, he could step up to penetration before mutilation."

"Then something's not right," Peyton said, her forehead wrinkled in thought.

The coffee cup halfway to his mouth, Taylor set it back on the table and asked, "Another vision, Miss Chandler? What's wrong? What you see doesn't match some creep yanking off over..." He stopped at the sound of Matthew's sharp intake of breath. "Sorry. In this business, you get a little crass about things. Go on, Miss Chandler."

"I'm not sure, but since we found Jackie, it's as though looking through a telescope, only backwards."

"Like a peephole in a door?" Fay Lundgren suggested.

"Perhaps. A bright light. The man with a mustache. Dark hair, attractive face, but something different from the other times. A collar, like a Catholic priest."

"If you think priests don't masturbate, Miss Chandler," Taylor said, "then you still believe in the tooth fairy, but you've been right so far, and I'll check it out. Anything else?"

"No, and I'm not sure I want to know more, not with Jackie. I don't think I could bear it."

"And you're certain there's nothing else you remember when you entered the house?" Taylor asked, looking first at Matthew, then at Peyton. "Anything besides the odor of candles?"

"Did you find candles?" Matthew asked.

"Two separate globs of candle wax on the mantel over the fireplace. Could she have been burning candles or incense?"

"Not while I was here," Peyton replied, "but it does sound like Chris Atwell's apartment?"

"Yes, ma'am. In between the globs, scratches where something heavy had been sitting."

Peyton stared at Taylor. "A cross. I saw the cross through Chris Atwell's eyes. It stood between two candles, and the..." Peyton stopped.

"What?" Dr. Lundgren asked.

"Music. Church music." Peyton turned to Matthew, her eyes fastened on his. "Lieutenant Taylor said it was also heard when the black girl was murdered."

"Yeah?" Matthew asked.

"The stereo. It was on when we got here."

"I turned it off."

Coffee sloshed across the table as Taylor shoved his chair back and jumped to his feet, the coffee cup spinning out of control and shattering on the tile floor. "Damn it, Berkeley! The stereo and church music. Miss Chandler, where are you going?"

"The tape deck," Peyton called over her shoulder as she moved toward the door.

Matthew found himself in a fight with Rich Taylor for the doorway, each trying to wedge through the opening when the word, "Gentlemen!" brought both to an abrupt about-face. "That's more like it." It was Fay Lundgren. "Miss Chandler," she called, "don't touch anything." To the men, she ordered, "Out of the way. Ladies first."

With Dr. Lundgren in the lead, Matthew and the lieutenant made their way single file to the family room,

Death's Bright Angel

Matthew determined not to let Taylor get past. "Who knows how to operate this thing?" Lundgren asked, pointing to the stereo.

"I do," Matthew answered.

"Then put these on." Dr. Lundgren pulled a pair of opaque rubber gloves from the pocket of her lab coat and handed them to Matthew. "Check both tape compartments. If there's a cassette in either, don't touch."

Matthew slipped the gloves over his hands while Dr. Lundgren did the same with a second pair, then eased himself to one knee in front of the stereo console and opened the left-hand tape compartment. "Empty." He pressed the *EJECT* tab of the right-hand compartment, and the plastic lid sprang open. "A cassette, but what do you want to bet it's Gloria Estefan. Jackie's got... Jackie had over a dozen of her CDs and tapes."

Dr. Lundgren moved next to Matthew and knelt. Very gently she reached into the compartment and removed the tape cassette. "If it's Gloria Estefan, the recording studio doesn't believe in labels." Holding the tape to the light, she said, "A little over half through. Rewind it a bit and let's see what your sister was listening to."

Matthew took the cassette, slipped it back into the compartment and closed the lid. With a push of the *POWER* switches on both the tape deck and associated amplifier, he pressed down on the *REWIND* tab, waited a moment, then hit the *PLAY* button. With only the slightest hesitation, the tape moved on the cassette spools and choir voices filled the room in midstanza.

> "... in Je-sus! far from thee
> Thy kin-dred and their graves may be;
> But Thine will be a bless-ed sleep,
> From which none ev-er wakes to weep."

The song ended, leaving only a faint whirring sound as the tape continued to roll across magnetic heads.

"Not very good fidelity," Lundgren criticized. "Like somebody holding a hand mike in front of a choir."

"Son of a bitch finally made a mistake," Taylor said, his mouth stretched wide in the first honest-to-goodness smile Matthew had seen on the man's face. "Seminal fluid and now, he forgot the tape. Rewind it to the beginning. I wanna hear —"

A loud burst of static cut him off, followed immediately by the voices of a children's chorus.

> *"There's a rest for little children*
> *Above the bright blue sky,*
> *Who love the bless-ed Sav-iour,*
> *And to the Fa-ther cry;"*

Matthew spoke above the chorus. "I know that song."

Dr. Lundgren put a finger to her lips. "Quiet."

> *"A rest from ev-'ry turmoil,*
> *From sin and sorrow free,*
> *Where ev-'ery little pil-grim*
> *Shall rest e-ter-nal-ly."*

Matthew looked at Peyton. "Remember?"

She nodded. "The children at the clinic."

Matthew pushed to his feet. "Somehow, some way," he said, shaking his index finger to emphasize the words, "the killer's involved with that group. Gotta be to have this recording."

"But if Miss Chandler's right," Fay Lundgren inserted, "and it was a Catholic priest, why —"

"If the killer's a priest," Matthew snapped, "I'm a Buddhist monk. More likely, he knew Jackie was a member of St. Paul's Catholic Church and he used the priest thing to get in." To Peyton, he asked, "The RV parked across the street from the clinic. Did you see it? There was writing on the side."

Peyton shook her head. "No. I was trying to get Jackie through the demonstrators."

"I've seen it," Taylor said, his eyes narrowed, his voice

heavy with anger. "I know who they are, and so do you."

"Who?" Peyton asked.

"The Children of Christ Reform Church. Truegood Foley and his wife, Mother Sam. You want antiabortion? That's their middle name, but like I told you, I can't touch 'em."

"So you said," Matthew answered with a knowing shake of his head and disgust on his face, "but you better damn well believe I can."

"Thought you were on their side," Taylor goaded. "Thought you didn't like abortion."

"I don't," Matthew shot back. "Except in extreme circumstances, never have, never will, but whoever's behind this is making a mockery of pro-life. Somebody murdered my sister, and I'm gonna do my damndest to get the son of a bitch, no matter who I have to step on."

CHAPTER 16
November 8, 1992
Sunday, Early Evening

Matthew and Peyton sat in the Jeep, studying the building and the few stragglers entering through the glassed double doors — families, mostly, with small children, none much older than seven or eight, as far as Matthew could tell. The cars in the adjacent parking lot — Chevys, Fords and a host of minivans and sports utility vehicles — indicated a middle-class, relatively affluent following.

"They must have quite a congregation," Matthew said as he surveyed the church on Atlantic Boulevard. With the exception of a narrow steeple illuminated by several spotlights and topped by a gleaming, chrome-plated cross, the structure's white brick façade and flat outline against the evening sky resembled an elementary school more than a church. The lighted sign on the shallow front lawn, however, was quick to dispel any doubt as to the building's use.

CHILDREN OF CHRIST REFORM CHURCH
The Reverend Truegood Foley, Pastor
Sunday Services: 10:00 A.M. & 7:00 P.M.

"Why's that?" Peyton asked.

"Can't be more than a year or two old, if that, and the

size of the building. Takes money, and that takes people. Wonder how long Foley and his wife have been here?"

"I don't know, but if we're going in, we really should go. We're late as it is."

"Yeah," Matthew agreed, glancing at his watch. "I only hope the man with the mustache is here."

• • •

The interior of the church was vast, larger than Matthew had imagined, an auditorium to seat well over a thousand people. Rather than pews, row upon row of padded, bronze-colored metal folding chairs arranged in semicircular fashion filled the sanctuary, all facing, not the conventional chancel, altar and pulpit, but a stage. The church was well over half-full for the Sunday evening service when Matthew and Peyton entered and took seats at the rear.

It was set up more for theatrical productions than religious services, or so Matthew thought, based on what he remembered of his parents' church. The stage was host to a small orchestra of strings, timpani and brass as well as a mix of children and adults in purple and white robes. It was the two downstage lecterns and robed speakers, however, that provided the focus of attention: Truegood Foley and his wife, Mother Sam. A broad banner floating high above their heads read:

Lo, children are a heritage of the Lord:
And the fruit of the womb is His reward.
— Psalm 127.3

"Yes, my friends," Foley said into the microphone, his arms outstretched to encompass the congregation, "You were a person in God's eyes long before you were recognized by your fellow humans. You were not just a fetus or even a 'potential person,' as many on the other side would have you believe. You were a 'full person,' and so too is any conceived child, at whatever stage of development."

Mother Sam picked up the message, her voice a rich contralto, sonorous, almost hypnotizing. "And when does 'ensoulment' take place in the womb? We know from the scriptures that body and soul cannot be separated, and to be alive in the mother's womb is to be both body and soul from the beginning. It is not the mother, neither is it the doctor nor nurse, that breathes soul into the newborn, but God from the instant of its conception."

"Because God is creator of all human life," Truegood Foley intoned, "all life belongs to Him. To destroy a child in the womb is to destroy a child who belongs to God."

From the congregation rose the words, "Yes," "God's child, our child," "Lord, save the children," and other murmurs in agreement. From the choir, a child's soprano voice cried, "Abortion is a selfish thing," met by a wave of, "How true, how true," from the congregation.

To his left, several rows away, Matthew heard an adult male voice call out, "The church must focus on saving the unborn and not the needs of the woman."

Farther away, a woman stood and shouted, "Yea, verily, the words of the Lord."

Matthew leaned close to Peyton and whispered, "The animals are getting restless."

"It's staged, isn't it?" Peyton whispered back.

"Absolutely, and it's gonna get better, you wait."

From around the auditorium, individual members of the congregation rose to their feet, one after another, faces distorted with suffering of the soul, voices brimming with the venom of hatred for those not embracing their faith.

"Elimination of abortion doctors is justifiable in the eyes of the Lord."

The congregation echoed, "In the eyes of the Lord."

"The life of one abortion doctor for the lives of a hundred babies. A fair trade."

"Yes, yes," the congregation cried, more than half now on their feet, chanting, "Fair trade. Fair trade."

Someone with a microphone shouted over the chant, "Stop the doctors. Cut off their hands." And now the crowd was in a frenzy, the chant becoming, "Off with their hands. Off with their hands."

Again, an amplified cry from somewhere in the auditorium. "A woman who dies from abortion deserves to die."

Matthew listened, thoroughly appalled, not wanting to believe what he was hearing as the congregation chanted the various phrases from different parts of the sanctuary. Some raised fists and waved them in the air, others pounded cadence to their chant on the backs of the metal folding chairs, while those remaining stomped their feet in a synchronized march to victory over abortion.

From near the stage came the chant, "Deserve to die. Deserve to die."

To Matthew's left, "Kill the doctors. Kill the doctors."

To his right, "Remove their hands. Remove their hands."

And from the center, "Save the babies. Save the babies."

Truegood Foley raised his arms for quiet. As shouts died to a low hum and the congregation returned to their seats, Foley said, "God knew the unborn child he was making, even before it took human form. That child is His creation. Man and woman serve only as the messengers. As God's offspring, it is imperative that the unborn be protected from its mother when that woman chooses to cast out the life inside her body. Should one prevail over the other, it must be the child that prevails. New life for old. Let us pray."

Mother Sam lifted her eyes to the heavens and prayed, "O God, direct our government and our courts to recognize the sanctity of the unborn. If not, guide us in our daily efforts to remove from the face of the earth, by whatever means necessary, abortion and those that worship at its altar, to cleanse the hearts of the evil ones, and to protect each babe nestled in its mother's womb. In the name of Jesus Christ our Saviour who loved the little children, Amen."

And the congregation repeated in unison, "Amen, and Amen."

"Talk about heavy," Matthew whispered to Peyton. "Mothers deserve to die, kill the doctors, cut off their hands. Regardless of where you stand on abortion, that's not what I learned Jesus is all about."

Truegood Foley held up a hymnal and said, "Join us in singing praise to the Lord. Page 236."

With the unmistakable snap and click of metal folding chairs, the congregation rose as Mother Sam turned and led the orchestra and choir in a rousing rendition of,
"What a friend we have in Je-sus,
All our sins and griefs to bear,..."

• • •

"Did you see him?" Matthew asked, as the last of the congregation filed from the auditorium, blank stares turned in their direction, but nothing said. On the stage, the only ones left were orchestra members putting away their instruments.

"No," Peyton answered, "and I paid particular attention to the orchestra and choir. In fact, not even a single mustache. Ready?"

Matthew nodded as he stood and moved into the aisle, positioning himself to help Peyton with her coat. "Guess we shake hands with Brother Truegood and Mother Sam on the way out, but I was so sure, if we came tonight,..."

"So sure about what, Mr. Berkeley? Or may I call you Matthew?"

Matthew immediately recognized the voice — Mother Sam. He turned. "Mrs. Foley. Yes, please do. Matthew or Matt, whichever you like."

Mother Sam smiled. "I did say we'd expect you, didn't I? And call me Samantha. We're old friends, aren't we?" She shifted sideways to allow room for Peyton in the aisle. "My grandfather's drug store in the early fifties," she said to Peyton. "If I remember correctly, we may have shared one of the store's famous Coke floats once upon a time, but," turning to Matthew again, "what were you so sure about?"

"The man with the mustache I mentioned when we met across from the clinic the other day. Based on things that have happened, I thought he might be one of your followers, but if he is, he wasn't here tonight."

The scarecrow figure of Truegood Foley entered the auditorium, kneading his hands as though they were in pain from excessive handshakes.

"Truegood," Mother Sam said, "Come meet Matthew and his friend." She looked at Peyton. "Afraid I don't know your name."

"I'm sorry," Matthew apologized. "This is Peyton Chandler."

Foley took Matthew's hand in a peremptory shake, then Peyton's. "The bookstore. Yes. This morning's *Times-Union*. It burned last night, and you're the owner. Terrible thing. Sam and I will pray for you."

"Thank you."

"But Matthew, the man with the mustache," Mother Sam urged. "Why would you think to look for him here?"

"From what we can determine, he appears to be, uhhh,... *very active* in the antiabortion movement, and since he was at the clinic during your demonstration, we thought —"

Mother Sam interrupted with, "Not to change the subject, but your sister. If I recall, she was the reason for you being at the clinic. How is she?"

"For an abortion?" Truegood Foley asked, surprised.

"Yes." Matthew looked at Peyton for help.

Peyton took Matthew's hand in hers and said, "She's dead. Murdered by the man with the mustache. Last night."

"Pity," was Truegood's only response.

"Did anyone see this man?" Mother Sam asked.

Peyton shook her head. "Not exactly, but we have reason to believe it was him."

"And the other murders you discussed in your television interview," Mother Sam directed at Matthew. "Do you think they were committed by this man with the mustache?"

"Yes, ma'am, but how did you know about the interview? It doesn't air until tonight." Matthew looked at his watch. "In fact, it's on now."

Truegood Foley looked at his own watch, quickly stating, "We were given an advance copy of the tape. A courtesy since the program would be on during the service."

"By the television station?" Peyton asked.

"No, but we have a number of other sources."

Matthew chuckled sourly. "I bet you do, but a question." Mother Sam and her husband stood in silence, waiting. "Your service tonight. People calling for the death of doctors and cutting off their hands. That women who've had abortions deserve to die. You certainly have a right to your own beliefs, but things like that can only serve to incite the fanatics and mentally deranged. Why do you do that? This is a church. I thought churches reached out to help, not hurt."

"We are reaching out, *Mr. Berkeley*," Mother Sam responded, her tone much more formal than before, the emphatic use of "Mr. Berkeley" rather than "Matthew" a signal of her sudden irritation. "We are reaching out to the unborn, God's children who have no one else to stand up for them. While we grieve with you over the loss of your sister, we will never condone abortion, nor those who participate in such acts of villainy."

"It's time we close up the church, Samantha," Truegood

said. "Nice of you to have shared the evening with us, Mr. Berkeley, Ms. Chandler."

"Thank you," Peyton replied, adding, "Your church is so impressive and looks so new, how old is it?"

"Our first service was last June, just after we arrived."

"So you've only been in Jacksonville since June?" Matthew asked. "Where were you before this?"

"Cleveland, Ohio," Mother Sam answered.

"Were you there long?"

"A little less than two years."

"And before that?"

Mother Sam looked at her husband. "Where, Truegood? We've provided witness for Christ and the unborn in so many places."

"Buffalo, New York, I believe, and before that, Kansas City, Missouri."

"Interesting," Matthew said. "And I suppose you have followers who move with you from place to place. Right?"

Truegood Foley's left eyebrow arched, his voice suddenly edged with suspicion. "Yes, quite a few, but why do you ask?"

"Makes sense," Matthew said. "The demonstrations, the service here tonight, everything scripted to perfection. For that, I'd think you'd need organizers that are well trained and experienced. Anyway, it's getting late, and you need to close up the church. Hope you enjoy your stay in Jacksonville."

It was Truegood Foley who answered. "I'm sure we will, Mr. Berkeley, and perhaps we'll see you and Ms. Chandler again some time."

"Who knows, Reverend. I don't think we normally walk the same path, but you might just do that."

William Kerr

CHAPTER 17
November 8, 1992
Sunday Night

"He knows, doesn't he?" Truegood asked as they entered the living quarters at the rear of the church. "Berkeley and the Chandler woman know that Azrael is one of our flock."

Mother Sam looked at her husband, read the fear in his voice and wondered why she continued to put up with him. Azrael wouldn't. If it hadn't been for her, Azrael would have abandoned Truegood Foley long ago. "You're a fool, Truegood. There's no way they could know for certain. Like that Lieutenant Taylor, they're grasping at straws."

"But Azrael told you he'd forgotten the cassette."

"He also said not to worry. There was nothing that could link the tape to us. He was certain, and Azrael's never been wrong. All they know is there's a man with a mustache. Nothing more."

Mother Sam watched Truegood take off his coat and tie and throw them on the back of a chair. She could see the ribs through his shirt as he unfastened the buttons and pulled his long, bony arms from the sleeves. What a hideous man, she thought, and weaker spiritually than she'd ever imagined. If she'd listened to Azrael's urging, she would have left years ago, but she needed Truegood, at least until now. Now, however, his weakness could be Azrael's undoing, and that she could not, would not allow.

"Azrael's done too much in too short a time," Truegood continued, sitting on the arm of a chair to take off his shoes. "What you did with him in August, September and October, I don't know, but it allowed a breathing space. Since he returned, three killings in the last week. And the bookstore fire. He'll drag us down. It's time for him to leave."

"No," Mother Sam said emphatically. "You know as well as I, neither of us can do without Azrael. You're being naughty, talking like that, and Mommy doesn't like it."

Truegood Foley's head swiveled slowly in Mother Sam's direction. Suddenly he was a little boy, his face puckered as though about to cry. "What are you going to do, Mommy?"

Mother Sam towered over him, the corners of her lips pulled down in a frown, her body drawn to its fullest height. "I think it's time for the secret place."

"I didn't mean to be naughty, Mommy," he pleaded.

"Go," Mother Sam ordered, pointing toward the large, walk-in closet at the far side of the room. "Put on what Mommy bought for you last week, and Mommy will be there in a moment."

"But I like my sailor suit."

"Mommy wants you to be a big, strong cowboy tonight."

"I like cowboys," Truegood said, the semblance of a smile stretching his face as he placed his hands on Mother Sam's thighs. "Cowboys with big cocks for Mommy. Can I watch Mommy undress? Please?"

Mother Sam slapped Truegood's hands away. "No. Mommy has to punish her big cowboy before he can play, now go."

She watched her husband pick up his clothes and slink

into the walk-in closet, a scolded child with shoulders hunched and head lowered. Thoughtfully, she stepped out of her shoes, turned to the mirror and watched herself as she undressed. Blouse, skirt, slip and stockings. Her body was large, but firm and smooth like those in a Botticelli painting. Her hands lingered at the top of her thighs, pressing the silkiness of her underwear into the soft valley of flesh beneath. Her fingers probed at lips hidden by the suddenly moist material, pushing deep enough to send delicious tremors through her body.

"Oh, Azrael, if only it could be you. If only —"

"I'm ready, Mommy." Truegood called from their secret place behind the closet. "I'm ready."

Without answering, Mother Sam removed the too-small bra which held her breasts tight against her chest and sighed as they fell free, the large, cherry-ripe nipples already swollen from the journey her fingers had taken between her thighs. She wanted to touch them, to rub them and tease them, even scratch them with her fingernails, but Azrael's needs had to come first.

Quickly wrapping a print housedress around her body, Mother Sam entered the closet and moved silently through a second door into what Truegood called his secret place. She stopped for a moment and looked around. She hated the room and the things she'd done for Truegood on the single bed, their actions always reflected in the mirrors on the walls, each mirror precisely angled to show the bed and its occupants at "play."

It was the nightstand next to the bed that she hated most of all, its open shelves and what Truegood referred to as his toys. The penis-shaped vibrators and dildos, the jars of flavored Slippery Jell, soft latex pleasure rings, leather straps and plastic handcuffs, wooden paddles and a coiled cat-o'-nine-tails with whips made from knotted strips of muslin. But tonight would be different. She had a mission, part of a greater plan, and the thought made everything bearable.

"I told you you'd like your cowboy suit."

"I do. I love it. The boots and the chaps. Real leather, and with no pants and no underwear, I feel so free."

She eyed his testicles and penis hanging free from the opening in the front of the chaps and chuckled. "So I see. What a naughty boy. Turn around."

Truegood turned so that she could see his bare buttocks. "I *am* a naughty boy, aren't I, Mommy? Are you going to spank me?"

"Come here," she ordered as she sat on the side of the narrow bed. "Across my lap."

Truegood hurried to the bed and draped his body across her legs, his feet and hands braced against the floor, his bottom, more bone than flesh, pushed high into the air. "Will it hurt? I want it to hurt, Mommy. Make it hurt."

Mother Sam reached to the top shelf on the night stand and retrieved a piece of wood, shaped like a Ping-Pong paddle and drilled with six large holes. Without warning, she slapped the paddle against Truegood's buttocks, lightly at first, then harder and harder, again and again.

"Oh, Mommy, it hurts so much."

"Have you had enough?"

"No, don't stop," he said in his little boy voice as tears spilled from his eyes. "I need more, Mommy. More."

Mother Sam could feel his penis against her leg, engorged by the sensation of pain. "I have a better idea. You've taken your punishment so well, it's time for Mommy to reward her big, strong cowboy. Pull your chaps down and get on the bed."

Truegood eased himself from Mother Sam's lap, untied the leather thong that held up the chaps and let them fall to the floor before crawling onto the bed.

"On your back," Mother Sam directed.

"Are we going to fuck, Mommy? I always wanted to fuck my real mommy, but she wouldn't let me."

No wonder, you skinny, incestuous little bastard, Mother Sam thought as she wrapped her hand around his erection, the head of the shaft already glistening with lubricant seeping like tears from its eye-like orifice. "Not tonight, but Mommy will take care of her cowboy. Does that feel good?"

Truegood's hips began to move with the up-and-down motion of Mother Sam's hand. Faster, tighter. "Oh, Mommy, Mommy."

"Hold it in, or Mommy will squeeze," Mother Sam threatened.

Truegood jerked sideways and upwards, his body movements primed to the same erratic rhythm pattern as his breathing. "I can't, Mommy," he gasped. "Please, let me."

Her hand squeezed tighter until the glans of Truegood's penis was swollen almost purple. Finally, "Now, my big cowboy," she ordered. "Now!"

Rather than allow the milky fluid to spurt freely, Mother Sam bent forward, wrapped her lips around the head of the shaft and caught Truegood's ejaculation, glob after glob, sweeping her tongue along the shaft to ensure that nothing escaped.

Dropping back onto the mattress, his erection already disappearing with the evacuation of blood back into the circulatory system, Truegood sighed, "Oh, Mommy. That was wonderful."

With the warmth of Truegood's semen tucked carefully into the hollow of one cheek, Mother Sam laughed softly as she pulled a blanket from the foot of the bed and spread it over her husband's limp body. "I'm glad you liked it. Now sleep. Mommy will wake you in the morning."

Truegood pulled the blanket farther up along the trunk of

Death's Bright Angel

his body, closed his eyes, and said, "Thank you, Mommy. Yes. I think I'll go to sleep."

Mother Sam eased off the bed and moved from Truegood's "secret place," closing the door behind her, and through the walk-in closet into the living quarters, going directly to the bathroom. After washing her hands, she slipped on a pair of latex gloves and took an empty medicine vial, removed the top and spit Truegood's viscous, milk-white seed into the container. Using the edge of the vial's opening, she scraped the surface of her tongue to collect as much of the remaining secretion as she could, then closed the vial and held it to the light.

"For you, Azrael. Once they know its source, we'll be rid of him, and then... only the two of us, together, always."

William Kerr

CHAPTER 18
November 9, 1992
Monday, Late Afternoon

It was the third magazine Matthew had thumbed through, every article on either prenatal care, the miracle of childbirth or how to prevent diaper rash on babies with overachieving bladders. Even worse were the sideways glances the plain, properly prim middle-aged receptionist had given him. Nothing flirtatious. More curiosity than anything else.

The nameplate taped to the top edge of her in-box read, *Agnes Pompio.* In between telephone calls, notations in the clinic's appointment book and the rapid tippity-tap of too-long fingernails against a computer keyboard, her eyes had been like scalpels, probing and dissecting. Matthew wanted to say, "No, Agnes, I'm not here to kill the rabbit or have an abortion, if that's what you're wondering," but instead, he asked, "Any idea how much longer?"

"Dr. Wagoner is with her last patient and Dr. Russo just arrived from County Hospital. A late afternoon delivery. Shouldn't be —"

"I'm so sorry, Mr. Berkeley, to have kept you waiting," Dr. Debra Wagoner said, cutting Agnes Pompio short as she entered the waiting room. "If you'll pardon my French, it's been one hell of a day."

Matthew stood and took the woman's hand. With an understanding smile and a nod toward the magazine rack, he said, "Except for the reading material which isn't exactly geared to the male gender, not a problem."

Dr. Wagoner's laughter was genuine, but Matthew could sense the weariness, not only in her voice, but on her face. "Your television interview last night and the resulting newspaper articles this morning have created a major problem for the clinic." She inhaled through drawn lips, then quickly exhaled her anxieties. "Agnes, here, has been on the phone almost nonstop since we opened this morning, and I understand you and a friend of mine, Peyton Chandler, are, uh, fairly close."

Matthew chuckled at the Wagoner woman's choice of words. "Quick change of subject, but yes, I guess you could say that." With a glance at his watch, he went on, "Almost six. Peyton said you had a number of questions. If we could go to your office, I'll be happy to answer what I can."

• • •

Debra Wagoner's office was comfortable, but not overly plush, furnished with a large mahogany-stained desk, a leather-bound chair and sofa, shelves of medical reference books, and a wall full of diplomas. The room reminded Matthew of Lieutenant Taylor's office, only here, the emphasis was on medicine and healing instead of police work and the law.

Matthew's eyes traveled from Dr. Wagoner in the chair behind the desk to Dr. Paul Russo at the window. A short, dark-complexioned man in his mid-thirties, or so Matthew guessed, Russo appeared nervous, his hands constantly on the move — straightening his tie, adjusting his watch, sliding a wedding band off and on his left ring finger.

"And that's as much as I know," Matthew said. "I'm sure Homicide has a lot they're not telling me, and I'd be surprised if they did, but Peyton and I felt we had no choice but to go public."

"I can't blame you for that, Mr. Berkeley," Debra Wagoner said. "I'm sure you —"

Russo interrupted. "Do you realize the problems you've created for the clinic?" he asked, his right index finger pointed accusingly at Matthew on the word *you*. "The number of appointments canceled this morning and afternoon? Eleven, and three of them much needed T. O. P. procedures."

"T. O. P.?" Matthew asked.

"Termination of pregnancy," Debra Wagoner answered. "The professionally acceptable euphemism for abortion these days."

Russo went on with his complaint without losing a beat. "Even those scheduled for prenatal care have canceled. They were afraid they might be mistaken for T.O.P. patients."

"I'm sorry, Doctor," Matthew answered, "but the safety of your patients from a killer, acting as judge, jury and executioner of women who've had an abortion, seemed a little more important than whatever inconvenience it causes you or the clinic."

Debra Wagoner looked at Russo and shook her head, then to Matthew, "Paul is tired and upset, Mr. Berkeley. Quite honestly, we wanted to talk with someone from the Sheriff's Department, but when I called, they gave me Chief O'Riley, of all people. He said there was nothing they could do for us, which wasn't surprising. For whatever reason, O'Riley and Sheriff Ryskowski have always been reluctant to provide assistance to the Women's Clinic. I also got the idea he didn't think very highly of you. His lack of cooperation is why I contacted Peyton and asked if we could meet. I was sorry to hear about the bookstore being destroyed."

Death's Bright Angel

"That's why she's not with me this afternoon, but I'm not sure what I can do other than recommend hiring your own security service. After what Peyton and I heard last night, there are a number of extremists in Truegood Foley's organization or church or whatever you chose to call it, and no telling what they might do."

"I don't know why they need to do anything," Russo said indignantly. "Your words have already done their work for them. Can you imagine how many women whose lives could be ruined by having a baby who'll now be too afraid to even consider an abortion? And what about the monetary loss to the clinic? My..." Russo caught himself, at the same time gesturing toward Debra Wagoner. "...*our* investment. Without a practice, we can go under just like that." Russo snapped his fingers.

"Better my words than some murderer killing and mutilating them after the fact," Matthew shot back. "Regardless of my views on abortion which are apparently the opposite of yours, I don't like extremists on either side, and sure as hell not one who's more worried about his investment than saving the lives of innocent women."

Russo turned toward the window and looked out into the growing darkness. "Forget what I said, Berkeley. I'm tired, and it certainly wasn't fair to Debra. It's just..." Russo's chin dropped to his chest. "Forget it."

Ignoring Russo, Matthew stood, ready to leave. "Wish there was more I could do, Dr. Wagoner, especially to catch the killer, but that's not my job."

"I understand," Debra Wagoner said as she stood and moved to the door with Matthew. "When is the funeral for your sister? I'd like to come."

"I don't know. Whenever the Medical Examiner releases her and her husband gets here from Saudi Arabia. I'll let you know."

"I'd appreciate it. Where are you parked?"

"In the lot out back."

"If you'll wait a moment and let me make sure everything's locked, Paul and I'll walk out with you. After dark, safety in numbers, I always say."

"That's why I recommend a good security service," Matthew said. "Safety for you *and* your patients."

• • •

Paul Russo pushed open the heavily insulated steel door to the rear parking lot and stepped into the chill night air. "Problem," he called back through the open doorway.

"What?" Matthew asked as he and Debra Wagoner followed close behind.

"Dark as pitch. Parking lot lights are out."

"I'll have Agnes call Jax Electric tomorrow morning," Debra Wagoner said, stopping next to one of two cars parked adjacent to the building. As she searched in the darkness for the car door handle and lock, she explained to Matthew, "We normally have three spot lights that keep the lot as bright as day."

Watching Russo head for the second car, Matthew said, "I can see why you need them. I'm parked at the back of the lot. Have a good evening."

"Thank you," Debra answered, adding, "Tell Peyton I look forward to her appointment on Wednesday."

Already halfway across the lot, Matthew stopped and looked back. "Appointment?"

"She didn't tell you?"

"No."

"She will, I assure you."

Matthew stood for a moment, watching as both Debra Wagoner and Paul Russo opened the doors to their respective cars, each caught in the glow of interior lights. Suddenly, movement from the far side of Russo's car. Shadows. Two

Death's Bright Angel

became four and four became seven or eight.

"Watch out!" Matthew shouted as something hard rammed against the back of his head. He staggered forward. Fireworks exploded inside his skull. Another blow, this time against his kidneys, the pain immediate, shooting through his gut and down into his testicles. He stumbled and fell to the pavement, doubled over. He wanted to get up, to fight, but the pain was like a paralysis. He couldn't move.

From across the parking lot, he heard screams, a woman's, and then a man's, both high-pitched, both filled with terror. Without warning, strong arms grabbed him from behind and pulled him to an upright position.

"You're into something that's none of your business, Berkeley," a voice growled in his ear. "Stay out of it or you're a dead man."

"Bastards!"

A fist smashed against his face. "Shut up and watch what we do to baby killers."

More cries for help, this time, Russo's voice. Matthew struggled to break free, but arms, two on each side and a fifth tight around his throat, held him firm as a flashlight suddenly snapped on, illuminating the hood of Russo's car. At the edge of the light, he saw Debra Wagoner, slumped between two large, shadow-like figures, both wearing ski masks to cover their faces. Whether she was conscious or not, he couldn't tell.

"Berkeley, help me!" Russo cried as two more figures forced the upper part of his body face down over the hood of his car. A third on the opposite side grabbed Russo's arms and stretched them across the remainder of the hood, then shouted, "The hands of Satan! Cut them off."

Matthew watched helplessly as another figure loomed in front of the car, its movements at lightning speed. One moment, the glint of light on steel, high above the figure's head; the next moment, a downward blur. Matthew had only a glimpse, but instantly, he knew. Machete! "No—o-o-o!"

The swing ended with the crunch of wrist bone and the sharp clank of machete blade against automobile metal. Russo's scream, like the high-pitched squeal of a baby pig caught in a trap, pierced Matthew's ears and echoed on the night air. Again and again until all at once, it stopped, replaced by the far-off sounds of police sirens and feet, running on asphalt.

In his ear, Matthew heard, "Keep out of it, or you're next," and then the loosening of hands and the impact of something hammer-hard against the left side of his head. Or was it the right? The force seemed to bounce back and forth, as though his brain was tethered to an elastic cord, ricocheting from one side to the other. As he fell, a set of RV headlights swung past him on their way out of the parking lot, leaving a blue-black darkness that folded around him like a soft-spun cocoon.

CHAPTER 19
November 9, 1992
Monday Night

Why doesn't somebody turn off the goddamn light? Matthew squeezed his eyelids even tighter. His feet were freezing and the air smelled like antiseptic mouthwash. The grinding whir of a nearby machine as it sucked or pumped air — he couldn't tell which — seemed to be on the same frequency as the pain he felt in his head and lower back. In and out, or out and in? *Dumb goddamn machine. Can't make up its mind,* he decided.

Matthew rolled his head away from the light and moaned, "Jesus Christ, that hurts."

"Doctor," an unfamiliar female voice called. "He's awake."

"About damn time."

Matthew recognized Lt. Rich Taylor's voice. Automatically, he shifted toward the sound, his eyes still shut tight. "Don't tell me!" he rasped, his throat and vocal cords coated with a shroud of sinus drainage. "Who the hell invited him? I can't even dream without —"

"Quiet." Two fingers separated Matthew's right eyelids and a face stared down, half of it covered by a circular mirror with a hole in the center. The mouth beneath the mirror formed words in a middle-to-lower octave baritone, "You had us a little concerned. Can you tell us your name?"

"Would you believe..." Matthew cleared the buildup of nasal crud from his throat. "What if I don't want to tell you?"

"Matthew, this is serious. We've been so worried."

At the sound of Peyton's voice, Matthew pushed the hand away from his face and opened his left eye. "Hi, sweets. Never know who's getting ready to poke you in the eye these days." He held his hand out to Peyton who moved quickly from the foot of the bed and past a nurse to take his hand in hers and press it tightly against her lips.

"How do you feel?" she asked.

"Like I was hit by a bulldozer, but what the hell was that noise? Some kind of machine?"

"A vacuum cleaner in the hall," Taylor answered. "The cleaning crew. Everybody else's gone home, and that's where I'd be if it wasn't for you."

"Well, gee whiz, Mr. Lieutenant. I'm sorry as hell, but you really didn't have to —"

"Gentlemen!" It was the baritone again. Matthew turned his head to the man whose tired, work-worn face looked better covered by the mirror. "I'm Dr. Tidwell. You still haven't told me your name."

"Berkeley. Matt Berkeley."

"Good, and do you remember what happened?"

Matthew lay very still, probing the back corners of his mind until, "Russo! They cut off his hands. Is he?..."

"He's alive," Tidwell answered, "but the EMT couldn't find his hands."

"Whoever did it must've taken 'em," Taylor inserted.

"He's in critical condition," Tidwell continued. "A tremendous loss of blood, but we think he'll live."

"And Dr. Wagoner?"

Death's Bright Angel

"A blow to the head. A concussion, similar to yours, but otherwise she's fine, physically. After what happened, it's her emotional condition we're concerned about, but only time will tell. She'll be released tomorrow morning."

Taylor moved from the foot of the bed to Peyton's side. "Backdoor neighbors heard screams and called 911. Sirens must've scared off the bad guys before they could finish the job. When our people got there, they found Dr. Wagoner unconscious, draped across the hood of Russo's car and covered with blood. Russo's, we think. Her arms were stretched out and wrists tied like they were gonna do the same to her."

"Did they find the machete?" Matthew asked.

"That what they used, huh?" Taylor shook his head. "No."

Matthew groaned as he tried to push to a sitting position. "Somebody help me up. I've gotta pee."

The nurse started for the adjoining bathroom. "I'll get a bedpan."

"Forget it," Matthew ordered. "I do mine standing up, and Doctor, if you'll give me something to stop the pounding in my head and back, I'd like to talk to Peyton and the lieutenant. Alone."

• • •

"I'm telling you, Berkeley," Rich Taylor said, "my hands are tied."

"And Paul Russo doesn't have any hands."

"Unfair."

"Bullshit! How many times have I gotta tell you, Peyton and I heard them with our own ears. 'Stop the doctors. Cut off their hands.' And half the goddamn congregation chanting, 'Off with their hands. Off with their hands.'"

"That doesn't prove they did it," Taylor insisted.

"Who the hell's pulling your chain, Lieutenant?

O'Riley? The Sheriff?"

Peyton put a finger to Matthew's mouth. "Calm down, or your head'll hurt that much worse."

Matthew leaned back into his pillow and shut his eyes as Peyton turned to Rich Taylor. "Matt told me what's in the 'Z' file."

"That's great!" Taylor exploded. "Who else did you tell? What about O'Riley? Then my ass would really be in a sling. If he thought I was able to access the 'Z' file and he couldn't, —"

"I wouldn't tell O'Riley the time of day," Matthew muttered, his eyes still closed, "and anyway, you told the medical examiner and probably Sergeant Bartelow as well."

"That's different," Taylor insisted before turning to Peyton. "What about the 'Z' file?"

"From what we learned last night," Peyton continued, "Truegood Foley and his wife moved from Kansas City to Buffalo to Cleveland and now here. The same cities listed in the 'Z' file. The same cities where all the murders have taken place."

"How come you haven't told me this before?" Taylor demanded, more of Matthew than Peyton.

Matthew shook his head, at the same time squeezing the muscles of his face against the increased pain. "When, for chrissake? She told you, we only found out last night."

"I can't believe you two," Peyton said, her voice filled with exasperation. "If you'd spend as much time working with each other as you do arguing, you might be able to accomplish something. As I was going to say, if you can determine the dates the Foleys were in those cities, you might find they coincide with the times of the murders."

"You saying you think Foley and Mother Sam are the killers?"

Matthew opened his eyes. "One of their followers, and I'll bet the name 'Azrael' we saw in the 'Z' file is what he calls himself."

Death's Bright Angel

"Without talking to the Foleys themselves or one of the church members, how do I find out? O'Riley won't let me get close to 'em if he thinks it's got anything to do with the abortion murders."

Peyton answered without hesitation. "Talk with Debra Wagoner and ask her to call the family planning clinics in Buffalo, Cleveland and Kansas City. If they experienced demonstrations when Foley and his wife were there, the clinic staff will know when and what happened. I got the impression last night the more people that know his name and cause, the better Truegood Foley likes it."

"Anything else we can do for you, Lieutenant?" Matthew asked. "We're trying to help, but you don't seem very appreciative, and by the way, am I still a suspect?"

Taylor walked to the door, then stopped. "Not to me, but O'Riley?... He hates your guts. If I were you, I'd watch my back, and yeah,... I do need your help." Taylor's face took on a grimace that deciphered to sheer frustration. "You two are the only ones who seem to give a damn. And Miss Chandler, I'll talk with Dr. Wagoner. Thanks for the idea."

Matthew watched the door close. "Thank God, I thought he was going to spend the night."

"Time for you to get some sleep," Peyton said to Matthew. "I'll come back first thing tomorrow morning."

Matthew took her hand and pulled her back to the bed. "Uh-uh. We'll get a cot, and you stay here tonight. They knew who I was and they threatened to get me, and you better believe, they know who you are, too. From now on, we stay together, and besides there's two things we need to talk about."

"What?"

"First, when I get outta here tomorrow, there's a newspaper morgue we're going to visit."

"Which one?"

"The *Beaches Gazette*."

"What are you looking for?"

"Not sure. Something clicked last night when we were talking with the Foleys. If it's there, I'll know. Otherwise,..." Matthew shrugged his shoulders.

"You said there were two things."

"Your appointment with Dr. Wagoner at the clinic on Wednesday."

"How did you know?" Peyton asked, surprised.

"Dr. Wagoner, but she wouldn't explain. Said you'd tell me."

Peyton turned loose of Matthew's hand, stood and walked slowly to the window. Opening the blinds, she stared out into the night. Matthew waited, silently, until she turned.

"During the first three years of my marriage, I was pregnant, twice, and each time, into the fourth month of pregnancy, I miscarried."

"I didn't know."

"No need," Peyton said. "Twenty years ago. That and the fact that my husband couldn't tolerate my psychic abilities led to a very unpleasant divorce."

"I'm sorry."

"Don't be. Best thing that could've happened, and besides, we wouldn't be together if it hadn't."

Matthew patted the bed for Peyton to return and sit by his side. As she did, he said, "The only reason you're telling me this is you think you're pregnant. Right?"

Peyton smiled and took Matthew's hand in hers. "Yes, but it's not only the miscarriages. I'm forty-nine years old, and that scares me."

Matthew pushed himself higher in the bed. "Why? If you're pregnant and unless there's somebody else you haven't told me about, that means we're in this thing together."

"You know there's no one else. I love you so much, but

after the way Tony acted about Jackie's pregnancy, —"

"I'm not Tony," Matthew said emphatically, at the same time, pulling Peyton closer. "I love you, Peyton, and you know damn well I'd never want you to have an abortion."

Peyton pulled away, laughing softly and tracing the lines of Matthew's face with her fingers. "It's not a sure thing, yet. That's why I'm going to see Debra on Wednesday. To make certain, but if I am, what about the miscarriages?"

"What about them?"

"I don't think I can go through that again. The growing emotional attachment to a child that might never be, to a life that's part of my own, only to lose it before it can take its first breath. And at my age, there could be even more complications. I just don't know."

"Let's find out if you're pregnant, first," Matthew said, "and then we'll discuss the future."

"Our future?" Peyton asked.

"Yes. One way or the other, our future. Together."

Peyton slipped off her shoes and snuggled in beside Matthew, her head on his shoulder. "Think we can do without that cot tonight?" she asked.

Matthew chuckled. "Did I say something about a cot?"

"I love you, Matthew Berkeley, with all my heart."

"I love you, too," he whispered.

As Peyton nestled even closer, Matthew closed his eyes, and the intense pain that had hovered over his body seemed to fade away.

CHAPTER 20
November 10, 1992
Tuesday Afternoon

Lettering on the wide expanse of plate glass window read:

ATLANTIC PUBLISHERS, INC.
BEACHES GAZETTE
VOICE OF THE JACKSONVILLE BEACHES
SINCE 1947

"We both know you needed at least one more day in the hospital," Peyton said as Matthew opened the door to the single-story frame and stucco building. "I could have done this, you know."

"I can hurt just as well here as I could there," Matthew answered. "And anyway, other than the name *Moreland*, I don't know what I'm looking for, so how would you?"

A gray, chest-high, Formica-surfaced counter ran the length of the office. At one end, a stack of that week's issue of the *Beaches Gazette* and a picket fence-type gate that lead to an array of desks layered with mounds of photographs and news copy, computer monitors and keyboards. Nearby stood the office's single occupant, an eye-catching young girl, early twenties, the listening end of a telephone hidden beneath

Death's Bright Angel

shoulder-length blond hair. The phone's chalk-white mouthpiece stood in sharp contrast to the girl's smooth, tawny-hued skin that reminded Matthew of billboard ads for Hawaiian Tropic suntan lotion.

"You wouldn't," the girl said into the phone. Her giggle gave an indication that her conversation had little to do with business, at least not the newspaper's. "My mother?" Another giggle. "Not if we don't tell her."

The girl held up an index finger and mouthed, "In a minute," before saying, "I've got to go, Bobby. I can't wait, either, and don't forget..." She looked at Peyton and Matthew, then half whispered, "... the uh... our little protection." She giggled again. "I love you, too. Bye."

"Nothing like protection, I always say," Matthew said to Peyton, a smile on his face as he watched the girl's suntanned cheeks turn a blushing pink. With a wink and a smile, he asked, "Where is everybody? No typesetters? No presses running at full speed?"

Regaining her composure and suntan, the girl returned his smile and answered, "We don't print the paper here. This is the business office, and the regular staff is at lunch. I work here part-time."

"Maybe you can help us," Peyton said, her voice telling Matthew to quit flirting and get on with what they came to do.

"How?" The girl's mouth hung open in question and her eyelids fluttered like butterfly wings. Matthew couldn't decide whether it was the "dumb blond" game she was playing or simple, out-and-out stupidity.

"Old newspapers from the early fifties," Peyton answered. "We're doing research for a history of the beaches."

"The morgue," Matthew added.

The girl drew back. "Oh, no. This is a newspaper office, not a —"

"I'm sorry," Matthew said, laughing softly at the girl's

ignorance. "Where you keep files of old newspapers."

"I don't think so. That would take an entire building. We're pretty old, you know."

Matthew and Peyton looked at one another, each with an eyebrow raised, before Peyton further explained, "Not the papers themselves. On computer, microfilm or microfiche."

"Not computers. What's microfiche?" the girl asked.

"Sorry. Like microfilm except not on a roll. Clear plastic slides with miniaturized pictures of newspaper pages and articles and a viewer that magnifies."

The girl scratched her head, then said, "Is that what that is? There's a room in the back with something like that. I've never used it, but..."

"If we could look," Matthew said, at the same time taking out his wallet and flashing his U.S. Naval Reserve identification card as though it was some kind of official passport to secrets of the past. "It wouldn't take long."

• • •

The two microfilm viewers glowed grayish white in the darkened room. "Anything in '52?," Matthew asked.

"Nothing, other than a couple of advertisements for RxMore Soda Fountain and Drug Store. One of them even advertised their famous Coke floats. A free float with the purchase of a package of Carter's Little Liver Pills."

Matthew laughed. "Don't know about the liver pills, but I can sure attest to the quality of the Coke floats."

"And did you and Mother Sam share a Coke float during those tender years?" Peyton asked, a note of humor in her voice.

"She's either got a vivid imagination, or I've got a damn poor memory. I remember Doc Moreland's granddaughter. Cute, but I was into diving for golf balls at the local golf course and selling them back to the golfers for a dime apiece. No time for girls, and besides, in those days, she was bigger than me."

"She's not far from it, now," Peyton joked with a short laugh. "Her husband might be the mouthpiece in public, but at home, I bet she's the one that cracks the whip."

Matthew returned the last microfilm to the *1951* container and reached for the boxes marked *1953* and *1954.* "You do '53, I'll do '54."

"If my eyes hold out," Peyton said, rubbing both eyes before inserting the first 1953 microfilm into the viewer. Turning the knob, she moved the linear cursor across and down, back and forth until suddenly, she stopped. "I've got something."

Matthew turned from his own viewer and looked over Peyton's shoulder. "What?"

"Week of March 15, 1953." She fingered a point in the center of the viewer and a headline in bold print. " 'Local Druggist Arrested. Well known druggist and longtime beaches resident, 59-year-old Sam Moreland, was arrested Tuesday night in the attic of his home as he was about to perform an illegal abortion on a 17-year-old girl. The girl's parents learned of her plans at the last minute and called the police.' "

Matthew whistled softly. "I knew something happened, but I couldn't remember exactly what. That's gotta be it." He ran a finger down the front of the screen until he said, "Read that."

Peyton read, " 'Moreland's granddaughter, eight-year-old Samantha Moreland, who has lived with her grandparents since her mother and father, Gladys and Samuel Moreland, Jr., were killed in an automobile wreck two years ago, was removed from the home and temporarily placed with foster parents by the Florida Social Services Department. Though her grandmother refused to be interviewed, young Samantha stated as she was taken away, "I'm glad he was stopped. What he's (her grandfather) done is a very bad thing, and when I grow up, I'll do everything I can to keep people from killing their babies.' "

Peyton scrolled down several more lines until a photograph began to emerge.

"What's wrong?" Matthew asked. "You look like you've seen a ghost."

"I may have. My God, Matt, look at that picture."

"That's Dr. Sam. Sam Moreland, Samantha's grandfather."

Peyton sat back in her chair and swallowed hard. "It's him, Matt."

"Yeah, I know. It's —"

"No you don't, damn it!" Peyton swore. Her lungs grabbed for air as she stared at the photograph. "It's the man with the mustache. I've seen him. Through Chris Atwell's eyes, the woman killed at Fort Caroline and your sister. It's the killer, Matt."

"Can't be." Matthew laid his hand on Peyton's shoulder as he leaned closer to study Sam Moreland's halftone features. "Dr. Sam would be close to a hundred years old by now, or dead."

"It's the same face." Peyton placed her hand on Matthew's and held tight as though he might suddenly disappear, leaving her with a ghost from the past.

"I'm not disputing that, but the Sam Moreland my parents knew and I knew is not the man killing people in Jacksonville, Florida, in 1992."

"Did Samantha have a brother?"

"If she did, I didn't know about it."

"When her parents were killed," Peyton mused aloud, "he might have gone with the other grandparents."

"Could be, but at this point, I'm not gonna be the one to ask her."

"Don't have to," Peyton said, releasing her hold on

Death's Bright Angel

Matthew's hand and pushing back from the viewer. "Let's get our little blond bombshell in the front office to find somebody who can make a copy of this, and then call your friend, Lieutenant Taylor. He can check birth records at the County Court House, and if Samantha Moreland has a brother,...."

Matthew leaned down and kissed Peyton's cheek. "We might've just found ourselves a killer."

William Kerr

CHAPTER 21
November 11, 1992
Wednesday Morning

Truegood Foley finished his cup of coffee and pushed away from the table. "Will Azrael be there?"

Mother Sam shook her head. "He's afraid the Chandler woman knows too much. She sees things the others don't, but he'll know what happens."

"I wish he'd go away. He's become too dangerous. He won't listen to me. Make him leave, Samantha. Please."

Samantha Foley glared at her husband, her disgust for his weakness growing with each day. "Stop whining, Truegood. The pro-choice people will be at the clinic today. Ignore them. Simply do what Azrael has instructed, and everything will go as planned. Understand?"

"Yes, but —"

"Just do it, Truegood. It's what Azrael wants, and you know Azrael has never been wrong."

• • •

From the Jeep, they could see the line of demonstrators strategically spaced along the front of the clinic. Peyton looked at her watch, her eyebrows cocked at a worried angle. "Eleven-thirty. I didn't think they'd be here this early."

"But look at the signs they're carrying," Matthew said.

Peyton read the signs aloud, " '*Abortion. A divine and constitutional right.*' '*Keep abortion legal.*' '*Against abortion? Don't have one,*' " before breathing a sigh of relief. "Thank God, they're not —"

"Speaking of God," Matthew interrupted, "check out the one on the far end. '*I asked God and she's pro-choice.*' A little presumptuous, don't you think?"

"Perhaps, but over there." Peyton pointed toward an RV parked across the street, on its side the words, CHILDREN OF CHRIST REFORM CHURCH — SAVE THE UNBORN. Immediately in front of the RV was a police patrol car and a small crowd of people carrying signs lettered with antiabortion slogans.

"I'm not believing this," Matthew muttered. "Truegood, Mother Sam and their band of merrymakers. Well screw 'em. You're not here to have an abortion. You're here to find out if *we're* gonna have a baby. And whatever it is you've got in that paper bag you're carrying, you'd better hold tight if they head this way."

"A jar of urine."

Matthew chuckled. "Couldn't wait, huh?"

"No, silly. Has to be the first in the morning before having anything to drink. With this and a blood sample, there should be no doubt, one way or the other."

Matthew kissed Peyton gently on the lips and said with a wink, "Let's go check out that urine."

As Matthew and Peyton stepped to the sidewalk, two women and a man emerged from the clinic's entrance and hurried in their direction. Each wore what looked like a brand new yellow crossing-guard vest with the word ESCORT stenciled front and back. Like members of a well-trained drill team, the women took up positions at Peyton's side and rear. The man held out his hand to Matthew.

"I'm Ernie. Doc Wagoner told us who you are and why you're here, but thought we'd come out anyway since ol' Truegood and his flock got here earlier than usual."

"Thanks," Matthew said, at the same time, nodding toward the street, "and speak of the devil, here he comes with his own police escort stopping traffic for him. Let's get inside."

"And he's got that goddamn megaphone with him," Ernie groaned. "I just spent a night in jail and paid a five hundred dollar fine because of that son of a bitch."

"If he causes trouble, leave him to me," Matthew insisted. "Let's go." Taking Peyton by the arm, he started toward the clinic's double entrance doors, Ernie and the two female escorts close behind.

"I'm tellin' ya, Mr. Berkeley," Ernie said at Matthew's shoulder, "you so much as touch him, —"

"I'll handle it, Ernie."

Truegood Foley reached the sidewalk and stopped directly in front of Matthew. The two police officers hung back, waiting, for what, Matthew didn't know, but it was Foley who commanded his attention. He nodded to the man. "Reverend Foley." Matthew quickly realized Foley was not there to exchange polite conversation.

Foley raised the megaphone to his mouth and shouted, "You're doing the work of the devil, Mr. Berkeley. Take her home. Not into this cursed place."

With the exception of Foley and himself, it was as if the world had suddenly grown silent. Members of Foley's flock, pro-choice demonstrators, policemen — all waited, motionless, holding their collective breath, poised for the inevitable to happen.

"You don't need your megaphone today, Foley," Matthew said, his words spaced evenly, each syllable spoken slowly so there would be no misunderstanding. "We're not here to —"

"And you, Miss Chandler," Foley blared, ignoring Matthew. "The life inside you. For the sake of God, let it live." Foley drew closer until the megaphone was directly in Peyton's face. "If you kill your baby, God will curse you and drive you from his grace."

"Stop it," Peyton shouted, back-stepping to avoid the megaphone. "Leave us alone. Matt tried to tell you. We're not here —"

"I will never leave you alone, you wicked woman. You're like all the rest. A filthy slut sent from Hell, bent on serving your own whorish cravings and —"

Peyton stumbled. As she reached to Matthew for support, the bagged jar fell from her hand and crashed to the sidewalk, the urine quickly spreading a dark wetness across the concrete.

Matthew's response was bullet-fast. His right hand was a blur as it smashed against the megaphone, knocking it from Foley's hand and sending it flying between two of the pro-choice demonstrators. It slammed into the clinic wall and fell to the sidewalk, the bell of the horn crushed from the impact.

"Officers," Foley cried, "did you see? You are witnesses. This man destroyed my property."

Enraged, Matthew grabbed Truegood Foley by the shirt collar, gave the material a half twist with his hand, enough to shut off Foley's cry for help, and lifted him off the sidewalk.

"Matt," Peyton shouted, "Don't!"

Ernie tried to grab his arm. "Mr. Berkeley, he's not worth it. Stop!"

But Matthew was too far gone. Ignoring pleas from both Peyton and Ernie, Matthew swung Foley out past the curb and sent him staggering into the street. "Ever do that again, you skinny little bastard," he shouted, "I'll break your goddamn neck."

Hands grabbed him. A shoe came out of nowhere and

kicked his feet out from under him. He landed chest down. Before he could move, a knee in the back crushed him flat against the sidewalk. Simultaneously, a baton slapped lengthwise against the side of his skull. The weight behind the baton pinned his head to the concrete.

"Matthew," Peyton screamed, but he couldn't answer. From somewhere above, he heard, "Cuff him, damn it, cuff him!" The voice was familiar. He tried to turn, to see, but the baton pressed harder. And then his arms were jerked up and twisted backwards. Lightning bolts of pain shot through his shoulders and neck, ending finally with the touch of cold metal against each wrist and the double click of handcuffs snapping shut.

"Get him up and out of here."

It was that voice again, and Matthew made the connection. At the same time, hands grabbed his arms, dragged him to his feet and marched him across the street toward the waiting police cruiser.

"Let him go," Peyton pleaded from the clinic door.

The voice ordered, "Go home, lady, where you belong."

Straining to look over his shoulder as the two policemen shoved him toward the car, Matthew shouted at the voice, "What the hell are you doing here?"

Chief of Detectives James Michael O'Riley stood on the curb in front of the Jacksonville Women's Clinic for Family Planning and called back, "I told you I'd get you, Berkeley. When people like you create disturbances in public places, you leave us no choice." To the two police officers he shouted, "Get him out of here, lock him up, and throw away the key."

• • •

Wednesday Afternoon

"Welcome to the City of Jacksonville Pretrial Detention Facility," the black female officer greeted facetiously as the arresting policemen, one on each side, pushed Matthew through the door into the booking room. To Matthew, she added, "We don't get many in here that look and dress as good as you." Her smile was almost as broad as her bust line which, at any other time, would have been a source of amazement and admiration on Matthew's part.

"Knock it off, Lurlene," one of the arresting officers ordered, at the same time, tossing a plastic bag containing Matthew's wallet, car keys and money onto the counter. "This guy's bad news."

"Why so?"

"Cause little Jimmy O'Riley says so."

"Murder?" Lurlene asked, eyeing Matthew suspiciously.

"Naw. Simple battery. Destruction of the Rev. Truegood Foley's megaphone in front of an abortion clinic." The officer shook his head. "I hate this fucking duty."

"Sounds like that guy named Ernie the other week, but what the hell's O'Riley got to do with something like that?"

"Hey! Don't ask me. He wanted aggravated battery, a second-degree felony, till he realized after what Foley did, he could be charged with the same thing. As usual, Foley was actin' like a horse's patootie. If it'd been me, I'd a punched Foley from here to next week."

Lurlene studied Matthew for a few seconds, then said, "Uncuff him."

"You sure?" the second officer asked.

Lurlene laughed and shook her head. "How do you expect me to print him? Ink his hands, slide the card under his ass and let him sit on it? C'mon, guys. I worked the midshift last night. I'm already late gettin' out of here 'cause my relief called in sick and I gotta be back at eight tonight."

Spinning Matthew around, the policeman unlocked the handcuffs as the other officer slipped a no-carbon-required custody form onto the counter in front of Lurlene and said, "Sign it, and he's all yours. What time's court tomorrow morning?"

Lurlene signed the form, tore off a copy and answered, "Nine o'clock, and that's if Judge Tatorre can locate his glasses and find his way across the Main Street Bridge in time. If you're a witness to the dastardly deed, might as well plan on spending the morning in county court."

As the arresting officers turned on their heels and stalked out of the room, Lurlene turned to Matthew. "Name?"

"Berkeley. Matthew W., as in whiskey."

"Okay, Mr. Matthew W., as in whiskey. We're gonna take your fingerprints, a coupla beauty shots with the camera over there, a breath test, some urine and your personals. Give me any trouble, and I've got six guys sitting back there who can put you down in a heartbeat."

Matthew quickly surveyed the rest of the office, spotting the half-dozen officers at their desks, each as large if not larger than himself, and each looking at him as if he was a prime suspect on *America's Most Wanted*. "I believe you."

"Over here," Lurlene directed. "Right hand first."

As Lurlene inked and took impressions of the fingers of Matthew's right hand, she asked, "How come a class-looking guy like you jumped ol' Truegood? Your wife getting an abortion?"

Matthew shook his head. "He thought so, but she was there for a pregnancy test, and you mentioned Ernie a while ago."

"Left hand. You know Ernie?"

"Met him today. He apparently paid a visit to your fine establishment for pretty much the same reason I'm here."

"Poor guy. Trying to protect a young girl from Foley sticking a megaphone in her face, but sounds like you took care of the megaphone. Good for you. There's Gunk in the can there to clean your hands, then up against the screen for some snapshots."

Death's Bright Angel

Matthew cleaned his hands, then moved to the far side of the room and a scaled-down motion picture screen as Lurlene stuck letters and numbers on a mug shot ID board. "How do you want me?" he asked.

"Face forward and then your best side."

"When can I post bail?"

"Bail?" Lurlene laughed. "Not this time, honey. You're in here on a misdemeanor, punishable by not more than sixty days confinement or a five hundred dollar fine. By the time you made bail, you'd've already been to court and paid your fine."

"Five hundred dollars. That's what Ernie paid," Matthew said, remembering Ernie's bitter words, "but I need to get out of here."

"That's what everybody says," Lurlene said, snapping the first picture before adding, "You're our guest 'til tomorrow morning when you go see Judge Salvatore Tatorre, and a word to the wise."

"What's that?" Matthew asked, blinking his eyes from the flash and following Lurlene's motions to turn for a side-on shot.

"He hates abortions and anything to do with abortion clinics. I had one two years ago. When he found out, and I don't know how, he wouldn't speak to me for six months. Even tried to get me kicked off the force."

"What a guy," Matthew said with a sigh of disillusionment. "Think maybe he could have a fender-bender on the way in, and I could get a female judge who's high on women's lib?"

"Don't bet on it, honey," Lurlene said. "Around here, ain't nobody high on women's anything."

CHAPTER 22
November 11, 1992
Wednesday, Midafternoon

DUVAL COUNTY
OFFICE OF VITAL STATISTICS
(RECORDS OF BIRTH)

Sgt. Polly Bartelow paused in front of the plate glass door and read the words stenciled in semigloss black.

"Damn record searches," she mouthed to herself. "I hate 'em."

Pushing against the glass, she entered a world of floor-to-ceiling, gray metal shelves crammed with volume after volume of oversized, cloth-covered binders. The rows of shelves seemed endless, the odor of aging paper almost suffocating.

"Can I help you?"

Bartelow jumped, startled by the voice. "Mr. Walker?"

She'd never met Mr. Walker. He blended in so well with the shelves and binders, if he hadn't stood, she wouldn't have seen him at the desk, tucked behind a computer monitor. He was a mousy little man with mouse-gray hair, what there was of it, mouse-gray skin, and a mouse-shaped face, a creature who had lived too long among the county's aging archives.

Death's Bright Angel

"Sgt. Polly Bartelow," she answered. "Need to check birth records, 1940 through 1950."

"Court order, or can't do."

"You and I both know these are public records," Bartelow said as she plopped a manila envelope on the counter, "but just to keep you people happy, here's one anyway."

"Hummpphh," Walker grunted, lifting the flap on the envelope and pulling out the original and several copies of the order. "Moreland, huh? Lots of Morelands."

"Parents' names," Bartelow answered, pointing to a line on the court order.

Walker nodded toward the end of the counter and, in a tone Bartelow considered a bit condescending, said, "Come around the end. I'm short of help today, so you'll have to do it yourself. Nineteen-forty through 1945 in row eight, tier three. Nineteen-forty-six through '50 in row nine, top tier. Names alphabetized by year. There's a ladder back there if you need it for the top tier."

As she looked down on the little man, Bartelow wanted to say, "Except for the lowest shelves, I bet you need a ladder every time you go back there," but instead, she gestured toward the rows of binders and asked, "Why haven't all these records been put on computer disks or microfilm? Sure would save a lot of space and time."

"If you must know, Sergeant," Walker said with a sneer, "everything from 1954 is on microfilm, but when records go back to 1865 and you're limited in time and money,... If this isn't good enough for you, come back in five years and perhaps it will be more to your liking. If you'll excuse me, I've work to do."

With the rest of the mice, Bartelow thought as she rounded the end of the counter and counted the rows — six, seven, eight. She turned and moved sideways down the fluorescent-lighted aisle. One of the fluorescent bulbs halfway down the aisle flickered on and off, causing her to blink as she adjusted her eyes.

Directly beneath the flickering light, she stopped. "Nineteen-forty," she said aloud, more to keep herself company than anything else. "*A* through *AR*, *AS* through *BJ*," and on, from binder to binder, until, "*ME* through *MU*." Pulling the oversized notebook from the shelf, she laid the top against the edge of the shelf for support, ran the end of her moistened tongue over her fingers and thumbed through the pages until she found *Moreland.* Three of them, but none born to Samuel Moreland, Jr., and his wife, Gladys.

Nineteen-forty-one and five more Morelands, again not who she was looking for. Nineteen-forty-two, '43, '44, the volumes for each year thinner than those of the thirties and later forties. World War II and most of the men at war, Bartelow decided as she moved through the Morelands of 1944. Mary Lee Moreland, Roberta Anne Moreland, Samuel Barber Moreland, III.

"Gotcha!"

Bartelow's eyes followed her index finger as it moved across the page and down each line, her lips mouthing the words. "Samuel Barber Moreland, III. Born May 17, 1944, at 3:31 a.m., to Gladys Simpson Moreland and Samuel B. Moreland, Jr., County Hospital, Jacksonville, Florida, County of Duval."

It was the adjoining entry that also caught her eye. *Samantha Michele Moreland. Born May 17, 1944, at 3:39 a.m., to Gladys Simpson Moreland and Samuel B. Moreland, Jr.*

"I'll be damn. Twins."

• • •

"Lieutenant."

Rich Taylor glanced from the file he was studying to the small travel clock on his desk, then looked toward the door.

"It's 5:30. Where have you been?"

Bartelow tossed the manila envelope on Taylor's desk. "Where you sent me, Lieutenant, and Miss Chandler was right."

Taylor dropped his head and laughed. "Tell me something new." Looking up, he asked, "What's the name? And don't tell me it's Sam."

"You got it. Samuel Barber Moreland, III, born May 17, 1944, eight minutes ahead of his twin sister, Samantha. Makes him forty-eight years old."

"Twins. I'll be damn."

Bartelow laughed. "Same thing I said."

"Is he still alive?"

"So far as the State of Florida's concerned, yes," she answered, "or at least, there's no record of him dying in Florida. No police record, no listing as a licensed driver with the DMV. Nothing under Workman's Comp, either, and nothing on the Master Name Index."

"What about the National Crime Investigative Center? NCIC?"

"Nothing. I've asked Sergeant Grimes in the Intelligence Unit to contact Social Security for an SSN which I probably won't get until tomorrow. He's also checking with ATF in case the man ever purchased a gun."

"Legitimately," Taylor threw in.

Bartelow raised an eyebrow at Taylor's interruption, then continued, "Also Civil Service and Department of Defense to see if they have or had anybody by that name in their records."

"Just in case," Taylor reminded, "add IRS to the list. They'll at least give you the date of his last federal tax return if he had one and the address he sent it from. And don't forget the Veterans Administration. If he's used a VA medical facility recently, they might have a DNA readout we could compare with the M.E.'s semen sample."

"Yes, sir." Bartelow turned and started from the room when the telephone rang.

"Hold it," Taylor ordered over the second ring. "Might be Berkeley. I've been trying to get him." He picked up the receiver and said, "Homicide, Taylor."

Bartelow could barely hear the caller's voice, but she could tell it was a woman.

"Yes, ma'am," Taylor said. "I'm gonna put you on the speakerphone." Before switching to the speakerphone, Taylor cupped his hand over the mouthpiece and said to Bartelow, "It's Dr. Wagoner from the Women's Clinic. I want you to hear this."

Taylor pushed a button on the base of the telephone and said, "Go ahead, Doctor."

Debra Wagoner's voice filled the room. "First, I contacted the clinics in Buffalo, Cleveland and Kansas City, and yes, the Foleys were there during the times you mentioned. Second, Agnes Pompio, our receptionist, went home sick this afternoon. When I went into her desk for the appointment calendar, I found a piece of paper with names of patients and what I think is a phone number."

"This is Sergeant Bartelow, Doctor," Polly said in a louder than normal voice. "If the Pompio woman is your receptionist, why is that so unusual?"

"With exception of the last name on the list, the others were former patients. Justine Crowley,..."

Bartelow's head snapped to attention. "The Fort Caroline skeleton," she whispered as Debra Wagoner went on, '... Chris Atwell, Lavonna Mayes and Jackie Serafina, Matt Berkeley's sister, along with appointment dates."

"And each one murdered," Taylor muttered to himself before asking, "Those appointments, Doctor. For the days they had their abortions?"

"Yes."

"And the phone number?" Bartelow prompted.

"Seven-four-seven-C-A-R-E."

"Seven-four-seven-C-A-R-E," Taylor repeated as he wrote down the number, "as in care. Some kinda care. In other words, the Pompio woman's been feeding the killer with names and dates. No wonder he..."

Debra Wagoner's voice interrupted Taylor's thought process. "I've been trying to get hold of Peyton Chandler all afternoon, but —"

"And I've been trying to locate Berkeley," Taylor said, "and as usual, without success."

"You didn't know?" Wagoner asked, her words tainted with surprise.

"Didn't know what?"

"He brought Peyton in for an appointment this morning."

"Not an abortion, I hope," Bartelow said to no one in particular.

"No," Debra Wagoner answered. "I'm not at liberty to say what, but definitely not an abortion. When Truegood Foley tried to stop them, Mr. Berkeley smashed the famous Foley megaphone. They arrested him."

Taylor jumped to his feet. "Who arrested him?"

"Chief O'Riley and two police officers."

"What the hell was O'Riley doing there?" Taylor blurted.

"I'm sure I don't know, Lieutenant." Debra Wagoner sounded offended at Taylor's demand.

Bartelow leaned toward the speakerphone. "The lieutenant understands that, Doctor, and his question wasn't directed at you, but I've got a question."

"Yes?"

"You said with the exception of the last name on the list,

all were former patients. What is the last name?"

"Peyton Chandler."

"Oh, shit!" was all Polly Bartelow could say.

• • •

"Who the hell do you think you are, bursting in here and talking to me like this?" O'Riley shouted. "I run this division, and if I want to go out to some goddamn abortion mill, I'll do it, and I don't need your permission. And who told you I was there?"

Rich Taylor placed both fists on the front of O'Riley's desk and leaned into the Chief's face. "Dr. Wagoner told me, and I don't give a shit what you do or where you go, but Berkeley's part of my case and I want him the fuck outta jail." Taylor pounded a fist on the desk. "Now, goddamn it!"

O'Riley was on his feet. "Berkeley's where I want him, and after my discussion with Judge Tatorre this afternoon, that's where the hell he's going to stay. And I told you to keep away from the abortion clinic and anything to do with abortion. Didn't I?"

Taylor whirled around and walked to the window, trying to calm himself before he got into real trouble, but O'Riley had gone too far this time. He turned and faced O'Riley. "Until Berkeley forced the issue on that television program, you've been covering up the abortion link with every one of these murders. You couldn't or wouldn't get into the 'Z' file which show the same kind of killings over the past three to four years in Buffalo and Cleveland and Kansas City. Every time Truegood Foley's gone someplace to do his thing, women who've had abortions get killed. Every time —"

"You got into the 'Z' file, didn't you?" The sagging jowls of O'Riley's face went livid with anger.

"You gotta know the right people, Chief."

"Damn you, Taylor! And Berkeley. It was him. Him and his FBI friend, wasn't it? Last Saturday night, and you thought

I didn't know where you were and who you were with."

"What're you hiding, Chief?" Taylor asked, trying to control his anger. "Who are you protecting? Your friends at the Children of Christ Reform Church? You're Catholic, so I know you don't go to church there, but you know Foley's wife, don't you? You know Mother Sam. Your old man was Chief of Police at Jax Beach when her grandfather was arrested for performing abortions, wasn't he?"

"So that's why Berkeley and the Chandler woman were at the newspaper office," O'Riley said, as much to himself as to Taylor. "Dredging up the past, and of course, he told you about Dr. Sam and his granddaughter. You're off the case, Lieutenant."

"Who says?"

"I say. You've disobeyed every order I've given concerning this case. You've used Berkeley to get around me, and I *will not stand* for it."

"You're full of shit, Chief, and you can't throw me off the case just like that. I'll go to the Sheriff and —"

"I've already discussed you with the Sheriff and you've been relieved as Homicide Unit Commander. There's a body behind Wayfarers Mall. Last night. Shot six times. He's yours and Sergeant Bartelow's."

"And who takes over my job and the abortion murders?" Taylor demanded.

"Who do you think, Lieutenant?" O'Riley asked, a satisfied grin spreading across his face. "The Sheriff wants the best, so he's asked me to take personal charge, and until I can find somebody I can trust, that's exactly what I'm going to do. Now get out of here before I reassign you to garbage dump patrol, or better yet, kick your ass off the force for good."

William Kerr

CHAPTER 23
November 11, 1992
Wednesday Evening

Truegood Foley stood behind the lectern, alone on an empty stage before an empty, darkened sanctuary. A single bulb, like some cold, distant star, shone down from high in the ceiling, forming a cone of light around the tall, perilously thin preacher. Tear lines glistened along the sides of his uplifted face.

"Oh, children of Christ, we feel your pain and your loneliness," he cried, quickly glancing at the papers in his hand to cue him onward. "But you are not forsaken. We are by your side, God's army, prepared and unafraid, ready to —"

A door opened at the rear of the church, letting in the chill breath of a November nor'easter before slamming shut. The sound echoed against the sanctuary's walls. Truegood shivered nervously as he stared into the darkness for the source of the sound. "Who's there?" he called, automatically erasing the tear stains from his cheeks with the back of his free hand. Footsteps, barely audible, moved slowly along the center aisle. One set or two? Partway down the aisle, they stopped.

"I still can't see you," Truegood said loudly, a sudden wariness in his voice. "Is that you, Samantha?"

The voice was raspy, almost sepulchral in its coldness.

Death's Bright Angel

"Samantha says you wish I'd go away."

"Azrael!" The sheath of papers containing Sunday's sermon dropped from Truegood's hand as he grabbed the top of the lectern for support.

"Samantha says you think I've become too dangerous."

"I... I —"

"Have we not slowed abortion's march wherever we've been? Have we not brought justice to the wicked, you with God's word, I as God's hand?"

"It... it's just that..." Truegood stammered, "... the Chandler woman and Berkeley. Especially her. Her powers. Samantha said even you have felt them. The woman knows something, Azrael. All I want is to stop the killing, the... the punishments for awhile. Later, you could start again, but for now, you could go away. Couldn't you?"

"We are stopping the killing, Truegood. The killing of innocent babes who can neither speak nor fend for themselves."

"Samantha. Is... is she with you?"

Silence filled the church.

"Please," Truegood begged. "If she's with you, let me speak to her."

A slight movement in the darkness, then, "I'm here, Truegood."

"Thank God," Truegood whispered to the Almighty, his eyes flickering upward in relief at hearing his wife's voice. "Samantha, I beg you, don't go with him. I'm afraid. He's trying to take over, and if something goes wrong, everything we've worked for could be lost."

"I'm sorry, Truegood. Azrael leaves me no choice. I will ask him to delay further retribution, but for tonight, he...we have no choice if we are to survive."

"No, Samantha, I won't let you. I—"

"It's time to go, Truegood."

He heard footsteps, fading as they moved toward the rear of the church. The door opened. Wind sounds rushed in as a sudden draft swept against his face, colder than before. "Don't go with him, Samantha," Truegood cried. The door slammed shut. "Samantha—a—a!"

• • •

By the time he reached the family quarters, Truegood was panting, each breath pained by the knowledge that this was the only way he could save Samantha and prevent his own downfall. He grabbed the telephone and punched the first of six memory buttons and waited.

"Let him be there, God," Truegood prayed, "Let him... Yes, it's Truegood. I need your help." He listened, then, "You don't have a choice. We've got to stop them. If you refuse to help, it could ruin us all, and you know what that could mean, especially for you."

The clock on the wall seemed magnified in Truegood's eyes, its hands moving faster and faster. "I'll be in front of the church, and hurry. There's not much time."

• • •

"I don't want you staying alone." Matthew reached across the table in the Detention Center's visiting room and touched Peyton's hand. He could feel the eyes of the two officers standing near the open door, like laser beams, insuring nothing passed between them.

Two straight-back chairs and a light-maple-stained conference table with long-ignored cigarette burns scarring the edges of both sides were the room's only furniture. A white and red cardboard sign reading *NO SMOKING* was thumbtacked to one of the pea-green walls. A second wall held a large, rectangular mirror that Matthew felt certain, if all the old detective stories were true, provided a view of the room for watchers on the other side.

"I could go to your apartment."

Matthew shook his head. "No good. You'd still be alone. What about Helena?"

"I suppose, but I really don't see —"

Matthew squeezed Peyton's hand. "I'll feel a lot better knowing you're with someone. After this morning's run-in with Truegood and what he said to you, —"

"But I wasn't there for an abortion," Peyton countered.

"He thought so, and if he did, and he's tied into the killings,..." Matthew sucked in enough air to fill his lungs, then let the air escape as he half-whispered, "Just do it. For me."

Peyton smiled, stretched across the table and touched Matthew's lips. "For you."

"Ma'am," one of the officers said.

"I'm sorry," Peyton responded, immediately drawing back.

"You're already past your ten minutes," the second officer reminded.

"And I appreciate you letting me stay." To Matthew, she said, "I'll run by the house, put an overnight bag together, and call Helena. What time is court tomorrow morning?"

"Nine, if the judge can find the courtroom."

Peyton looked quizzically at Matthew. "I'll be there, but what's that about the judge?"

Matthew laughed darkly. "Forget it. Bad joke I heard today. Just remember," he continued as Peyton rose to leave, "I love you. Whatever the outcome of the pregnancy tests and whatever you decide, we're in this thing together."

Peyton patted her lower stomach and smiled. "I know, and I love you, too. For that, and everything else."

• • •

The remote control clicked through one channel after another: the local weather channel and a warning of extensive beach erosion from the season's first nor'easter, ESPN and

Golf's Greatest Heroes, CNN's *Larry King Live* with Ross Perot and "Why I Lost the Election," a three-hundredth rerun of an episode of *Gilligan's Island* on Nickelodeon, *The Bill Cosby Show*, Public Television's *Pavarotti Sings Puccini*, and back to *Cosby*.

Anna shook her head. "You're driving me crazy, Rich Taylor. Give me the control and go do what you know you oughta be doing."

Taylor tossed his wife the control. "What I oughta be doing, I can't. Why don't you understand that?"

"You could if you really wanted to."

"You know what I want, Anna? I want to stick a gun barrel up O'Riley's rear end and pull the trigger, but I'm not."

Anna pointed the remote at the television set and pushed the *POWER OFF* button, sending the room into silence. "You were getting there, Rich. You and Polly Bartelow and that man, Berkeley, and Miss Chandler. This is the biggest case you ever had, and you're gonna let that fat puke of a white man take it away from you and get all the credit? It's hard enough for a black man to make it to the top, but you're throwing it away. Get Berkeley and —"

"He's in jail, I told you, and I want to get to the top as bad as you. I got dreams, too, but bein' black, I've gotta stick to the rules more than anybody else. No matter how many *atta boys* I've got, one *aw shit* mistake, and I'm out, with O'Riley's footprint square in the middle of my ass."

Anna pushed up from the sofa. "I'm gonna find something to drink. You want a Coke? We've got Dr. Pepper, too."

"Rather have a beer. A cold Bud might —"

The doorbell cut him short. "Who the hell could that be?" Taylor looked at his watch. "It's already after ten o'clock."

"I'll get it," Anna said, hurrying to the front door. Taylor heard the foyer light snap on, the door open, and Anna say, "Why, Polly Bartelow," her voice accompanied by the sound of wind whistling through the doorway. "Come on in. He's in the living room."

"I know it's late," Bartelow said as Anna led her into the living room. "As I was saying, —"

"I know," Taylor said, mimicking Bartelow's voice, "It's late, but it just couldn't wait." In his own voice, he added, "If it's about the abortion murders, Polly, we're off the case, and you know it."

Anna shook her head, her lips pursed tight, visibly irritated with her husband. "Rich has forgotten his manners, Polly. Have a seat. I was about to get something to drink."

"Not for me," Polly answered. "I thought the lieutenant would want to know what I found, but..."

"Damn it, Rich," Anna cursed, "listen to her. She came all the way over —"

"All right, Polly, goddamn it, what've you found? As if it's gonna do us any good."

Bartelow sat on the edge of the sofa where Anna had been sitting, pulled a sheath of papers from her purse and handed them to Taylor. "Samuel Barber Moreland, III. Lived with an aunt on his mother's side after his parents were killed. Waycross, Georgia. According to the Department of Defense, joined the Army at eighteen. Served in Vietnam as a cook."

"Probably where he got so handy with a knife," Taylor said, sarcastically. "Join the Army and learn a trade. How to butcher women."

"You don't know that for sure," Anna scolded. "What else, Polly?"

"You takin' over the investigation?" Taylor asked Anna. "Thought you were gonna get us something to drink."

Anna ignored her husband. "Go on, Polly."

Bartelow tried unsuccessfully to hide the smile on her

face before continuing. "He retired from the Army after twenty years with a thirty percent VA disability. They're checking to see if they might have preserved any blood or tissue samples. Probably not, but should know tomorrow."

"What kind of disability and where'd he retire?" Taylor asked.

"Something from Vietnam. Constant headaches and vision problems. Not with his eyes, but having visions, from what the VA said. Flashbacks of Vietnam, I guess, and religious things. Sometimes thought he was God."

"And maybe an angel," Taylor tossed in, "like the angel of death."

"He retired in Kansas City."

Taylor sat back in his chair. "No shit!"

"According to the IRS, he submitted his last income tax return for the year 1988, which would have been submitted in 1989."

"And according to the 'Z' file, the year the killings started. In Kansas City, no less. Anything else?" Taylor grunted as he forced himself out of the recliner and to the window, not wanting Bartelow and his wife to see the increasing excitement on his face. "Nor'easter's startin' to really get wound up," he said, trying to retain an air of disinterest in his voice as he watched trees in the front yard bend before the wind.

"In February of '89, he bought a Smith and Wesson .38 Chiefs Special revolver from a licensed dealer in Kansas City, according to the ATF." Bartelow hesitated as she watched Taylor's face mirrored in the window pane. "What's wrong?"

"Ex-Army. Buys a five-shot revolver. Why not a semiautomatic? Something big with a lot of firepower."

Bartelow shrugged her shoulders. "I'm only telling you what ATF told the Intelligence Unit and what they told me. After that, neither the VA nor the IRS ever heard from him

Death's Bright Angel

again. When his disability and retirement checks weren't cashed after a year, VA and the Army went looking for him, but —"

"He was gone," Taylor said, anticipating Bartelow's words as he turned from the window. "Disappeared. No record. Right?" He didn't wait for Bartelow's response. "I'd be willing to bet the farm he was gone to Buffalo and then to Cleveland with his sister and good ol' Truegood Foley. And now here. Anything else?"

"Not about Moreland, but I think you'll be interested in what Intel got from Southern Bell security about 747-CARE."

Taylor saw the I-told-you-so smile on his wife's face, but he had to know. "Well, go on," he said anxiously.

"An unlisted number. To get that kind of number, he had to —"

"Damn it, Polly, who does it belong to?"

Bartelow hesitated. Taylor knew she was building the suspense. Finally, she said, "John Azrael. Three twenty-seven Mickelmeyer. Off Monument Road near Craig Airport. I checked. A duplex belonging to a man named Watson. Watson lives in one side, so Azrael must be renting the other."

"Goddamn," Taylor breathed. "Goddamn!"

"Too bad you're not on the case, Lieutenant," Anna said to her husband, her voice coated with mock indifference. "With what Polly's told you, you might be able to solve the case and keep another woman from being killed, but I guess you can pass it on to Chief O'Riley. Tomorrow morning ought to be soon enough."

"No damn way!" Rich Taylor spun on his heels and rushed to the hall closet, pulled down a shoulder holster with a Glock .40-caliber semiautomatic pistol, and a jacket. Returning to the living room, he stopped cold, staring at Anna and Polly Bartelow. Each had an impish little grin spread across her face. "What the hell's so funny?"

Anna threw her arms around his neck and said, "You, Rich Taylor. When Polly walked in this house, I knew you'd be back on the case." She kissed him and pulled away.

Already on her feet, Bartelow asked, "What do you want me to do, Lieutenant?"

"I want you to stake out the duplex until I get there. Don't do anything but watch. If you need me any sooner, call the beeper from your car, and I'll get back to you as quick as I can, but no matter what, *stay in the car*. The son of a bitch is a psycho, and killin' a cop won't bother him one damn bit."

"Where are you going?"

"To get backup."

"Backup?" Bartelow asked, surprised. "Everybody in the department knows we're off the case. I was lucky to get what info I did from Intel before they cut me off. You try to get backup and O'Riley'll know quicker than you can say kiss me, I'm gay."

Try as she might, Anna couldn't help but laugh. "I'm sorry, guys," she said, still chuckling to herself.

"You take care of the stakeout, Sergeant," Taylor ordered, an index finger directed at Bartelow, "and I'll take care of the backup. If I've got anything to say about it, the death angel's about to get his wings clipped."

CHAPTER 24
November 11, 1992
Wednesday, Late Night

With the unmarked cruiser's headlights already darkened, Polly Bartelow eased the car along the curb beneath the overhang of a massive live oak tree. The crunch of fallen acorns beneath the tires were like tiny explosions, each one a signal that she had arrived. Limbs, silhouetted against a yellow-orange streetlamp several houses farther along, danced forlornly in the wind. Lonely trees along a lonely street.

It was Bartelow's first time to handle a stakeout by herself, and like the street, she felt desperately alone. Each sound, each sight, the blustery northeast wind against the car — their combined effect like a conjurer's wand creating nightmare visions of the man called Azrael.

Dark shadows stretched toward the car, ready to claim her as their next victim, then faded as if carried away on the wind. Without thinking, Bartelow pulled the Glock semiautomatic from beneath her coat. It was smaller than Taylor's in both size and the number of rounds it held, but as her firearms instructor used to joke, primarily to embarrass her in a class of twenty-three males and herself, it's not always how big it is, but how you use it.

William Kerr

Bartelow's laugh at the memory was more a sarcastic grunt as, with expert precision, she retracted the slide, allowing a 9 mm Black Talon Hollow Point to spring upward from the magazine with a sharp, metallic click, then pushed forward, shoving the round into the chamber. Just the feel of the weapon in her hand and the sight of its dull black outline as she laid it on the seat beside her gave her an increased sense of security.

Except for a few cars parked at random intervals in front of dark, single-story frame houses and the rush of wind through the crack in the window next to her ear, Bartelow's world was deserted. Across the street, the duplex — 327 Mickelmeyer, its design like two narrow, old-time shotgun houses shoved together to make one. There were no lights and no signs of life.

Removing her bifocals, Bartelow lifted a set of night vision binoculars she'd signed out from the SWAT team and held down the automatic focus button until the building's form took shape. Everything fused into shades of yellow and green. Slowly she moved her line of sight across the front of the house. There was nothing to indicate a heat source other than what remained of the sun's warmth stored in the building's paint-peeled, wooden façade from the previous day.

Ignoring what she knew to be the owner's side of the duplex, she concentrated on the left-hand apartment. A raised concrete stoop, reached by two steps and covered by an aluminum awning, led to the front door. On either side of the stoop stood a window with its shade pulled down; at the side of the house, a graveled drive. Unless hidden at the rear, there was no garage.

Bartelow lowered the binoculars and shifted to a more comfortable position, ready to settle in for a long night, or at least until Taylor and his backup arrived. She craved a cigarette, but she knew the glow of embers would alert passing drivers or anyone watching from the duplex.

Suddenly, headlights. Slipping her bifocals back on, she followed through the rearview mirror as an automobile turned onto the street and moved in her direction. Automatically, she slid down in the seat, waiting for the lights to pass, but they didn't. They stopped alongside the cruiser, the glow of red brake lights entering the rear side window. She heard the low purr of an engine idling; felt invisible eyes searching the interior of the car.

"Oh, God," she prayed, "if it's Azrael, don't let him see me." Her hand inched along the seat until she felt the pistol's handle. Scarcely breathing, she pulled it closer. Using her left hand to support both weapon and wrist, she wrapped the fingers of her right hand around the grip, curled the index finger over the trigger, pointed the barrel toward the passenger's side window... and waited.

It seemed forever until gears shifted and the car pulled away, leaving the *pop, pop, pop* of acorns beneath its tires as a reminder of its presence. Lifting her head just above the dash, she watched as the car turned onto the driveway and disappeared into the darkness behind 327 Mickelmeyer.

A sigh of relief escaped Bartelow's lips and she whispered, "Thank you, God. Thank you."

• • •

"What the fuck have I done to you," the scraggly old man shouted at the policeman as Rich Taylor pushed through the double doors of the Pretrial Detention Center's booking office. "A man has a coupla drinks in Hemmin' Plaza, an' you drag him in here like he's a criminal or sump'n'."

"It's yourself you're doin' it to, Jake," the officer patiently explained as he guided the man toward the block of detention cells in the back of the building. "Stop drinkin' and we won't have to —" The cell block door slammed, cutting off the officer's explanation.

"I'm not believin' this," Lurlene said, looking up from the paperwork on her desk. "Hey, you guys," she said to the other officers sharing the Detention Facility late night shift. "Look who's here."

Taylor nodded as he let the doors close behind him.

Lurlene pointed a finger at the sulky teenager seated beside her desk. "You stay in that chair and don't move 'til I get back. See how big I am? You blink, and I'm gonna sit on your ass 'til you're nothin' but a grease spot on the floor." The boy nodded sullenly, shifting his feet for Lurlene to get by.

As she reached the front counter, she asked Taylor, "What's the matter? Anna kick you out or something? I wouldn't blame her."

"If you weren't Anna's cousin, Lurlene, I'd —"

"You wouldn't do a damn thing, Rich Taylor, and you know it. I'm too likable. What're you doin' here?"

"Prisoner release."

Lurlene grunted her surprise. "At a quarter 'til midnight? Which one and why?"

"Man named Berkeley. Simple battery."

"You crazy? That's O'Riley's boy. The arresting officers said O'Riley wants his white ass under the jail, not out of it."

"Here." Taylor pulled an envelope from his inside coat pocket and tossed it on the counter. "Let's just say that O'Riley and I had a meeting."

Lurlene opened the envelope and unfolded the release form. "I'll be damn. An R.O.R.? Who'd you sweet-talk into goin' along with releasing Berkeley on his own recognizance? Bet it wasn't Tatorre."

"Tatorre's not the only judge in Jacksonville."

Lurlene leaned her massive breasts on the counter and pushed her face toward Taylor's. "What I want to know, cousin, is why?"

Keeping his voice low, Taylor said, "The case I've been

working on."

"Those women?"

Taylor nodded. "All murdered because they had abortions. I don't have time to explain, but I need Berkeley if I'm gonna stop another one."

"You know what you're askin' me to do?" Lurlene demanded. "You wanna screw up your job and your life, that's your business. I've got two kids and nobody else but me to bring home a paycheck. I do this and O'Riley's gonna —"

Taylor grabbed Lurlene's arm and threatened, "You don't honor this release, another woman's gonna die. I remember a girl who had an abortion. If I hadn't stood by that girl, Judge Tatorre and O'Riley and the rest of 'em would've kicked her outta here faster than she could say good-bye. You remember that, Lurlene? We're family, and this time it's me needing *your* help."

Lurlene pulled her arm free and stared at Taylor for a moment before saying, "I hope you can earn enough money to support your family and mine."

Without waiting for a reply, Lurlene swung around and stomped back to her desk. "Get your legs outta the way, boy," she ordered the teenager.

With the thump, thump of a date stamp in two places on the form and the scratch of her initials on the "action completed" line, Lurlene turned back to Taylor and said, "He's yours, Lieutenant, but you'll have to get him. Officer Ward's back there tuckin' in a drunk. He'll open the cage."

• • •

Matthew and Taylor reached the car on the far side of the parking lot. Matthew pulled the collar of his jacket tight and shouted above the wind, "I appreciate you getting me out, but when O'Riley finds out, as they say back home, you gonna be in a heap a trouble, boy."

"Not your problem, *boy*," Taylor responded as he

unlocked his door, opened it and pushed the button unlocking the passenger's side. "Get in."

"I need to call Peyton."

"No time."

As Matthew edged into the passenger's side, he asked, "Where are we going?"

Taylor started the car and turned the wheel toward the parking lot exit. "To find Azrael. We've got an address."

"Where?"

Taylor whipped the car onto East Adams Street and headed toward the Hart Bridge over the St. Johns River.

"Out close to Craig Airport."

"That's a helluva long way from here," Matthew said. Eyeing the grim determination on Taylor's face, he added, "And if there's some kind of time factor you haven't told me about, I'd strongly recommend you tear ass all the way."

• • •

With the nor'easter swirling about the corners of the house and dreading the drive to Helena's apartment, Peyton placed the overnight bag and car keys on the chair, picked up the phone and tapped out the numbers. After the third ring, a voice answered, "You've reached 247-8383. We can't come to the phone now, but you're welcome to leave a message at the sound of the tone. Have a great out-of-body experience. Bye, now." *Bleeeep.*

"Helena, this is Peyton. Was wondering if you could put me up for the night, but since you're not home, not to worry. I'll call tomorrow."

Peyton hung up the phone and sighed. "Nothing like home, sweet home." Leaving the overnight bag and keys on the chair, she walked back through the house, checked to make sure the doors and windows were locked, then made her way past the kitchen to the master bedroom, unbuttoning this and unzipping that as she went.

Death's Bright Angel

Five till twelve. Peyton turned from the clock and switched on the television. A&E. She recognized scenes from the 1940 movie, *House of Seven Gables*. "That ought to put me to sleep," she said to herself as she slipped out of her skirt and into a cotton nightie.

• • •

Bartelow pushed the button on her watch and the face turned a bluish tint — three minutes before midnight. What she normally would have called the beginning of a drizzle sounded like a machine gun barrage of water pellets, driven almost horizontally by the wind against the windows. Even through the night vision binoculars, the duplex had become a blur.

Where was Taylor? Damn him! If O'Riley had been tipped off that she and Taylor had ignored his orders and were still on the case,... She didn't want to think about it, but with each minute that dragged by, Azrael could be closer to slipping through their fingers. Moving on to another city and another abortion clinic, or worse yet, preparing for another murder.

A single light burned somewhere in the back of the house, faintly visible against the shaded front windows, its glow more pronounced on the graveled driveway through a window near the rear. What was the man doing? Playing with his souvenirs? The thought sent shudders through Bartelow's body.

If she could only... Bartelow remembered Taylor's words. "...no matter what, stay in the car. The son of a bitch is a psycho, and killin' a cop won't bother him one damn bit."

Again, the proverbial rabbit ran across her grave as she reached for the semiautomatic on the passenger seat. Safety in numbers, she thought. One in the chamber and nine big ones in the magazine. Holding the pistol close to her body, she caressed the top of the barrel and rationalized that the power she held in her hand as well as her training, the storm, the cover of night and the element of surprise made her more than equal to some crazy who hated women.

"Goddamn you, Taylor," Bartelow cursed out loud, "If you don't get here, we're gonna blow it." She sat for a moment, breathing deeply. The air rushed in and out of her mouth through drawn lips as she stared through windows stippled with rain beads, their ranks driven in one direction, then another, by the force of the wind. "And I can't let that happen, damn it."

The sound of her own voice helped push back the fear that she knew would never be far away, but with the decision made, every thought and move had purpose and, at the same time, held the fear at bay.

Jacket — zipped tight against rain and wind. Interior light — switched off for opening the door. Pistol — round in the chamber and ready to fire.

With a quick downward movement against the door handle, Bartelow shoved the door open. The wind fought against her, holding her in, but she pushed with hand and shoulder until the opening was large enough for her to drop to the ground. She grabbed the outside handle before the wind could slam the door shut.

Easing the door closed, Bartelow crouched behind the front fender for a moment, catching her breath, then, head down to keep the rain off her glasses, weapon close against her jacket, she ran as fast as she could. The street, the shallow front lawn, weeds snapping at her legs, past the narrow stoop and front door... she pulled up when she reached the corner of the duplex.

Breathing heavily, Bartelow stuck her head around the corner and rapidly scanned the driveway and the splash of light from the window at the rear side of the house. She looked back at the cruiser parked across the street. For an instant, the protection it represented gnawed at the mental bindings holding back her fears, but she shut her eyes tight and hissed at herself, "Just do it, Bartelow. Do it!" With the Glock semiautomatic raised in a two-handed firing position, she turned from the cruiser and slid around the corner of the house.

Her back against the wood siding, eyes darting back and forth, Bartelow quickly sidestepped toward the lighted window, careful to keep her feet from the edge of the graveled driveway. Even with the roar of the wind in her ears, she was afraid the crunch of gravel might alert the man called Azrael. Closer and closer. When she reached the window, she ducked beneath the sill, hesitated only a moment, then raised her head to eye level.

The shade, age-yellowed with spidery cracks stretching across its width and length, was drawn, but there was a space of at least three inches between the bottom of the shade and the window frame. Bartelow blinked the dampness from her eyes and studied what she could see of the room. A kitchen. A table and two chairs. On the table, a telephone and an answering machine, a black leather case and a silver cross. Above the sink, cabinet doors stood open, upper shelves removed, the lower shelves laden with gallon-sized Mason jars, neatly lined, one after another, cabinet after cabinet. Each jar was labeled; words hand printed. Bartelow squinted in an effort to determine the contents and read the labels.

The sudden blow to Bartelow's right lower back forced her hard against the side of the house as a gloved hand ripped away her glasses and sent them flying. The same hand clamped tight over her mouth and yanked her head backwards. She tried to scream, but only a muffled whine came out. She couldn't move, her body jammed against the building, her hands crushed between the wooden siding and the pistol. The weapon's muzzle gouged painfully against her breastbone.

Another blow, this time near the center of the lower back, slicing, penetrating, burning, and again and again. The realization raced through her mind. *Dear Jesus, I'm being stabbed!* A voice at her ear growled, "You've delayed God's work long enough."

She wanted to beg, to plead for her life, to say she was sorry for the delay. Anything, but the hand held firm over her mouth. Another blow, and her legs turned to rubber. Urine ran warm down the length of her thighs. "Bad girl," her mother would have said. *I'm sorry, Momma. I can't help it.*

Polly Bartelow slipped to her knees; the pistol dropped from her hands into the forest of water-soaked weeds next to the house. Her body felt sticky and warm, like molasses on hot buttery pancakes, but her mouth was suddenly free.

"Scream, Polly, scream," her mother's voice demanded. Polly wanted to scream. Oh, God, she wanted to shout as loud as she could, to hear her voice carried on the wind, but for some reason, she couldn't. *I can't, Momma. I can't.*

CHAPTER 25
November 12, 1992
Thursday, The First Hour

The rain had stopped, but the nor'easter's fury rocked the car as they sped along St. Johns Bluff Road. With only the deserted landing strip and aircraft hangers of Craig Airport to his right, Matthew was able to concentrate on street signs on the opposite side of the road as they whipped by, each caught in the loom of the automobile's lights for a matter of seconds, then gone. Lone Star, Akers, Prim, Causey, Michelle and finally Mickelmeyer. "There."

"Got it," Taylor acknowledged, at the same time, hitting the brakes and turning onto Mickelmeyer. "Three-twenty-seven. You look for the house. I'll look for Bartelow's car." Taylor turned off the headlights and slowed the car to a crawl.

"You better find the car," Matthew said, straining to see numbers on homes and curbside mailboxes, " 'cause I can hardly see the houses, let alone house numbers."

"That's it." Taylor pointed to a black Chevy Caprice parked on the side of the street, as he eased in behind the car and stopped. "And there's the duplex across the street."

"Interior lights?" Matthew asked before opening the door.

"No problem. Disconnected."

Matthew shoved his door open against the wind, got out and watched as Taylor approached the Chevy. "What's the matter?" he asked, his voice raised loud enough to be heard above the wind.

Taylor motioned with his head and hand.

Matthew hurried forward, searching for movement inside the Chevy, but there was none.

"She's gone, goddamn it. I told her to stay in the car, and she fucking well ignored me."

"Maybe she didn't have a choice."

Using his body as a shield from the duplex, Taylor switched on a flashlight and quickly swept the inside of the car with the beam, then turned the light off. "No blood, no struggle and the doors are locked. She had a choice. C'mon." Taylor turned off the flashlight and handed it to Matthew, drew the Glock semiautomatic from inside his jacket and started across the street.

"Slow up," Matthew commanded, his words caught on the wind and gone almost as soon as they left his mouth. He grabbed Taylor by the arm and stopped him in the middle of the street. "You can't just bust in there and start shooting."

Taylor jerked loose from Matthew's grasp and warned, "Don't ever do that again, Berkeley." Turning back toward the duplex, he added, "If Polly's in there, I gotta get her out."

"We'll do it, but if Azrael's in there, storming the place will only get her killed... if she isn't already dead. This way."

Matthew moved quickly across the weed-choked lawn to the side of the house, Taylor close behind, muttering, "Fucking Navy pukes. Think you know everything."

Any other time, Matthew would have hit back with a dumb-cop remark, but his mind was concentrating on Polly Bartelow and the man called Azrael. He counted the windows. Three, each spaced equidistant along the side. No screens.

Death's Bright Angel

Dark. He tried each. Locked, or cemented shut by layers of paint. As he rounded the rear corner of the house, the wind hit him full force, tearing at his face and shirt and sending shivers through his body. "Lieutenant."

Taylor stopped at his side. "What now?"

Following the curvature of the graveled driveway, Matthew used his right index finger to draw a quarter circle in the air, then a straight line to the middle of the back yard and a flat, concrete pad the shape of a one-car garage. "What used to be a garage, or a carport."

"So?"

"Two bits says Azrael doesn't hitchhike, so where's his car?" Matthew moved quickly to the pad, knelt down and felt the edges, then the center. Taking a quick glance over his shoulder toward the duplex, he flicked on the flashlight.

"Jesus, Berkeley. Why don't I just knock on the door and tell him we're here?"

Ignoring Taylor, Matthew ran the beam quickly around the pad, then turned it off. "There was a car here."

"You a fucking Indian scout or something?" Taylor hissed.

"Edges of the concrete are still wet from the rain. The middle is dry, and here's a warm spot." Matthew patted the right side of the pad.

"The ol' campfire-still-warm trick, huh?"

"More like heat from a catalytic converter. A car's been and gone, and it hasn't been long."

"Shit!" Taylor hissed, shaking his head.

Matthew got to his feet and hurried to the rear door. "Time to go in. Don't guess you've got a search warrant?"

"No."

"After springing me, your troubles probably can't get any worse, so..." Without waiting for a response, Matthew placed his body at an angle with the door, took aim at the area just below the knob and kicked. Once, twice, and the door splintered inward. "Now you've got an excuse. You just found a clear case of breaking and entering, so what are you waiting for? You first."

"Jesus fucking Christ," Taylor cursed as he burst through the door, the semiautomatic ready to fire at the first movement. "Police! On the floor. Police!"

Silence, until Taylor order, "Gimme light."

Matthew flicked on the flashlight and worked the beam around the room. "Kitchen," Matthew said, noting the table and chairs, telephone and answering machine.

Taylor headed for the next room. "Keep moving." Matthew followed with the light through what could have served as a bedroom, with a quick glance into an empty front room.

"Except for the kitchen," Taylor growled, "no furniture, no nothing." He nodded toward two doors leading off the bedroom. "Open 'em. I'll cover you."

"Thanks, Lieutenant. You're a real sport."

Matthew inched his way to one of the doors. Holding the flashlight in his right hand, he very gently wrapped his left hand around the knob, then, as fast as he could, turned the knob and jumped out of the way.

"Closet!"

"Yeah," Taylor said, following the beam of Matthew's light through the doorway. "A man's suit, a shirt and tie. Interesting. Try the other door."

Matthew moved to the second door, turned the handle and pulled. "Locked," he said, stepping back and gesturing with his hand. "Your turn, Lieutenant. I did the back door. This one's yours, and if you —"

Click!

Taylor put his finger to his lips, "Ssshhhhh," then pointed toward the front room.

Death's Bright Angel

Matthew nodded, switched off the flashlight and waited in the dark, ears straining, body tense.

Another *click*, followed by metal sliding against metal and the low growl of hinges as a door swung open. A sudden blast of wind swept the room. The door slammed, and the wind was gone.

"Azrael?" a voice called. Matthew knew that voice.

"I told you we'd be too late," a second voice grumbled. "It's all your fault."

"Shut up, Truegood, and turn on the lights."

A light clicked on in the front room as voices and footsteps got closer. A hand reached around the doorway and switched on the bedroom ceiling light.

"You could've stopped him at the church if you —"

"Good evening, Chief O'Riley," Taylor said, his weapon leveled at O'Riley's chest as the man stopped cold in his tracks.

Matthew laughed sourly as Truegood Foley tried to back out of the room. "Don't be bashful, Reverend. Join the party."

"What the hell are you doing here?" O'Riley exploded at Taylor.

"I might ask you the same thing, Chief," Taylor said, his voice low and menacing.

"And him," Foley sputtered, pointing at Matthew. "You promised you'd get him out of the way."

Matthew challenged, "Out of the way of what?"

A loud pounding came from the adjacent apartment and a muffled shout, "Shut up in there, or I'll have you evicted."

"You're supposed to be in jail," O'Riley directed at Matthew.

"I got sprung, Chief, and how about answering Foley's question."

"I'll ask the questions," O'Riley shot back.

Rich Taylor shook his head. "Not this time. You know

the man called Azrael. You've known all along, you and Foley, and now you're gonna —"

"Lieutenant," Matthew said, grabbing Taylor's arm.

"Goddamn it, Berkeley, didn't I tell you —"

"Shut up and listen." Matthew pointed toward the locked door. A moan, and then another.

"Key to the front door. Who's got it?" Taylor asked.

Foley held up a simple skeleton key.

Taylor waved the pistol at the locked door and ordered, "Try it."

Foley inserted the key, turned it and the lock clicked. He looked back at Taylor, fear in his eyes about what might lie behind the door.

"Get out of the way," Matthew snapped. He shoved Foley aside, grabbed the knob and yanked open the door. The moan was suddenly louder, a plea without words. Matthew found a switch and turned on the light. From behind the shower curtain, another moan. He grabbed the curtain and ripped it away. "It's Bartelow! There's a phone in the kitchen. Call 911."

• • •

Matthew watched as the emergency medical team lifted a blood-soaked Polly Bartelow to the stretcher, an IV already in her arm. He shook his head, not understanding how the hell she was still alive nor how she could stay alive much longer. Taylor's voice forced him to turn away and walk past two police officers into the kitchen.

"How the hell can you two just sit there," Taylor shouted. "Azrael was here. You saw what he did to Bartelow." Taylor stuck an index finger in Truegood Foley's face. "He's Mother Sam's brother, isn't he? Where is he?"

Matthew stared hard at Foley. "You know where he is, don't you? He's gone to kill again." Matthew punched the *PLAY* button on the answering machine.

Death's Bright Angel

The voice was deep and raspy. "Hello, Chris. I know how deeply you hurt. Just say, 'help me,' and I'll lift this burden from your shoulders." A beep, and then a whisper, "Help me."

Matthew hit the *STOP* button and the machine began to rewind. "Taylor's already played it once. How many more times have you got to hear it? He ripped her apart. Rammed a goddamn fetus doll up her gut after he cut her open. Is that what he's doing now? Slicing up some woman because she had an abortion? Because she did something he didn't like? Something you and that asshole of a cop don't like?"

Taylor turned on O'Riley. "Big headlines. Asshole cop accessory to murder. Your family's gonna love that one. If you know something, tell us now and maybe —"

"The cabinets," Truegood said, the blood drained from his face.

Matthew raised an eyebrow. "What cabinets?"

Truegood nodded to the cabinets above the sink and counter. "Those," then buried his head in his hands.

Matthew walked to the sink and opened the first cabinet and drew back. "Holy shit!"

Six glass jars, gallon-sized, lined the bottom shelf. Inside each jar, pieces of flesh, some recognizable, some not, immersed in a yellowish liquid. Each jar was neatly labeled.

Harriet Wegland, June 1989, Kansas City, MO
Juanita Moses, October 1989, Kansas City, MO
Mildred Blanding, Christmas 1989, Kansas City, MO
Cynthia Roberson, February 1990, Buffalo, NY

Matthew stopped reading.

Truegood raised his head. "Two more cabinets, Mr. Berkeley."

Matthew opened the second cabinet and counted. "That's twelve so far."

"Kansas City, Buffalo and Cleveland," Taylor added.

As Matthew opened the third cabinet, O'Riley gagged and dashed to the sink. Vomit splattered the linoleum-covered floor before he could get there.

"Five jars," Matthew said. "Chris Atwell, Lavonna Mayes,..." He hesitated, then continued, "Jackie Serafina, Paul Russo... Jesus, it's the guy's hands." Matthew closed his eyes for a moment, then continued, "And two fetus dolls, ready for implantation."

Taylor interrupted. "Hey, O'Riley, Jackie Serafina's Berkeley's sister, but I don't guess you give a shit, do you?" O'Riley's head jerked spasmodically as he dry heaved into the sink.

"Fifth jar's empty."

Truegood nodded. "There's a label on the back, Mr. Berkeley."

Matthew turned the jar around. "Oh, no. Oh, God!"

"What is it?" Taylor asked.

"*Peyton Chandler.*" Matthew grabbed Truegood by the collar and lifted him from his chair. "She's next, isn't she? Answer me?"

Truegood nodded. Matthew dropped the man and fumbled for his wallet, pulled out a card, lifted the telephone receiver and punched out seven numbers. Three rings and a recorded voice answered, "You've reached 247-8383. We can't come —" The recording was interrupted by, "Hello, I'm here."

"Helena?"

"Yes?"

"Thank God. This is Matt Berkeley. Let me speak with Peyton."

"Peyton's not here."

Matthew's mouth fell open. "What do you mean, not there?"

"I just got home a little while ago and found a message

on my answer machine from Peyton. She's at home."

Matthew slammed the receiver down. "He's gone after Peyton!"

"The clinic list," Taylor gasped.

"What clinic list?" Matthew asked.

"A list Dr. Wagoner found. Names, dates and times of appointments of the four murdered women. Miss Chandler's name was on the list."

"Why the hell didn't you tell me?"

"Because she hasn't had an abortion," Taylor tried to explain, "and I didn't think..."

Shock spread across Truegood Foley's face as he stammered, "But she was at the clinic. She —"

"If you'd listened to me," Matthew blasted, cutting Foley off, "you would've known. She was there to have a pregnancy test, not an abortion, damn it."

"Don't hurt Samantha," Foley pleaded.

Taylor grabbed Foley's shirt. "She with Azrael?"

"Forget Samantha," Matthew demanded. "Let's go."

Giving a quick head nod toward Foley and Chief O'Riley, Taylor directed the two officers, "Get these two slime bags to the Detention Center and book 'em. Accessory to murder."

As he reached the door, Matthew shouted over his shoulder to the officers, "And if they try to get away, shoot the bastards."

William Kerr

CHAPTER 26
November 12, 1992
Thursday Morning, The Dark Hours

Peyton's eyes blinked and her head shuddered momentarily as though trying to sort out the brain's inner wires and connections. Everything dark. The television? She remembered the opening credits for *House of Seven Gables*, intermittent snatches of black and white scenes, but now... It dawned on her. The music and the dialogue, gone; the screen blank. With the exception of the northeast wind racing about the corners of the house, a numbing silence had settled over the room. She realized it was the absence of sound that had awakened her.

How long had she been asleep? She reached toward the electric clock on the night table and pushed the button to illuminate the face. Nothing. The lamp. Again, nothing. "Damn power company," she muttered to herself. "If only they'd bury the lines."

Sighing away her inability to check the time, Peyton closed her eyes and allowed her head to sink back into the pillow. Wind sounds, rain pellets against windowpanes, nature's lullaby until... Peyton jerked upwards, pushing herself to a sitting position. She heard it again, this time closer.

Death's Bright Angel

A human sound. Footsteps on the hallway tile. Soft, yet audible.

"Matthew?" she called automatically before remembering the detention center. Her eyes sought the doorway, but, with curtains drawn, the blackness of the night was too deep. As quietly as possible, she felt for the phone on the night table and brought the receiver to her ear, her finger ready to punch out 911. Dead! The thought struck home. The TV, the lights, the phone — it wasn't the work of the storm.

The footsteps stopped at the doorway, and she knew. "You're Azrael, aren't you?" she said to the darkness.

The voice was deep-pitched and malignant with hate. "Yes, God's hand to punish the wicked."

"Why?" Peyton asked, not believing the calmness of her own voice. "If it's for an abortion, I haven't had one."

"You lie." The voice was closer. "You were at the clinic."

"For a pregnancy test, only. Not everyone goes to the clinic for an abortion."

"But their presence perpetuates the evil. God knows what's in your heart. Selfishness. An unwillingness to carry your child. God's child."

Peyton clutched the edge of one pillow. She had to hear his voice to know where he was. "God is mistaken, but I know what's in *your* heart."

"What?" The voice was closer, almost to the side of the bed.

"Bloodlust. To fight abortion might have been your original aim, but now, it's only an excuse. As for me, you're afraid I know who you are."

"And do you?"

Peyton felt his nearness. She could also feel the hatred, reaching for her like an aura expanding from his spirit center, its desire to enfold and smother her life's spark as real as the night around her. She sensed a knife, raised, its tip pointed at her chest.

"Yes, I know who you are," she answered. Gripping the edge of the pillowcase and with every muscle tensed, Peyton aimed at the responding growl and swung. She felt the impact of the pillow against his body, heard the tearing of cloth and knew the knife had struck the pillow instead of her. She tried to pull the pillow back, but couldn't as the knife continued to jab and tear.

"You're fighting God's will, Peyton. You cannot escape His retribution."

"I can try," Peyton shouted as she spun across the bed and swung her legs off the side. The sheet caught one foot, and she crashed against a chest-of-drawers. Pain shot through her shoulder, but she willed herself to ignore it, to keep moving toward the doorway. Her arm snagged the pointed edge of the dresser. Again pain, but she knew she was headed in the right direction. The cry of "Damn you," reached her ears as she caught the doorframe and propelled herself into the hallway.

Peyton ran. Where? Her only chance, outside. The street. Neighbors. Behind her, footsteps pounded against the floor, closer and closer.

"You can't escape, Peyton," Azrael called. "God will find you."

She reached the living room. Suddenly there was streetlight through the windows, enough to see the large, mahogany-stained coffee table as she hit it full stride. A sudden fire erupted in her shin. Her arms shot forward to break the fall, but too late. Her head slammed full force against the side of the table, throwing her sideways and trapping her between table and sofa. She lay there a moment, dazed yet aware of the syrupy warmth on her eyelid and cheek as blood flowed from a cut just above her left eye.

Gasping for air and using only her right eye to guide the

way, Peyton pushed to her knees and aimed for the front door. Mentally, she knew what she had to do. Physically, her body refused to respond. The carpet undulated beneath her like a raft at sea. Arms and knees wobbled like Jell-O. Her left eye was swollen nearly shut while the other was blurred and unfocused. Sobs of helplessness and fear came spontaneously as she realized she would never make it. *Oh, Matthew, I wanted so much for us.*

The blow just above her right shoulder blade drove her into the floor. She felt a knee in her back and heard a grunt as the knife pulled free. "I told you, Peyton, there is no escape from God or from Azrael, but you wouldn't —"

The squeal of tires and the wail of a siren cut off Azrael's words. With pain tearing through her shoulder and down her back, Peyton prayed, "Please, God, help me."

"Get up," Azrael growled.

Peyton tried, but she couldn't move.

"I said get up!"

With the siren growing louder, Peyton felt a hand on her head. Its fingernails raked her scalp as it grabbed chunks of hair and yanked. Her head snapped back and up. She screamed. Another hand on her arm, the power of its grasp enough to pull her to her feet and drag her through the house to the kitchen.

"What are you going to do?" Peyton gasped as the siren wound down to a low moan. Car doors slammed. "They're coming. Why don't you leave me?"

"Oh, no. You're coming with me."

"But why?"

"Because you know who I am."

"Where are you taking me?"

Pocketing the knife, Azrael jerked her toward the back door, answering, "If you can see through the eyes of a dead woman as they say, you should already know."

But which woman? Justine Crowley, Chris Atwell, Matt's sister, Jackie? Peyton's mind swirled around the names and the memories they represented when, suddenly, her hip rammed against an island counter in the middle of the kitchen, stopping her forward movement. An instant of pain, like a punctuation to her thoughts, and then, as she wiped blood from her left eye and cheek, she knew.

Fists banged against the front door. A shout. "Peyton! Are you in there? Let us in."

"Matthew!" Peyton cried, at the same time, trying to break loose, but Azrael held tight as he turned the knob on the back door and shoved Peyton out into the wind. The rain felt like ice picks against her skin, the cotton nightgown immediately soaked and plastered against her body. Wet grass, bare feet. Tremors sped from her toes to the base of her skull like waves on an ocean's surface, but all at once, feelings of pain and fear and anxiety were gone, replaced by an empty, floating sensation. It was as though mind and body had separated, each cognizant of the other, yet apart. Why? The blow to her head? The stab wound in her back? The loss of blood?

With a strength that Peyton could hardly believe, Azrael forced her through the backyard to a car parked in the alleyway that ran behind the homes on her street. For the first time, Peyton recognized a revolver in Azrael's hand as he looked hurriedly over his shoulder toward the house.

Azrael opened the driver's side door. "Slide across," he ordered, his voice urgent and commanding.

Peyton stared at the man called Azrael for only an instant. Even in the dark, she sensed the message hidden behind his eyes, and yes, she knew his secret. She knew who he was.

The barrel of the revolver jabbed against her ribs as Azrael demanded, "Get in!"

Death's Bright Angel

• • •

Two blasts from the end of Taylor's Glock semiautomatic echoed through the neighborhood as the front door lock exploded in a shrapnel burst of wood and metal. The heel of Taylor's shoe forced the door inward.

"Peyton!" Matthew shouted as they bolted through the doorway. He hit one light switch, then another. Nothing. "Azrael cut the power," he yelled, automatically swinging the flashlight beam from one side of the living room to the next, crisscrossing the path of a second light jammed next to the weapon in Taylor's hands. Both lights settled as one on the overturned coffee table.

"He was here," Matthew said, "and there's blood."

"Where?"

Matthew spotlighted the stain between the table and sofa. "On the carpet," then pivoted on the ball of one foot, snapping, "The bedroom!"

Both men lunged for the hallway, Matthew edging past Taylor as they ran. Matthew slapped a door as he moved past. "Bathroom. Check it."

Matthew heard Taylor's fist smash against the bathroom door as he rounded the corner into Peyton's bedroom. "Nothing here," Taylor shouted. "What you got?"

"Feathers!" Matthew directed the flashlight toward the bed as Taylor entered the room. "Goddamn feathers, everywhere. She tried to fight him off with a pillow."

"I don't see any blood," Taylor said, swinging the beam of his flashlight around the room.

"Me neither. She must've got as far as the living room before... C'mon. You check the bedrooms on the other side of the house. I'll check the kitchen."

The closer Matthew got to the rear of the house, the louder the sound of wind. He could feel the increasing draft against his face. A door swung on its hinges. *Bang!* It slammed shut. "Peyton!"

Matthew charged into the kitchen, the beam of his flashlight moving rapidly from corner to corner before steadying on the floor. Blood drops. He followed their trail to the counter in the middle of the kitchen. They stopped, then continued around the counter to the back door.

"Aw, Christ," he whispered. "Taylor! He's taken her."

Taylor ran into the kitchen. "Where?"

"Out the back. After that, how the hell do I know?" Stepping over drops of blood, Matthew pushed open the back door and looked out as the wind lashed across his face. "There's an alley out back. That's why we didn't see his car." He slammed the door and stepped back into the kitchen.

"If I..." Matthew stopped in midsentence. "The counter top." He leveled the flashlight on two dark red, finger-drawn letters, still wet, and a small reddish splotch on the counter's white surface, the splotch tailing off into a wide smear as though the writer had been pulled away. "Peyton's blood!"

Concentrating on the letters, Taylor said, "Capital F and little t."

Matthew touched the blood smear with one finger and repeated, "F and t... and if the spot after the t was meant to be a period,... It's Peyton. She was trying to tell us where he's taking her. $F, t,$ period. It stands for fort. Fort Caroline!"

"You're sure?"

"You got a better idea, Lieutenant?"

Death's Bright Angel

CHAPTER 27
November 12, 1992
Thursday Morning, Predawn

Wind chills ran through Peyton's body as she struggled along the sandy path, her arms pulled tight behind her back, wrists bound with picture frame wire twisted tight enough to draw blood. The muzzle of Azrael's revolver, jammed hard against spinal vertebrae in the middle of her back, prodded her forward beneath a dripping canopy of oak trees and pines. Her way was illuminated only barely by lights from an electric power plant across the river, reflecting pink off low flying clouds driven by the storm.

Feeling had returned, and the throbbing pain of the stab wound in her shoulder was like a fireball, pulsating with a fierceness she could never have imagined. Jagged edges of fallen acorns and pine cones, partially buried in the sodden earth, pierced the skin of her bare feet. Clumps of waist-high palmetto, crowded along the narrow path, their bayonet-shaped leaves whipped by the nor'easter's force, sliced menacingly at her legs and tore the bottom hem from the cotton nightgown that provided her only protection.

"Faster," Azrael ordered, jabbing the revolver with even greater force into Peyton's back. "God is waiting."

Peyton felt her wrists and arms pulled up and away from her back, almost straight out, and her body pushed forward. She gasped at the added burst of pain in her shoulders and wrists and stumbled sideways against the trunk of an oak tree. The roughness of its bark gouged and scraped pieces of skin from her face and breasts.

A voice from deep inside cried, "Break away! Run! Hide!" But how? And where? *If you really are waiting, God*, she prayed through a veil of tears and pain, *help me now*, but God's response, if there was one, was lost on the wind.

• • •

The police cruiser's high beams swept the parking lot as Taylor spun the steering wheel, sending the car in a narrow circle, its tires sliding on the wet asphalt.

"There." Matthew aimed a finger at a lone car parked next to the Fort Caroline Memorial visitor center. "It's gotta be them. They've taken the footpath down to the fort. We'll take the work road."

Taylor braked the cruiser to a halt. "Which way?"

Matthew pointed. "Far side of the parking lot."

"Hold on," Taylor warned as the engine roared and the cruiser spun forward.

Matthew kept his left arm pointed toward the ink-black opening in the trees, his right hand wrapped tightly around the handhold protruding just above the door. He watched the speedometer. Thirty, forty, fifty! "Oh, shit!"

His body left the seat when the car shot off the edge of the asphalt and took to the air, then dropped as the tires hit the dirt road and slammed against the top of the fender wells. Trees and bushes, only inches from the window, flew past. The sound of tree limbs lashing the side of the car screamed in his ears.

"You're gonna kill us, Taylor," Matthew shouted, his voice bouncing up and down with the movement of the car over tree roots washed out by the rain.

"Who's driving the fucking car?" Taylor yelled back, at the same time whipping the wheel one way, then the other, as the car plunged headlong through the trees. "You wanna save that woman of yours, shut up and hold on."

Matthew held his breath as the car entered the clearing in front of the fort. He felt Taylor jam on the brakes and the car careen in a sideways skid over the wet grass and sand. "The moat!" he yelled as the car continued its slide toward the four-foot-deep, water-filled trench that protected the front of the fort.

With the car's front-wheel drive screaming for traction, the right rear wheel spun out over the edge of the moat. The car's undercarriage dropped with a bone-jarring crunch onto the wooden timbers that lined the moat. As the rear bumper, muffler and tail pipe tore loose, crushed beneath the floorboard, Matthew tensed in anticipation of a ruptured gas tank and explosion, but it never came. How and why, he didn't know, but with an abrupt jolt, the car stopped, engine dead. It leaned in his direction, but thank God, it was still upright. He had only a moment to catch his breath before Taylor shouted, "There they are!"

Matthew followed the dual shafts of light from the car's high beams through the sheets of rain that suddenly swept in from the river. He saw the quickly disappearing outlines of two people for only a split second, one pushing the other forward around the side of the fort and onto the narrow levee that separated the river from the marsh.

"He's taking her to the excavation."

• • •

The rain and wind-driven spray from the river, like frozen ice pellets, cut at Peyton's body as savagely as the pain from her wounds. She could see the piles of dirt, their silhouettes rising against lights from across the river, and she knew, once there, the only thing left would be the razor-sharp blade of Azrael's knife.

Though physically numbed by cold and pain, Peyton's mind raced ahead, searching for a means of escape as Azrael pushed her along the shell-encrusted levee. Had Matthew deciphered the message she left on the counter? If he had, would he get to the fort in time? If not, she needed options, but what?

To her left, the marsh, knee-deep mud and even deeper pools of water, its tall grasses bent flat by the nor'easter. To her right, the river, its wind-flung white caps crashing against jagged riprap at the base of the levee. If she could get past the rocks, could she manage the river's turbulence?

• • •

Matthew tugged at his door. "It's jammed!"

Leaving the headlights on, Taylor swung open his door and shouted, "This way."

Carrying the flashlight as a potential weapon rather than for its light, Matthew slipped under the steering wheel and burst from the car, immediately running as fast as he could. As he caught up with Taylor at the side of the fort, Taylor yelled, "Stay behind me. He might be armed." The words were hardly out of his mouth when two shots rang out. Both men hit the ground. "That's two," Taylor shouted.

"So?" Matthew asked sarcastically while hugging the dirt. "I guess you know how many rounds he's got?"

"Five-shot, thirty-eight revolver. Bought in Kansas City. Any more smart-ass questions?"

Ignoring Taylor's put-down, Matthew sputtered, "Three to go," before pushing to his feet and sprinting along the side of the fort toward the levee and the river.

Ka-powwwww! Another shot. Matthew dropped to his knees, did a quick roll, and was off again. Turning onto the levee, he saw the outlines of two people and the dirt piles

Death's Bright Angel

against lights on the distant shore. "Peyton!"

Two more shots and a cry from behind.

Matthew stopped long enough to look over his shoulder. "Taylor?"

"My leg," Taylor called out. "Take my weapon."

The voice was too far back. "Keep it. If you're right, he's empty. If you're not..." Without waiting for a reply, Matthew turned back toward the dirt piles and started running. This time, however, only the silhouette of a single person was visible against the lights. "Peyton-n-n-n!"

The silhouette turned in his direction, arm raised, knife poised. Matthew measured the distance as he ran. Twenty yards, ten, five. With only the smallest fraction of time separating the two actions, he threw the flashlight at the figure and hurled his body through the air, hitting the silhouette in midtorso. Whether the flashlight hit or not, he didn't know, but he felt the knife bite into his side as his right shoulder drove deep into soft flesh.

Azrael's cry was like an animal, low at first, turning to a terrible growl as he struggled to break free. Matthew jammed his elbow hard against Azrael's throat, at the same time grasping for the constantly moving knife hand, but the man's strength surprised him.

Azrael, only slightly smaller than Matthew, seemed possessed with superhuman power. With a single lunge, Matthew felt his hold broken, his body thrown off and over the side of the levee. He smashed against the rocks, felt water cascade over his body, then suck at his clothing as it pulled away. Azrael's figure disappeared, and Matthew knew automatically what was happening.

With Peyton's scream in his ears and pain shooting through his side, Matthew clawed his way over the riprap and up the loosely packed dirt of the narrow levee. Halfway up, he shouted, trying to divert Azrael's attention, "Why, Azrael? She hasn't had an abortion."

Azrael turned from the dirt pile and cried, "She knows who I am."

Matthew stopped. He had to keep Azrael talking. If Taylor could limp or crawl, maybe... "So do I. You're Samantha's brother."

"Wrong! Samantha's brother was weak. He threatened to expose us to the Kansas City police. I killed him years ago."

Matthew was stunned. He'd been so sure Azrael was the brother. "What have you done with Samantha? She's supposed to be with you."

"Samantha can't come out. I won't let her."

"What are you telling me? That you killed her, too? Where is she? I need her. Truegood needs her."

With the wind tearing at his voice, Azrael shouted, "Azrael needs her more. Azrael is the hand of God, but it is Samantha's life force that provides that hand."

Azrael's words were lightning bolts, piercing Matthew's consciousness and sparking a firestorm of revelation in his brain. Even though the rasping voice and the face behind the mustache resembled those of a man, suddenly he knew. "Then you're —"

"No-o-o, damn you!" the figure before him cursed above the wind, its fists bared to the heavens. "*I am Azrael*, death's bright angel. Only Azrael has the will and the strength to cleanse the wicked." Azrael pointed at Matthew. "Like your sister and all the others, you and this woman are wicked, and death is your only salvation."

Matthew knew from Azrael's voice that he couldn't stall any longer. "Then kill me, son of a bitch." Matthew motioned with his hand. "Come get me and kill me."

Azrael was suddenly a blur against the clouds as another rainsquall blanketed the night sky. Where did he go? Matthew started toward the low mound of the levee, but the impact

Death's Bright Angel

drove him back onto the rocks. He lashed out blindly. His knuckles smashed against flesh and bone, again and again until Azrael rolled away.

Wave after wave washed over Matthew. He held onto the rocks, trying to keep from being swept into the raging river.

"Help me!"

Matthew swung around. The cry came from the water. "I can't swim. Help me." He saw the head for only a second, but the voice wasn't Azrael's. It was a woman's.

"Azrael?" Matthew called.

Peyton answered his call from the top of the levee. "There is no Azrael," she shouted. "There never was. Only a means of killing without guilt."

Again, from farther out, "Help me."

Without thinking, Matthew dove into the river in the direction of the voice. At first, the strokes were strong and steady. One, two, three, breathe. One, two, three,... but with each stroke, the pain from the knife wound in his side ate at his strength. The current tugged at him. The wind forced water into his eyes and mouth each time he raised his head to look.

"To your right," Taylor called from the levee.

Matthew wanted to shout, "About time you got here," but that would have used just that much more energy. He did a half-turn and pushed forward with a breaststroke, the current carrying him downstream, the wind shoving him sideways toward the levee.

From only feet away, he heard, "Help me, I'm drowning." He twisted around and grabbed for anything he could find. An arm, a wrist. He felt a head just beneath the surface. Hair! He took hold and yanked upward, trying to get the head above water, but the hair came loose.

"A wig!" Matthew slung it aside and shouted, "Where are you, goddamn it?" He searched with his hands, groping blindly above and beneath the surface. He felt something.

"Gotcha!" It was soft and rubbery, but the weight behind it was real. Azrael!

Unable to bring Azrael to the surface, Matthew turned on his side and scissor-kicked as hard as he could toward the levee until, suddenly, the weight behind the object in his hand slipped away. "Azrael!" There was no reply. Matthew called again, only this time, "Samantha—a—a—a!"

A flashlight beam fanned the waters, picked up Matthew, then swept farther out. Matthew looked back at the shore to see Peyton and Taylor, both struggling on the rocks at the base of the levee to keep up with his downstream movement.

"It's no use," Peyton called. "She's gone."

Taylor reached down and grabbed Matthew's shirt. "Give me your hand," he ordered.

"I had her, and I lost her," Matthew panted, bracing himself against the rocks. "Here. She was holding this."

Matthew gave a small rubbery object to Peyton, pulled himself out of the water with Taylor's help, and rested a moment. To Taylor, he asked, "Your leg?"

"I'll live," Taylor said bitterly, but his attention was focused on Peyton and what she was holding. "I'll be damned!"

"What?" Matthew asked.

Taylor pointed the beam of his flashlight at Peyton's hands.

"A doll," Peyton whispered.

"Yeah," Taylor groaned. "A goddamn fetus doll."

Peyton looked at Matthew. "It was meant for me, wasn't it?"

Very gently, Matthew touched Peyton's hands, avoiding her badly mangled wrists, then took the doll and held it in the circle of Taylor's light. "Not anymore, it's not. Whoever Azrael was, whether real or something created in Samantha's mind, it's finished."

Death's Bright Angel

Matthew pushed to his feet and threw the doll as far out on the river as he could. At the same time, he shouted into the wind, "And so are you, Azrael. Finished."

William Kerr

Epilogue
November 13, 1992
Friday Evening

Though not as confining as the television studio, the portable lights added enough heat to the hospital's conference room to create a dribble of sweat in the hollow of Matthew's chest, its downward path along the center line of his stomach and onto the wide swath of adhesive wrapped tightly around his waist. At least this time, he thought, he wasn't fighting a callous bureaucracy. He was glad Sheriff Danny Ryskowski had declined to appear on the program.

"This is the first time I've seen you since they brought us in yesterday morning, and we need to talk," Matthew whispered to Peyton during a commercial break.

Peyton smiled from her wheelchair. "After the show, and Matt..."

"Yes?"

"I've missed you."

Matthew leaned across the wheelchair's arm and brushed Peyton's cheek with his lips before chuckling and saying, "I've missed you, too, but if you think sharing a hospital room with Rich Taylor is fun,..." He nodded in Taylor's direction before adding, "try sleeping in the same

Death's Bright Angel

room with a cement mixer. That guy can snore like a —"

"Five, four, three, two, one, you're on." The program's producer pointed a finger at Kevin Richards, the show's host.

"This is Kevin Richards and we're back with the final segment of our special edition of *Jacksonville Talks*, live from the conference room of the Duval County Good Samaritan Hospital. We'll continue our questioning of Dr. Fay Lundgren, the Duval County medical examiner.

"Dr. Lundgren, it's understood that at one of the murder scenes, there was the trace of seminal fluid. If Azrael was a woman, how and why did this happen?"

"Quite simple, once you think about it," Fay Lundgren answered. "First, from information he's provided, we're almost certain the semen came from Truegood Foley. We're running tests to confirm that. A small vial of semen was found in Peyton Chandler's home, presumably dropped by the murderer during their struggle."

"But why?" Richards asked again.

"You must remember we're talking about multiple personalities, a condition characterized by the existence within the individual of two or more distinct identities each of which is dominant at a particular time. The personality of Azrael was very much a separate being and very much a man. For lack of any other explanation, several psychiatrists I've talked to over the last two days feel that Azrael was, in a sense, a revitalization of Samantha Foley's grandfather, Sam Moreland.

"This served several purposes. One, following certain very traumatic childhood experiences surrounding Sam Moreland's involvement in illegal abortions, Samantha was determined to punish, not only the memory of her grandfather, but all those who sought or performed abortions. She found, however, that she was psychologically unable to carry out the extreme sanction. In order to do so, Azrael was born."

"In other words," Kevin Richards said, "Azrael was little more than a coping mechanism. When Mother Sam found that killing was more than she could tolerate, she avoided the problem by splitting off a part of herself to do what she couldn't do. Though much more drastic, similar to the multiple personalities found in the *Three Faces of Eve*."

"Exactly. In this case, however, the Azrael personality happened to be the opposite sex from the basic individual which was not the case with Eve. Hence, the need for seminal evidence to enforce the belief the killer was a man. There's also the strong possibility it was used as a self-defense mechanism to falsely direct law enforcement toward Truegood Foley as the killer should the police get too close."

"You said Azrael served two purposes."

"In addition to being the instrument of punishment and death, these same psychiatrists think Azrael was a way of seeking forgiveness for Sam Moreland's sins, or what Samantha Foley considered to be the sins of a man she once loved."

The program's host turned to Rich Taylor. "We've been advised that Mother Sam's body has been recovered."

Taylor nodded. "This afternoon. Off the Coast Guard piers in Mayport."

"There was also something about a doll."

"Yes. The replica of a human fetus, caught in her clothing." Taylor glanced quickly at Peyton and then Matthew before adding, "It's my understanding the doll was not in her possession at the time she drowned. How it came to be, we'll probably never know."

Despite the warmth of the room, a cold chill ran the length of Matthew's spine as Kevin Richards continued, "We've also been told, Lieutenant, you'll be James O'Riley's replacement as Chief of Detectives in the Jacksonville Sheriff's Office."

Death's Bright Angel

Rich Taylor smiled. "On an interim basis as long as I can drag this leg of mine into the office."

Matthew interrupted, "And if they don't make it permanent, they'll be missing a great opportunity. I might even hang around and help the lieutenant run for election for sheriff in a couple of years." Matthew looked straight at the television camera as a broad grin spread across his face and asked, "You listening, Sheriff?"

Polite laughter filled the room, cut off by Kevin Richard's question to Taylor, "And Sergeant Bartelow?"

"Talked with Polly this morning. Still in intensive care, but the doctors say she's out of danger. I look forward to having her back on the force."

"Miss Chandler," Richards said, "you've been unusually quiet. What are your thoughts?"

Peyton touched the abrasions on her face, thought for a moment, then said, "Thankful to be alive. It's difficult to express how much I owe Matt," she nodded toward Matthew and, at the same time, took Matthew's hand in hers, "and Lieutenant Taylor for refusing to give up and being at the right place at the right time. I'm also thankful that the women of Jacksonville can now make their own very personal decisions without the threat of death hanging over their heads."

• • •

Matthew eased the wheelchair through the doorway into the hospital's solarium. "Careful with your side," Peyton said.

He laughed. "Looking at you and me, you'd have to say, Azrael was a real cutup."

"Oooohhh," Peyton mouthed. "Bad joke."

"Sorry 'bout that," Matthew said as he pushed the wheelchair to a broad expanse of windows overlooking the St. Johns River and Jacksonville's nighttime skyline. "Jackie would've appreciated it, but I guess she and I grew up on the darker side of humor. Anyway, Dr. Wagoner stuck her head in the door this morning and said hi, but didn't stop other than to say she was going to see you."

"That's right."

"Social call, or did she have the results of the pregnancy test?"

Peyton took in a deep breath before answering, "Both, and the test was positive."

Matthew dropped to his knee beside the wheelchair and took Peyton's hands in his. "You're pregnant?"

"Very much so, and from an ultrasound scan the hospital ran at Debra's request, everything appears normal. No damage done."

"Fantastic!" Matthew brought Peyton's hands to his lips and kissed them. "That's the best thing I've heard in..." Matthew stopped in midsentence. "What's wrong?"

Peyton pulled her hands free of Matthew's and spoke very softly. "The two miscarriages and my fear of another one. I've done a lot of thinking this afternoon and I've made a decision. I hope you'll understand."

"You know my feelings, but in this case, I'll go along with whatever you feel you have to do."

"I want to try. I want to have the baby. Our baby."

A smile swept across Matthew's face. "And you will. Whatever it takes, whatever —"

"What about us?" Peyton asked, eyes focused on Matthew.

"I always did want to be married to a psychic."

"You... you really mean it? Us married?"

Matthew grinned. "Got a problem with that?"

"God, I love you so much," Peyton said, her face radiant with emotion. "I only hope..." Peyton stopped, her mouth open in shock.

"What's wrong now?" Matthew asked.

"I just remembered. Today's *Friday the thirteenth*."

Matthew laughed. "So who cares? We'll remember it as one of the best days of our lives. You, me and,..." He touched Peyton's stomach with loving gentleness. "... and whatever the future may bring."

Peyton patted his hand still resting on her stomach. "A girl."

"A boy."

"A girl," Peyton said emphatically. "There's one thing you must learn, my love."

"What's that?" Matthew asked, looking up warily.

With a mischievous grin on her face, Peyton answered, "Whatever you do, never, ever, argue with a psychic."

THE END

William Kerr

Read
The Collector

A sinister web of greed and murder set against a backdrop of southern charm in the Carolina Low Country, and the islands of Bermuda in the Atlantic, was the first in a string of Matthew Berkeley novels being published by Narwhal Press.

The book's hero, Matthew Berkeley, is Director of Security for NAARPA (the North American Archaeological Research and Preservation Association). Berkeley made his first appearance in Kerr's best-selling novel, *Path of the Golden Dragon* (by Commonwealth Publications Inc., Edmonton, Alberta, 1997).

In this adventure, Berkeley, a former Navy Special Warfare officer, pits his wits and skills against a murderous "Collector" of rare and priceless historical artifacts, who does not hesitate to kill to advance his collection.

The targeted item is a unique, solid gold casting of the Great Seal of the Lords Proprietors of Carolina. The seal had been stolen and buried by the legendary "Gentleman Pirate," Major Stede Bonnet, shortly before he was captured and hanged at Charleston's famous "White Point." The discovery of the giant gold seal some 270 years afterwards at an archaeological site near Beaufort, South Carolina, brings the past and present together in a unique and compelling mystery.

The ruthless Collector seeks to possess the Great Seal, not only for its intrinsic and numismatic value, but as an ancestral right, justified only in his own twisted mind. To his ire, Berkeley stands between the Collector and this blood-stained relic from the past.

Narwhal Press, already internationally known for its non-fiction books on shipwrecks, chose this as its first real foray into fiction. Read *The Collector*, by William Kerr, Narwhal Press, copyright 2001, and you will understand why.

William Kerr

Read
Judgment Call

Best-selling novelist and award-winning author, William Kerr does it again. This time Kerr makes his hero weigh everything, the good and the bad, then make judgment calls that can spell life or death, not only for him, but for those whose trust and love he holds most dear.

Fifty-one seconds – the time it takes to carjack an automobile at knifepoint. In the car, a child, the fifth victim in a string of unsolved kidnappings. A mother's cry for help, and Matt Berkeley, former Navy Special Warfare officer, now head of security for the North American Archeological Research and Preservation Association (NAARPA), finds himself confronted with one of the most depraved, yet cunning and elusive adversaries of his career.

Berkeley's return to Charleston, South Carolina, the city of his youth, is further influenced by: Ashley Peake, a beautiful and savvy, private investigator determined to enlist his help in finding the missing children; the kidnapping of his "adopted" nephew; the terminal illness of his elderly stepfather, a man he has despised for the last ten years; and threats against his mother by a callous bureaucracy for seeking whatever means, legal or illegal, to alleviate the intolerable suffering of his stepfather.

Each event forces Berkeley into another judgment call. Each a judgment call he would rather not have to make.

As usual with Kerr's novels, *Judgment Call* has plenty of twists and turns, most caused by deceit and betrayal. It is fast paced and its ending is both explosive and satisfying.

Whatever your preference – suspense, mystery, action, drama – you should definitely read this compelling Matt Berkeley mystery novel by William Kerr. Published by Narwhal Press, Charleston, South Carolina, copyright 2001.

William Kerr

AWARDS FOR WILLIAM KERR

Death's Bright Angel –
  Finalist, 2001 America's Best Screenplay Contest (winners not yet announced, as of the date of this publication)
  Winner, 2000 Crystal Reel Award Best Screenplay, Feature Film, Florida Motion Picture & Television Association
  Finalist, 1999 Bad Kitty Films Screenplay Contest, San Francisco
  Honorable Mention, 1998 Novel Competition, National Writers Association
  Honorable Mention, 1998 Writer's Network Screenplay Contest

Dragon Path –
  Finalist, 1999 Hollywood Symposium Screenplay Competition

Night Scream –
  Finalist, 1999 America's Best Screenplay Contest
  Finalist, 1999 Screenwriting in the Sun Contest (sponsored by *Scr(i)pt Magazine* and the 14th Annual Fort Lauderdale International Film Festival)

The Red Hand –
  Winner, 1997 Quantum Quest Screenplay Competition

Night of the Angels –
  Winner, 1997 Novel Contest, National Writers Association

Path of the Golden Dragon –
  New York Times Paperback Best Seller List, 9/97
  Finalist, 1996 Florida 1st Coast Novel Competition

Lightning and the Tempest –
  Winner, 7th Annual Screenwriters Competition (sponsored by Universal Studios Florida)

WILLIAM KERR

William Kerr spent much of his life at sea as an officer in the U.S. Navy. Among Kerr's most memorable assignments were serving as Chief of Staff for the Navy's Readiness Command in Charleston, and as the Liaison Officer to Congress for the Chief of Naval Operations.

A recipient of both the Legion of Merit and the Navy Commendation Medal, Captain Kerr retired after nearly 25 years of service.

Kerr and his wife, Rebecca, now live in Ponte Vedra Beach, Florida. They are avid scuba divers and have explored reefs and shipwrecks in the waters of Florida, the Bahamas and the Caribbean.